THE BOOK OF SCIENCE
AND ANTIQUITIES

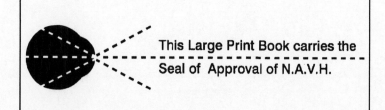

This Large Print Book carries the
Seal of Approval of N.A.V.H.

THE BOOK OF SCIENCE AND ANTIQUITIES

THOMAS KENEALLY

THORNDIKE PRESS
A part of Gale, a Cengage Company

Thorndike Press® Large Print Basic
The text of this Large Print edition is unabridged.
Other aspects of the book may vary from the original edition.
Set in 16 pt. Plantin.

LIBRARY OF CONGRESS CIP DATA ON FILE.
CATALOGUING IN PUBLICATION FOR THIS BOOK
IS AVAILABLE FROM THE LIBRARY OF CONGRESS

ISBN-13: 978-1-4328-7234-2 (hardcover alk. paper)

Published in 2020 by arrangement with Atria, an imprint of Simon & Schuster, Inc.

Printed in Mexico
Print Number: 01   Print Year: 2020

*To my friend Jim Bowler,
and to Mungo Man, 42,000 years old,
who found each other on the shore of
Lake Mungo in 1974*

AUTHOR'S NOTE

I have said in the past that, given the many brilliant Aboriginal writers presently at work, it would be gross fraternal impoliteness for a white fellow to horn in on Aboriginal tales. Yet I hope I am forgiven for writing about 42,000-year-old (or older) Australian ancestors. This is because the Paleolithic humans from Lake Mungo speak of all our human ancestries, black or white — even though I believe the community at Lake Mungo lived a far more desirable existence than my own ancestors in Central Asia or Eastern Europe. Mungo Man, the novel's Learned Man, is a treasure of three great surviving peoples, the three groups enumerated and, I hope, honored in the book. But in a secondary sense, and though our leaders are as yet indifferent to him, he is a possession of all humans, a phenomenal treasure, a prophet for us all.

I must thank again the amiable Professor

Jim Bowler for his tolerance and vision, and a number of patient members of the New South Wales Department of Environment and Heritage who gave assistance with this book.

This book returns to the Horn of Africa, the scene of an earlier novel of mine, *Towards Asmara*. I wanted to assure anyone who by chance has read that earlier work that material from that long-ago book is not recycled here; that this tale makes use of journeys I made to Eritrea after 1989, the date of publication of *Towards Asmara*. The establishment of peace between Ethiopia and Eritrea in 2018 was good news for the noble citizens of both states. But Eritreans are still overrepresented in the boatloads of hapless people fleeing across the Mediterranean to Europe.

I would like to insist on the fictional nature of all the characters of this book, and though some of them were instigated by real people, the novel is not a roman à clef. The character Ted Castwell, for example, bears resemblance to the late visionary Fred Hollows, but is entirely fictional within the limits of this novel, as are all other characters, including Shelby Apple himself.

Two Old Men Dying offered my publishers significant editorial issues, given its two

8

tales, parallel and yet individual. In resolving these, I owe much to my wonderful agent, Fiona Inglis, and to Nikki Christer, Meredith Curnow, and Karen Reid at Penguin Random House. As for my wife, Judith, I did not ask you when we first met whether, amongst your other notable merits, you were a good editor, but it turns out that you were, thus impelling once more my abundant gratitude.

■ ■ ■ ■

I
THE BOOK OF
SCIENCE AND
ANTIQUITIES

■ ■ ■ ■

FINDING LEARNED

At the time of the discovery of the astonishingly ancient Learned Man, some decades back, my friend Peter Jorgensen, a scientist from Melbourne, was testing dried lake basins and their sediments for records of ancient rainfall oscillations. In modern times this area is marginal country in terms of rainfall, and the Learned Lakes are dry these days. They are not lakes in the European sense, not lakes that assert their lakeness by brimming and thus accommodating the eye. However, the lakes did hold water in the day of Learned Man, and accommodated *his* eye.

Ironically, twentieth-century heavy rain had kept Jorgensen bound to the homestead of the old Lake Learned Station on that historic day of his discovery. When the rain did stop and a brightening landscape and a firmer surface presented itself, Jorgensen set off on a motorcycle to investigate the

13

sediments of the long lunette or semicircle of sand dunes and hills that marked the former eastern shore of the lake. After he abandoned the motorcycle and trudged up the hill, he walked over layers of the past, as exposed by millennia of winds and rain. He ascended from the eighty-thousand-year-old sediment level to the seventy-thousand-year-old layer and so on up to the fifty-thousand-year-old sediments. He was now not far from where, five years earlier, he had discovered the remains of a young *Homo sapiens* woman he'd dubbed Learned Woman, who had until that day represented the human who had the oldest formal burial we had knowledge of. Before her flesh was burned off her bones, it had been adorned with ocher, which the sediments around the bones of the woman were full of. This ocher did not come from the lake area but from hundreds of miles away. It had been deliberately applied in reverence to her. Her remaining bones had been broken up and even partially ground for whatever cause by her people. But her skull was still intact to assert her humanity.

Dating methods were in their infancy when Learned Woman was found in the early 1970s, and she was initially thought to have lived about thirty thousand years ago.

However, there had been technical advances in subsequent decades: from thermoluminescence dating to electron-spin dating, uranium-thorium, carbon 14, and so on. Don't ask me to explain any of them, or how they were applied to her. But they ultimately proved that Learned Woman had lived forty to forty-two millennia ago.

The young paleontologist who worked on Learned Woman's remains and removed them to the Australian National University in suitcases was a friend of Jorgensen's named Harry Spurling, who became well known because of his work on Learned Woman.

Though of course Jorgensen had suspected there must be other ancient remains in the vicinity of Learned Woman, he was not looking for them as he strode up the slope on the day of discovery, though he was willing to register them if they presented themselves. And thus he stopped when he saw what appeared to be a white disc shining through a mantle of clay and lightly cemented sand. Looking at it more closely, he saw that it was the side of a skull uncovered by the rain. Though Jorgensen did not know the skull's gender on first sight, it would prove to be the remains of Learned Man.

Late afternoon, and one of the ancients had chosen to resurrect himself! Even as it happened it had the flavor for my friend of a willed meeting on both sides. Indeed, Jorgensen would come to believe what a female elder of the Barkindji people later told him: "You did not find the Old Woman and the Old Man. They found you!" Another elder observed, "The Old Man knew what he was doing. He showed himself to a man of science."

I was already a documentary filmmaker of what could be called either note or notoriety when I met and became an admirer of Peter Jorgensen. I visited Lake Learned one year on a road trip and was captured by the vast dry lake of semidesert lushness and encountered the tale of Learned Man and the man who had found him. Jorgensen explained he was a geomorphologist when I first contacted him. That is, he was a researcher of what the earth looked like once, in ice ages past, and of how the rain fell on it, the ice shaped it, and long-gone waters occupied and honed it. Now, these are very technical issues and ones that stand aside from the question of humans and human action. We weren't numerous then, and our species trod lightly upon the earth. We lacked the power and ambition to weigh upon it heavily. So the earth was still supreme when the rains Jorgensen was interested in fell. And Jorgensen, grandson of a Norwegian mariner who came ashore in Melbourne long ago for the sake of an Irishwoman, was a student of the supreme earth as it then existed, within its carapace of atmospheres and its veins of current and wind.

I felt too, for reasons that will become apparent, that in trying to make my film on Learned Man, I might lead Jorgensen to think me a chancer. I'd been depicted in that way because of the controversy over a documentary I'd made with my late friend Andy Mortray. That had made me edgy enough to suspect I was mistrusted, which is why I was reluctant to ask my new acquaintance Jorgensen straight out, from the first hour of our filming at Lake Learned, whether it was all a matter of technical concepts for him; all a matter of the rainfall of, say, 43,757 Before the Present Era, and whether Learned Man was only of technical interest to him?

In order not to offend him, I first asked him the question off camera.

"Oh," he told me, "I'm a familiar of Learned. No question. There are three men

17

I dream of, Shelby. They visit me when I'm asleep." The great scholar swallowed. "One is my drowned brother, Herk. He was strong, but sometimes I get nervous that he died to bequeath his strength to me.

"The other is my father, whose life was marred by a wound he suffered at Pozières on the Somme."

Already the geomorphologist had confessed to a greater human sensibility than I had expected.

"The third," he said, "is of course Learned himself."

"So what does Learned Man tell you?" I asked glibly.

"Well, he says that to be human is to have business to attend to, to be on a quest. He was honored, you see, by those who buried him, as if he had been on a quest on their behalf. His people recognized what he'd tried to do, whatever it was. He says to me that we say we want an easy life, but without a pilgrimage, a dangerous search, we don't live a life worth having. He tells me something a bit creepier too. He definitely says to me that being human is a test that kills us."

"That's a rather despairing idea," I said, with the cinematographer's everyday piety.

At this Peter Jorgensen smiled and said, "I

don't believe my friend Mr. Learned failed his test. He was buried like a hero, the first burial of a hero we have. But he tells me that not only do we face tests but there's something in us that welcomes them. That's the way we were in the time of Learned Man, and it's the way we are now. At least I can tell you that everything the human brain was then, it is now. If you and I are poets and questioners, he was too. He prodded at the universe the way we prod at it. He felt overwhelmed by it, but had the human urge to encompass it. He chased love with the same sacred and profane mix of motives we do. At the end of it, he was you, Shelby."

And so Learned Man was, according to Jorgensen, not a phantasm on the edge of the imagination, or a tepid taint of humanity over ancient terrestrial facts, but a personage of the present.

I was delighted to hear all this.

Then Jorgensen lowered his voice. "On top of that, Shelby, there is a white hyalite stone amongst Learned Man's bones. What was it doing there? Maybe an emblem of authority. The stone comes from hundreds of miles away and is particular to Lightning Ridge up near the Queensland border."

This was when I got the paleontology bug and began to make the first of my documentaries about Jorgensen, Learned Man and Woman, and the lakes region.

Learned Man stayed with me too, from the day I encountered him through Jorgensen, and in the end stayed with me longer than most things. He straddled time, and was the guessed-at past in an undiscovered future; the reconciling phenomenon between Australia's geological antiquity and its societal juvenility. He hung suspended between the layers of our contradictions: Lake Learned had brimmed with water at the time Learned Man was there; it was his mare nostrum, his Mediterranean, his ministry, his dream, and his kindly shore. What must it have been to be human then, when to be human was so marginal an experience, a world in which we were not yet the dominating force but had mere elbow room amongst a wealth of other species?

LEARNED ARGUMENTS

When he first encountered the remains he called Learned Man, Peter Jorgensen made note of the location and summoned Harry Spurling and another leading paleontologist. Spurling and his colleague excavated the site and took the remains back to a laboratory in Canberra for testing. Henceforth, the bones became the archaeologists' business, since Jorgensen was not one of their company.

As clearly as Jorgensen sensed that Learned Man might have something revolutionary and explosive to say, so too did the leading paleontologist, Harry Spurling, who studied Learned Man as he had studied beforehand the female skeleton of shattered bones Jorgensen had found in the sand dunes.

Dating by radiocarbon testing in the 1970s being chancy, what Harry Spurling discovered with the skull of Learned Man, as earlier with that of Learned Woman, was that the measurement of its thickness indicated it was *Homo sapiens,* if an archaic version. None of this surprised Jorgensen, who had long believed Learned a brother of his, having decided the issue not on scientific grounds but for profound reasons of the heart, as Pascal had defined the heart when he said, "The heart has its reasons, which reason cannot grasp."

Meanwhile, from studying Learned Man and other research, Spurling became renowned for questioning the "replacement" theory so commonly held by scientists. This theory posited that in Africa, and wherever *Homo sapiens* went from there, they *replaced* all other human strains. They did not make the other human species disappear by interbreeding with them. They were not their lovers on the savannahs of the past, but may have been their murderers, an uncomfortable but realistic possibility. Thus, according to the replacement theory, by the time Learned Man's ancestors reached Australia, they were the only human species.

On the other hand, Harry Spurling was charmed by the elegant bones of Learned Woman, the young wife who had been cremated and whose fractured remains he chiseled forth with a dental drill from the ochered sand that adhered to them. And from her, and then from assembling Learned Man, Spurling decided on a new theory — that if *Homo sapiens* had not spread out of Africa until around two hundred thousand years before, there wasn't time for them to have turned up where Learned Man and Learned Woman were encountered by Jorgensen. That, he declared, was one problem with the replacement theory and its idea of one mother, the Mitochondrial Eve from Africa, the woman whose line survived daughter by daughter by daughter — who made the modern human, her mitochondria snuggled in the cells of all her descendants. The woman who gave birth to Learned Man could not be a daughter of that one African mother, said Spurling, because there hadn't been time for Learned's mother to have got to Lake Learned if she came from the African Eve.

So, said Spurling, the story must be that modern *Homo sapiens* had developed in parallel in a number of places on earth, interbreeding with other human species on the way. Harry Spurling once said to me, "The *replacement* men and women say modern humans replaced Neanderthals without interbreeding. That's what I don't

23

get. No interbreeding. Does that sound like the humans you know, Shelby?"

By then my first documentary on Learned Man had been screened on television to some acclaim via the normal route of the ABC, BBC, PBS, and I found myself attending archaeology and paleontology conferences, where people would ask me about Jorgensen and Spurling.

Though I knew Jorgensen had great affection for Spurling, nonetheless he had warned me, "Don't spend too much film on Harry. I can tell you he's wrong."

"How can you tell?" I asked him.

He didn't give me a scientific answer, but rather, "Learned Man didn't go whoring after hominid women on the way to making us what we are. His ancestors entered a continent empty of other humans. Imagine this, because it's what my friend Spurling imagines. Two different kinds of people came down from different places and settled near Lake Learned. One was from Java and was made up of hominids, and another had its roots in China, and were on their way to becoming us. The two parties were encamped and they began to crossbreed." At this point he laughed indulgently. "That's how *Homo sapiens* got to Australia, in Spurling's view."

Then he hastened to say, "I've got nothing against Harry. I recall him asking for a moment's silence in honor of the first Australian after we excavated Learned Man. And he let only the wind speak then. His heart's in the right place."

Harry Spurling's theory would indeed come to be disproved by advances in genetic science. He took it well; and Jorgensen was not vainglorious when his fraternal instincts about Learned Man were proved right. Learned, it would be proved in time, was the child of our kind of humans, and no other hominids were in the vast Australia his ancestors had entered, and which he no doubt took for granted as the ordained place for him.

LEARNED REVISED

By the time I made the second Learned film, we knew how long ago old Learned Man really had lived — a cool forty-two thousand years! And the three tribes whose land abutted Lake Learned knew that the remains of Learned Man and Learned Woman were treasures which had been taken from them. A number of Aboriginal elders from the towns of Mildura, Balranald, and Ivanhoe — speaking under the Anglo names their forebears had picked up from nineteenth-century sheep stations or missions — had made reasonable complaint that they had not been consulted by Jorgensen or Spurling or anyone else over the removal of their ancient forebears. It was the sort of mistake scholars had traditionally made, and Jorgensen was repentant but motivated to come to an arrangement with the elders, that there would be no more removals of their dead unless by permission.

I covered this compact as part of the second documentary.

Amongst other matters, I wondered about speech in Learned's day. The organization of his burial seemed to have demanded that speech existed between the people who buried him. Though one brave commentator had granted ancient humans the capacity, as distinct from the communicating sounds of other apes a hundred thousand years before the present, there were those who cast doubt on the idea of speech being as ancient as the time of Learned Man.

Jorgensen and I were out in the sand dunes of the lake's lunette again, the light fading on the site of Learned's Paleolithic Manhattan, on the lake's rumor of fullness, on the memory of the beasts of Learned's time, and on the long, low undulations of the place, when Jorgensen said to me, "None of what was done at the burial was done by a pack of well-meaning primates with howls and groans.

"They could talk all right, believe me," reiterated Jorgensen, like a grandchild defending the grandparents from charges of incoherence or stupidity.

I was a man holding a camera and aged almost seventy when he said this, and it was a matter of wonderment to me to hear such a claim. At this stage of history Learned Man and Learned Woman were still waiting, on museum shelves, by permission of the elders for the time being, between layers of expectation and indifference, and always with the expectation they would come home in the end.

At the time of the second documentary, Jorgensen still considered all the other manifestations of ancient civilization, whether mummified or present in identifiable bone or flesh fragments, as mere contestants, with Learned Man supreme upon his tower of age. For *he,* Peter Jorgensen, had confronted the most ancient of the ancient, something almost too good for a display case; something, he argued, worthy — if the elders permitted it when they brought Learned home — of a cenotaph, a world focus; a place of interpretation, wonder, reconciliation, and pilgrimage.

Indeed, Jorgensen believed that the three language groups whose country converges on Lake Learned were waiting courteously for a management plan to be made final for Learned's return to his dry ghost of a lake. And if they wanted Learned Man to be reburied secretly in the Lake Learned lunette, and the reburial site to remain secret from the world, they were entitled to do that. "A treasure greater than Ramses waits on the shelf at the National Museum!" Jorgensen said as he expatiated on his concept. "And the traditional owners certainly know it. But because we, the others, are only dimly interested, just to protect him from the indignity of shelf life the elders might give up on us and bury him secretly. And I wouldn't bloody blame them."

But he believed they wanted more than that. So that was also part of the business of the second documentary, as well as the idea that Learned could heal the country's history.

"What's been our predominant attitude?" Jorgensen would say with genuine pain in his eyes. "Disrespect. Worse than gunpowder. In fact, the two are connected. At every turn, we disrespected the old people. We called the country 'No-Man's-Land,' *terra nullius.* And that was the legal fiction that allowed us to take a continent. And when *they* claimed land, we laughed, and when the court overturned *terra nullius* and decided the country was really theirs, we went stark bloody crazy, as if *we* had been invaded."

But Learned was Jorgensen's cure. "He'll calm our souls, teach us respect a busload at a time. Learned Man will heal us. He'll undermine our contempt. He'll alter the history we carry in our heads."

Learned Man, manifested, would be a memorial too, for all his children who in the nineteenth and twentieth centuries were killed for persisting in the belief that the land was theirs — for the thousands of Aboriginals who had died by high-muzzle velocity rifles while defending or standing on their country. Learned Man, with the mass and majesty of his years, could also carry their commemoration. And though my dreams were not as invaded by Learned Man as Jorgensen's, I too listened to the elders' idea that, as one of them, Clarence Millet, put it, "Learned Man went out in the world to let whites learn something very big." And this would be best appreciated if his country became a place of visitation for all of us, run by the elders, by their permission. This was a version no one in government had ever offered the elders. Jorgensen was determined that one day someone in power would.

Meanwhile, Jorgensen and I began years of letter-writing to politicians of every stripe to support Learned Man's children in their quest for the return of Learned Man to his original home, and to do it with whatever seriousness of purpose they allowed.

■ ■ ■ ■

Another thing about Learned Man. His teeth were worn but in decent condition, so his missing upper incisor seemed something ritual, as it was in later Aboriginals. With his good, if worn, teeth, he ate the flesh of the giant fauna of his day, and the flesh of what we call Murray cod, as well as the varieties of shellfish and wild poultry. He was a man who lived on the lunette of the lake a little like a householder, and who traveled for the same reasons we do: romance and education, pilgrimage and trade.

O My Hero

O my hero, I devote this account of my latter days to you, so that you understand how well I love you and love the earth, and know my duty to them, to all the Heroes, to all the beasts and to all the people.

I am thinking pleasantly of the wrestling that comes at the start of the cold season, when we occupy equal days of moon and sun, the days when the half of everything yearns for the half of everything else, when ice sings to light, and when there should be efforts made at wholeness. So we come to the equal day-night wrestling, and its banquet. First off, on our side of the camp we have already had seven sets of wrestlers face each other, skin group contesting with skin group, all splendid boys. That's the thing about these young men, they don't know they are perfect. Initiated into adulthood this winter, they have the dewiness of their new knowledge, and they'll try anything, and don't even know they shouldn't. That's how we come to my sister's son, one of the Short-Faced Bounder people to which I belong — the lovely people, lovely at least to each other, the smilers and singers and lovers of the tall Bounder.

My sister's son is in some ways a hard young man to watch. He is rather like my Son Unnameable, though a little shorter. My nephew has fought the young men of the four clans who make up our side of the people, is the champion of our half. Indeed, he's rangy and quick like my sister's husband used to be before a curse struck him speechless and brought him down. And oh, but he is as well set as anyone living, except for one old wound in his calf that has weakened the tendon. Yet we are all pleased to have our half of the people's wrestling spirits in Redder's hands.

He is a young man just short of marriage whose beloved, as far as we know, is still the Lake country itself. A wrestler should have a wide zeal for life and all companionship, and not as yet for any particular woman. A woman is going to follow in a visible way soon, I would say, particularly now that women from the other four clans will get such a good look at him today. After the wrestling and the celebration meal, girls will

33

dance for the wrestlers and console them for all the tearing of flesh and hair-pulling and strained sinew. But before the banquet, and first, he must contest for our half of our world, to make a claim of enduring strength for us and, my Hero, for you, and so to mediate an evenness and completeness for all the Lake peoples.

I love wrestling as much as I love any sport. Clearly now I am set aside for other tasks, and my shoulder is home to a recent and painful constriction that would inhibit reaching for a ball, the great bladder of the dome nose. But I, being of taller form and more solid than my nephew, *used* to wrestle at this time of the year on the edge of this same shore. I *used* to strive to reconcile the earth's halves to each other by reconciling my opponents' backs to the dust, and having them in turn reconcile mine. It was easy then. In other words, I had a few victories, which meant I was given commensurate duties, since the rule is there should be time for enjoyment, but not a lot for vanity. A young man is flattered when it happens. He does not understand in full that the world is a world of kindly obligation. Without the obligations, no man would know who he was.

So, if you prevail you are given tasks. It's

the way we live in these latter days, since the Heroes left the earth to us. There was once an earlier playful time when men and women lived as heedlessly as children, but that couldn't be sustained.

In any case, as often at the end of the time of heat, the Lake's shore has receded too far, and Redder is the sort of sprig designed by high influences to attract the wraiths with his contest, and restore things with a decent full pelt of replenishing rains.

I am a man of great good fortune, and that is why I sing to you of these things. We are all a very lucky people, our crowd, as long as things go well and cycles are reliable, and our young wrestlers draw favor. Now, I admit we would wrestle anyhow, but we have a command to do it from you, Our Brother of the Clouds, and from all the other Heroes.

We know where this command came from: the great perentie who lost too many of his kin to ritual war and who chanted in grief to the Father of Heroes and had him appear as a giant, terrifying snake. And this great, fluent snake, of heavenly derivation and ancestral probity, said simply, "Watch the bounders!" And watching them, the lizard saw how those tall beasts fought, grooming, then chasing, engaging, sitting back on their tails and kicking at each other with powerful hind legs, causing the other's fur to be gouged forth but then, at close quarters, taking each other in a head-grasp. And once a buck bounder was thrown to the ground, the victor adopted a casual pose, relenting of all vainglory, and the loser gave up and at once vacated the wrestling ground. And hence, wrestling rather than blood was recommended for all our people!

Yesterday my brother-in-law Sandy brought in a butchered long-faced bounder his team had caught. It was seven arms high, a splendid buck, a creature to sing about. When I saw them carrying the butchered haunch — for no man can carry the unbutchered meat — I and all the people of our shoreline were reminded again that between the Lake and the earth, and the plains running away to our Morningside, we are beautifully provided for. Fish and perentie, roots and seeds and fruit, and the giant beings who provide the mercy of meat.

So those who muttered during the hot months when the water was taken up and the Lake shore extended by spear-lengths upon spear-lengths upon further spear-lengths, are now pacified by the size of the reward of meat. The meat of the giant creature is being slowly cooked at the edge of the wrestling and game ground, at the place set aside for ovens. It lies covered with clay and is baking away in layers of aromatic leaves and the bark of the shred-tree. My wife, Girly, is there, a judge of how the cooking progresses and when it will be ready. Younger women — my daughter Shrill amongst them, a wonderful net maker, but today a helper to the older women — are cooking tubers and seed-bread in shallower fires on the side. And despite the onshore sunrise breeze, all the people can smell the slow-cooking flavors, as the older women earnestly plug the steam from the oven with hard clay slabs carried between sticks. Despite the onshore sunrise breeze, we can smell it all. The people are graced by this foretaste of the wrestling and the banquet.

I have been sluggish today, but now I am awake. As I draw near the wrestling field, the wrestling council are there smoking the ground already, rendering it clean and dis-suading mischievous spirits with stinging smoke and prohibitive songs. They do their feather-racer dance, advancing over the ground with the all-cleansing fumes rising around them and the smoldering branches in hand. This smoke too is an exciting promise of large events. The sun is full now above great tendrils of white cloud. No one is cursed today, though I feel small curses in my shoulder and slight traces of my early weariness. Everyone's face seems lit. Women walk by me and my gaze is drawn by their passage to the fire, and the senior women, including Girly — a better talker than me — are chortling, and with plenty to say. These women have gone double foraging over the last few days in order to leave this morning free to servicing the oven.

I see Girly's large eyes swing and attach to me. She is an enchanter. Her eyes are deeper than the earth and promise to take a person to the outer edge of things. Sometimes when I sleep with her she releases me amongst unpredicted stars. That is her. This loud woman. How I like loud women, though they are loud in fury too, and when they bang at your ankles angrily with the digging stick that was given to women for the delving of earth and the punishment of men. It is better for a man not to carry scars on his ankles or other men will call him eagle-bitten. Some men carry the insult for phase upon phase of seasons. Always pecked by their eagle. "Haw, haw, haw!" cry the other men, who delight to see when a man's scars are reopened by his woman. The eagle has been at him again.

Girly is my second wife. My wife when I was young, She Unnameable, did not look at me in the way of Girly. A more placid soul with a slower smile, she would sit back on her haunches, her stick slack in her hand. No eagle. A less hungry, more companionable bird.

My daughter Shrill, the weaver of nets, is now attending to yams in a side fire. I see her assiduous shoulders, well muscled by her work.

When I emerged from my mother's womb, a visitor appeared where my mother and I lay wrapped in fur by a fire, and he bent down singing and found my small foot amongst the skins. Then, almost without my mother knowing, as if plucking a small root from the earth, he dislocated my little toe. I screamed of course and he departed, but no one tried to reset the little toe, since it was meant to suit me for some future office. My toe remains thus to this day. I have always been treated with respect by people who read my tracks and who know that in my human habiliments I am not simply a man with a malformed foot, but also one to be feared only when the law enters me. That dislocated toe was a message that I had been picked up as a weapon of the law and that I would be directed to protect it, that it will be still dislocated when I pass skywards and am laid in the dunes.

Thus I know, for instance, where the awful fluid from the dead man is stored, the fluid in which the long bone of maintenance and restoration and punishment must be steeped. But now, going to the wrestling ground in my normal clothing, the gracious fur and the leather clout, I am simply another fellow walking in the dunes, not on any other enterprise than to relate to the elements of the day and to my fellows. This seems a day appointed to mere breathing and no complex duty. The sanctifying smoke and the first rumor of the succulence of the bounder haunch suggest exactly that.

The people of the clans are now gathering in from all sides. I love the ever-shriller chatter of the women, which is of a higher order even than the chatter of the birds but comes from the same source. The birds' task is to sharpen the dusk to a point of sound, the pink-wings and the curved-beaks who are so strident and the loudmouthed honey-eaters and all the rest, of whom the rosy hook-beaks are the greatest honers of the point of their song. Meanwhile the task of women is to sharpen the day to a point, which they are doing now amidst the smell of meat and the cleansing smoke.

I am grateful today for my kindly skins, the fur on my shoulders and chest and on my loins. My shoulder hurts, but I can walk as if it doesn't. The dunes I climb are washed with red and yellow and gray and blue, and the sand pillars the wind makes stand up solid around us. I know they say, the people of the many clans, that I am as tall as one of those piles of formed clay and earth, and am sometimes to be mistaken for one. People tell me I take on that form though I am not aware that I do. I will not be suspected of it on a plain, joyful day like today.

I see the man named Clawback walking with children skipping around him, three and three, and they're laughing and he pretends to be a wily spirit, first ignoring them and then chasing them. The children skitter, arching their backs to avoid his grasping hands. Clawback is a teaser and a man with a quick tongue, likable to all, familiar to all. He is, however, also a violator of blood and, it seems, to be marked in the place of the law to die. He does not know that, nor do the children or the women at the fire under the warm influence of which many of them have slipped off their furs. Like every man besotted with a

41

woman, Clawback believes his passions are not legible. He still thinks that his transgressions with a forbidden woman of the Earless Lizard clan are unknown. But they have been perceived and weighed upon by the aged men. Even some of the women at the fire might have discussed them. He does not know that the killing bone is meant to go down the base of his handsome laughing throat. Being who I am, of deformed foot, I know how much it is to be regretted that so often the great violators are the best loved of the people and the ones who light up the faces of people.

There was a time on earth when people were so few and manners so unrestrained that the Heroes of heaven did not need to enact law as exactly as they have in this latter age. That world would have suited a playful sinner like Clawback. Yet, in the world as it is now, such people vanish like clouds and are — afterwards — not spoken of.

Soon it seems all the people are at the contest ground. I look away towards Morningside. There are pleasing banks of silver-green honey bush, waist-high, stretching off towards stands of river trees, red and gray and very high, which mark the course of the wandering streams that flow into our lake. I have not yet reached the contest ground myself when I see a party of men coming out of those far trees, as if they have just crossed the water, wading through the morning skin of ice on the surface. They are now walking in the long grass towards us. Though they are still so far off, a person might see they are carrying burdens, and weapons, both old and freshly acquired. I know at once it is Baldy's party returning from their long mission to the Upper Waters. They have the look of men, even at this moment, perhaps especially now, who've been through many meetings and transactions off in that direction, of those who are weary but conscious of carrying news which will enlarge our world, even as they seek us again. The smell of the people's meat on the breeze from the Lake draws Baldy and his men in towards their home.

In the meantime, the wrestling matches are proclaimed to be ready to start by an old councillor, who seems unconscious to the approach of the party. As the champions of our clans draw closer, I can see they are cunningly marked in white clay. It is grand to see them — impeccable young men, delineated by the tension of their muscles, empowered by spirit paint and beside themselves with intent. The Otherside clan's upholders are at the other end of the ground and are given leanness and spirit by their yellow clay. They have assumed some of the strength and everywhere-ness of ghosts. They clap their hands and in a yellow mist their spirits move.

Even when I had my first wife, Girly used to run in to tease and howl at me. The mockery of seduction. No one is better at it than her. Some of the neighbor girls of ours with fancies of their own to marry into the Otherside now run in, hallooing in delicious scorn, hoping to win the benefactions of ancestors and implant themselves enchantingly in the memory of the Otherside wrestlers. And though the real contest has not yet begun, already the wives and children of the members of the Baldy party are breaking away from the feast and running, hooting, to greet the returning men.

The wrestling councillor, in his great hat of council, goes on instructing his wrestlers. And the young wrestlers listen, now and then stamping and raising impatient dust. Soon, at a moment the old man and they know chiefly from having so often magicked themselves into the role of wrestlers, wearing the pigments fit for their gifts, they will separate out into four different two-men contests. The two sides of earth and lake must bind, white to yellow, and in their grappling is delight and healing. I see Girly in her group of women, walking amongst others, a light-boned woman herself. It is pleasant to see her shape amongst the massed shoulders.

I am now older than most of these women. My own shoulder tells me I am older. But I delight more in the simple sight of a young woman's shoulder slipping the limits of pelts than when I was young. Once, I could not find the seconds of rest to relish such simple sights in the tumble of my present wishes and tasks. Now that I can so relish plain things, I believe I am being prepared for my journey by the powers of the air and the old councillors sitting together at the midpoint of the wrestling ground. The first journey is solemn though usual, yet I have never before had such a potent sense of pending journeys to be made in earth and sky, in body and in spirit.

The wrestling councillor has still not been distracted by the remote appearance of Baldy and the others. He finishes his instructions, and at the sound of a clap the young men, the white and the yellow, enmesh themselves in each other, making fretful unions of muscle. The women shrill as the men's first sweat cuts small runnels

45

in the decorative clay of their wrestling bodies.

It is already happening then, the wedding of powerful shoulders, and legs grinding in the dust to find hoist. They are magnificent legs, legs to sing of, as some of the women do, rejoicing in the power of those legs on the upthrusting earth which represent a future for the Lake people.

The councillor has already drawn a chart of the wrestling ground, and now he keeps a count of the falls, for he understands wrestling and its numbers. He marks the wrestlers' falls with chalk on a tablet of bark as the eight contestants contend for us all.

The count is important insofar as it reflects the future health and numbers of the eight clans. So no one can say that the old man is indifferent to the arrival of Baldy and his party. In these circumstances everyone has his duty. But the sad thing is that Baldy and his returning party will not be permitted to lie with their wives until tonight, since they did not know that the wrestling ceremony, the balancing of the earth by young, striving limbs, was due for the morning of their homecoming. They have been gone many days, many times three and many times four, traveling towards the Morningside and the Upper Waters, returning the long way Nightwards to us.

The wrestling continues mightily. Yellow backs are pounded into the dust, then white backs. A pleasing and promising toil, seamless limbs in the most earnest contest, regular, to be expected yet still marvelous, the union and the splitting of the earth, the embrace, then the halves hurling each other to the dirt. The women are now shrilling like one creature. Girly, a woman who likes display, stands up, free of her skins now, her breasts painted white, howling a bird-like chant to recognize and celebrate the contest. I can see the scars of mourning slashes on her long ribs and beneath her breasts. She is so proud of these scars she inflicted on herself when her mother died, and her uncle, and our Son Unnameable. The scars are a warrant, visible to God and man, that she grieved them fully and dutifully and still in some way possesses them. Occasionally she turns Morningwards to check on the progress of the returning party. She liked Baldy when they were young.

I like to fancy I can read the land, but Girly is a remarkable assessor of all things within the circle of her view. Within the circle of my view, Clawback and the children are still playing the game of them pestering him and then squealing at his mock rage and reachings-out. I look across the wrestling field to the place where the Earless Lizard women, streaks of yellow on their breasts, are standing — where only the oldest still sit. There, following Clawback's movements and clowneries with limpid eyes, is the broad-faced girl of great beauty forbidden to him. I know the somber man, Crow, for whom the girl is intended. Yet Clawback wrongly gave her his poisonous consolations, endearments that blight us at our source, the source where man meets woman to make the world.

Clawback was a member of my own hunting squad. Younger men like him often distinguish themselves with close passes at the beasts, and Clawback was brave enough, though he generally played the role of the joker who enacted the hunting as a comedy afterwards. Unless someone was killed, as was my Son Unnameable when we went on an ordained hunt for the thumbed slicer, the one that is a test of every skill and every sharpness of eye and spirit. Even Clawback could not make a joke of the slicer, since when it pounds in at you it takes away the choice of hunting or running. The hunters must remain, singing mercy and driving our spears into the armpits, and flinching and hiding behind our blinkings as we wait for someone in our party to have the thread of his life ripped from his throat, or else to find and pierce the heart of that grand killing creature. Not many jokes from Clawback on those days.

On normal days, however, hunting allows relentless jest. And as Clawback dances amongst the children, the eyes of that girl from across the ground still follow him with her criminal adoration. Honey is her name, and she glints like nectar. I feel a stir of sorrow for her and for Clawback. But more for her. She is young, and Clawback knows better. Men of my clan can marry and have affections for women of the Small Lightning clan, which is Girly's own clan. That is the mercy of things, and any other arrangement clogs and drowns the mercy. One could feel one's own vain pity though for the girl casting her eyes in Clawback's direction. The only way she could be cured of it is by marriage. Marriage is the great cure for forlornness and hapless dreams. But Clawback's Parrot clan cannot have women from the Small Lightning crowd, or from the Earless Lizard clan either.

I notice that my nephew Redder, who has had a number of wins, has just been thrown by a young man from the Tan Hawks who is

49

far broader-shouldered but squatter than Redder, and fit to throw Redder once he grew tired, as now, after many successful assaults on the yellows. The wrestling continues because tiredness is intended by the wrestling councillor and is prized for its capacity to even the earth out, and give both sides of the people, each side with its four striving clans, a proper ratio of triumph. And the women get shrill as they see young men who have been thrown earlier in the contests now becoming the equals of the wrestlers from the other side. It is only when things are equal, when the shouting of old men and women advising the exhausted not to let them down or praising those with remaining strength for not doing so has reached a point of equivalence, that it will all end. Only the councillor, a noted wrestler himself from the old days, can tell when the earth's hunger for the even and the composed will be satisfied. But that will take hours yet.

Meanwhile, Baldy and his party draw nearer still to the wrestling ground. Old men claw their way up to full height to greet them. I notice even from this distance that though Baldy looks somber and tired, his eyes are unresting and alive and they are searching. When he sees my figure — I am

50

still alone on the fringe of the clan — he raises both arms, irrespective of any plans his wife might have, and makes a slow gesture that says he has plenty to tell me. But the time for it is not now, in this turmoil of return and wrestling and cooking.

I watch as my nephew is thrown again. Redder accepts it, but when he rises I see in his eyes a bleak desire for more strength or else the close of the contest. The wrestlers will change opponents soon, and his next opponent might enable him to find an equalizing vigor. Meanwhile, Girly and a group of women, hallooing, have now drifted from the wrestling and surrounded Baldy and the other men, who by now have reunited with their women, children, aunts, uncles. Clawback leads his trail of children into the midst of the reunion and makes it more playful still. Through all this, Baldy's eyes remain bleakly on mine; I remain in place like a man interested in the contest, for Redder's sake.

JACK THE DANCER

I still remember vividly the morning in 2015 when my doctor called me with the news that I had small tumors on the lowest section of my esophagus. I was surprised, but something else as well. I was instantly and crazily fascinated. I thought, *So this is what will do it. This is what I will spend my last days with, a cancerous assault on my esophagus, an organ to which I have paid so little mental attention.* That day, as Dr. Gleason reported the sighting of the cancerous tumors to me and recommended I see a further specialist, a professor of the gastroenterological craft, was a day of particular sharp winter light, and I felt something unaccustomed: specifically, a profound sense of what a good life I'd had! I also thought of Andy, dead by accident in youth, my doppelgänger in the shades, someone who had endured the nullity of death on my behalf. I have never taken much time to be a counter of blessings, nor do I believe the gods are interested in showering them in any way equally. But some of us are lucky. And I'd been one of them. I felt above all grateful that I would have time to make peace — not with the world, because it's unappeasable — but with my daughters and grandchildren and, above all, with my enduring wife, Cath. Well, "make peace" is too dramatic. We were already pretty much at peace in those days. That too is my good fortune.

"That was Dr. Gleason," I told Cath when the call was over. "I'm sorry, but she says the scans I had showed a few tumors on my esophagus."

I reached out my arms to her then — a compact woman a bit over midheight, her hair dyed an attractive reddish-silver, the underlying silver having an impact of fashion statement rather than the decline of age. Cath entered the embrace so simply, but not compliantly, never compliantly, full of questions and plans. I could feel her breasts through the sweater. At eighty years, bespeaking shelter.

"Oh, Shel, what's the prognosis, for heaven's sake?" Cath asked.

"She wouldn't give me one. She's recommended another doctor for that. A professor of gastroenterology. She did say I can afford to be hopeful."

Indeed, Dr. Gleason had been a little staid in her recital of the news. What the tumors meant I was to discover, so she told me, from the professor she was sending me to.

From the day Dr. Gleason called, Cath had a better sense of the peril I might face. She did not take a pessimistic view. But she knew of the standard treatment for what ailed me — a serious, old-fashioned excision of the esophagus, large surgical wound side and front, the fashioning of a new, alien esophagus out of stomach tissue. Long convalescence. And the fact that the operation brought on that state of vulnerability and frequent accompaniment of old age — "morbidity"; death's door.

Cath has always proved calm at times of true peril. When our children were young, it took domesticity to make her hysterical — a messy room could do it. But big emergencies left her clear-eyed and wise, ready and brave and generous. At any crisis in our marriage she'd adopted a steely air of waiting for reason to dawn.

"You might have to cancel that meeting with the premier," she said, thinking of the diary which I had forgotten. Every human dies in the midst of a diary of some sort.

But not necessarily with the sort of composure I kept feeling.

"Bugger it!" I told her. "We're still going skiing!"

I suppose that given our age, that was a brave assertion. Cath had found it hard to tolerate turning eighty. Older than me, she still has fine features, and is very beautiful in a way that — at least I think — resists age and asserts itself in a face. Her complexion, for an Australian, is still composed of milk and Celtic mist, a sort of ivory remembrance of another place. As far as I can work out, this enviable complexion came from a convict woman named Kate Heaney, transported pre-Famine to New South Wales. If you're old enough you've probably seen me on TV exploiting the fascinating connections I possess through Cath, in what the exhibitors called "groundbreaking documentaries." One of the headings that had to be filled in on the convict ship's muster in Cork was "complexion," and the clerk had written of Kate's that it was "fair and milky."

Not that I would like to imply Cath is entirely a creature of vapors. She is solid and healthily but not excessively tanned, all to a wise antipodean level, though she complains of the unevenness the sun has

55

brought to hers as to most European-Australian skin. She is used to people telling her she doesn't look a day over fifty-five, though she secretly thinks of fifty-five as a tragic enough age. And, Mother of God, she didn't want to turn eighty! It was not fear of death. It was as if she worried she would become disentitled to being spry in demeanor and movement.

For once she didn't want her children and grandchildren round her. She didn't want to have a party. She harbored a murderous hostility to anyone who might tell her on that day that she was marvelous for her age! She did not want to celebrate her survival either, her "making it" to eighty. We were both aware of the delusion most people harbored that life had time to amend itself, to emerge on a serene plateau, and that by eighty that's where you were: arrived and completed in soul and destiny. She knew she was still arriving, that despite our mutual good luck the plateau was the same mountainside as ever, and that she was still Miss Sisyphus with her rock. In any case, she didn't consider turning eighty a triumph and didn't want any friends, especially the four women she normally delighted to spend time with, to get their jollies out of toasting her.

Instead she and I had driven to Victoria's haunted, beautiful Wilsons Promontory, the furthest south you can go in Australia without actually leaving the mainland. In the country behind us the dispossessed Highlanders and islanders of Scotland, brought here on bounty ships, had slaughtered the Kurnai people in the nineteenth century, all according to Jorgensen's proposition; disrespect equals gunpowder in the end. And the bush was so melancholy and underpopulated you could nearly hear the protests of the dead or the suggestions of screams from the unmapped massacre sites. The deep sclerophyll forests were full of ghosts who did not feel fully content. The rough, vivid sea of Bass Strait ran so potently, a water road that traveled south of Cape Horn, and was on its way uninterrupted by landmasses to southernmost South America.

It was also de rigueur that we had to have sex on the night of her birthday. That was as important as the Nordic skiing. She had some black lingerie that always demanded I take notice. She leaned over me. With her girl's smile.

In my reckless life, I presumed my esophagus, humble and functional organ whose purpose I had never before inquired into, was invulnerable in a way that I never attributed to my visible outer skin. I had not even known I possessed an esophageal valve, which until recently had prevented stomach acids reentering and scalding the esophagus and taking my breath — an experience I'd had more commonly just lately. At the time Dr. Gleason first gave me the news about what she called "Barrett's syndrome," my esophageal valve had been working for humble decades in the dark — unnamed and unappreciated by its owner. But it was under threat now, and if I was unlucky it might cease its steadfast work of conveying nutrition into my body altogether. For somewhere down in the dark was a new player, or a colony of new, dark players. Jack the Dancer had moved in.

I told Cath that despite the news I'd just received I would still like to take my daily walk. Our house is a short walk from a bold set of honey-colored cliffs above a boisterous Pacific. The mass of the headland is a grand lump of Gondwana upsurged from the pre-Pacific with all its antipodean oddities intact, and now returned to the use of folk like me. One found on the bush tracks around where we live young travelers from Japan or Germany or Brazil or Spain. When

I was a child, Australian beauty spots like this were not frequented by the people of the world, only by one's aunts and relatives. Sydney in the old days was a secret only we possessed. Now it is, delightfully, the world's.

When I set out for a walk on the day of Dr. Gleason's pronouncement, I was still in an equable condition, still a citizen of the world, likely to point out an echidna to a foreigner who saw its spines and thought it a porcupine instead of being one of two survivors from an ancient megacontinent. A mammal that nonetheless lays its eggs duck-style to produce its young, whom it then suckles. I loved to encounter this sturdy, industrious long-snouted and spiny creature. A being from before nature clearly worked out who should do what, and consistent rules for warm-blooded beings.

This oddly beautiful landscape still felt like home to me, and the pre-Flood bushes named banksias held the same charms as yesterday. I think if Monet had ever met the banksia he wouldn't have wasted time on pallid irises. Banks was the first European we know to have encountered this splendid plant and its big flowering cone. He must have thought, when he saw it on the shores of Botany Bay down where the airport is now, that he had hit the naturalist jackpot. Here was a shrub which grew serrated leaves and the most exquisite golden upright stems of filaments, providing a fountain of nectar for birds and bees, a candle on the altar of the life machine. The cones shone in that robust winter afternoon sun, as they did in light, and so did the glossy side of the leaves.

Stopping for a while, I took out my mobile and looked up case histories of esophageal cancer. I still felt I was doing research for a relative rather than myself. Some kindly chemistry prevented me from feeling doomed in my bones and my waters.

None of the cancer blogs made for happy reading. Most of them had not been written by the sufferers, but by those who observed a harsh decline in father or spouse. I learned that by the time you noticed the symptoms — the digestive problems, the pain, the heartburn, the vomiting of blood, the episodes of choking, the exhaustion, and the loss of weight — your adenocarcinomas, the kind of tumors that grow in the lining of the esophagus, had probably already invaded lymph nodes and made strategic claims on other organs. In these accounts, gross discomfort turned quickly to appalling pain. There were tales of throw-of-the-dice chemotherapy and radiation, and of operations to remove the esophagus and form a new ersatz one from stomach tissue, leading to the chance of a permanent state of fragility and ill health.

There will be a time, I thought, dizzied, *when in the universe of atoms I too will have been gone for forty-two thousand years. And as the nuns of my childhood would have said, "Eternity will have just begun."*

At the time of the diagnosis I wanted to tell my friend Peter Jorgensen, who was more ancient than me. Eighty-six years of age and his Scandinavian hair a firm thatch still on his head. He could have passed for the champion of antique bodies. In the gentlest and least hubristic way, Jorgensen was somewhere between a seer, a remaining living brother, a Dutch uncle, and a man who seemed, like Learned Man, to gaze calmly on the limitless sea of death. And though I was not gripped by fear, that still seemed a nifty trick and I wanted to be near it.

The relationship between these descendants of two ancient people — Learned and Jorgensen — was fraught; the discovery, like the discovery of our own clan at birth, was a blessing and a curse, but in any case inescapable. Jorgensen and I had spent so long fussing together over remains rendered holy by passage of time, by the effort their people had put into their burial, and by our quest to convince politicians to have Learned Man's remains brought back to his country. And because there was such composure in those ancient bones, I had looked at them and thought, *Oh death, where is thy sting?* Maybe that was the sort of message I wanted reiterated by Jorgensen.

"Are you busy, Peter?" I asked when I got through. I didn't know if I would actually tell him my news of the day.

"Not hugely. I'm filling in teaching grad students for a friend. They're so . . . *young*. So blatantly young. These blokes and damsels!"

"Yes," I agreed. " 'Blatant' is the word."

"I'm going to Canberra to talk about Learned to a new crop of Heritage and Environment people," he said.

Sturdy lad, I thought. Eighty-six years of age, but a boy from the bush — one of those three-mile-walk-to-school kids. And still, at his age, well and truly up to a schlep to Canberra. "I'll take my wife," he assured me. I believed she was a little younger than him, a sylph of seventy-eight.

I had come to love this man, for whom the effect of weather on ancient lake sedi-

62

ments had a poetic and humane resonance. He was still active in the International Union of Quaternary Research. But in a parallel world he might well have won the Nobel Prize for Literature. "I sing the Pleistocene Époque" could have been one of his songs. "The cold nights of 41,000 BP, and those who woke that morning, before the months had our names, / And cried, 'The world is old. We must repair it with a song.' " That's the sort of thing he would have written.

"Are you well, Shelby?" he asked as if he might suspect I was not.

I took in the luscious sky above the spider bushes and *Banksia serrata* that lay in my path. "Yes," I lied, though was it a lie when I felt so alive? "How about you?"

"My doctor's told me to give up white wine," he said. "It pains me that we've been writing to ministers, state and federal, for decades to no avail, Shelby. I sometimes fear you and I will be buried before Learned Man goes home."

That chilled me a second.

He told me again, "They're insisting I give up wine."

"I think my highly technical second opinion on that, Peter, is to tell them to *get fucked!*" I replied, though I could not deny

63

that boozing had made my mucosa prone to what had now befallen it. I remembered my ninety-two-year-old father's response to doctors who were advising wariness and new habits of care. "How old and bored do you bloody well want me to be?" he challenged one physician. Yet at the same time he knew ninety-two years wasn't enough. A breath.

There was a chuckle over the phone. "I like your second opinion," he said.

"I'm going to write to the prime minister again," I told Peter, like a man with decades at his disposal. "I'll let you know what happens."

It was clear that Learned Man, from his repository shelf in Canberra, had reached out to me and become something I wanted to discuss on this significant day, the beginning of the great passage I knew I was on. Well, he was a Time Lord who had consumed millennia, and still lay tranquil and with dignity, his hands on his thighs. Like the poet Shelley, he was not only half in love with easeful death, but had eaten its grim provender three times a day for tens of millennia, and was still undefeated. Maybe the dream of seeing Learned Man return to his home and reassume his country would make the prospect of death more tolerable for me and somehow dent the thoroughness of what it did to us. The gagging, the starvation, the vomiting, and the pain recounted in the online confessions of the sufferers' relatives meant that when it came to the day of departing, there would be no such thing as "easeful death," or merely denting death's surface or lying tranquilly thereafter.

I said a routine goodbye to Jorgensen.

The sea or the vast southwards-running harbor of Sydney were never far away anywhere on this walk. In fact, the ground I walked on was elevated sea bottom, sand that had once renounced the sea and risen under pressure to become headland. I went home through a hanging swamp, a sea-pond elevated above the sea and squawling with frogs. Amongst its winter-moist grasses I heard them warn each other of my approach. And then fall silent. The bushes and grass trees ran away up a rise I needed to climb to get home.

I jogged up it.

The End of the Wrestling

As a crowd assembles for the feasting that is to come, I cannot hope to find out from Baldy what his gaze meant. And when the councillor calls an end to the wrestling, Redder lopes towards our clan and I greet him shoulder to shoulder. Young people and children are still milling around the wrestlers.

"You did some mighty work," I tell Redder, though half my mind is still on Baldy.

"I did some work," Redder agrees with an askew smile, and as if it has just occurred to him that he did. His eyes, in the size of his pupils, still carry signs of the purpleberry plant that, mixed with ash of the wattle tree, enlarges strength and endurance. Though young, he was allowed to chew it during the wrestling. He is still full of its effect, and for a tired man has much purpose, for purple gum makes it easy to see purpose in every direction.

As a child Redder was always much taken by what befell my Son Unnameable, though he seems to be less weighed by that horrid event these days. I always had the sense that his plain conversation had a secret space in it, as if he had something to say about his kinsman's death that would give me the power to see it in a new way but he did not have the means to frame it. His smile slews into a grin that says something simple now, "The earth's restored and now I can get up to some fun." Tonight, girls might contest for him.

The three-quarter moon is on the Morningside of the night sky. Girly and I lie entwined in the cold. We are awake to each other in a way, but we are not awake to the world. Tiny icicles have grown on the hairs of the fur skins we are covered by. Indeed, waking now and then, I brush my hand across the surface of our skins and am somehow delighted to find that they are frozen upright, and yet we, close and tangled beneath the furs, are safe from the cold kiss of the air around.

Such a point of the night is time for gratitude to those who gave us all we have, and this sharp impulse to be thankful is more common to me now than when I was young. It is what the old do before they leave. They . . . we . . . praise. Girly, my blood-warm wife, snuffles. She snuffles, indeed, in a way that foretells her appetite for the day to come, her impatience with the state of repose that has overcome her after a day of feasting on the great bounder and accompanying treats. She is already preparing herself, without knowing it, to speak. I know her nature. She is preparing to sing in the day, to spread her body from its raw core at dawn and yell with satisfaction. How I love her I cannot say, but the idea of her causes laughter to rise in me, and what there is of sap to rise too. I first saw her when she was a girl, and with her stringent aunts beside her and rejoicing in her, by the fire of the Small Lightning clan. I saw her dance after she had first bled and she looked at Baldy. She is impudent by nature, and I have always welcomed a measure of insolence in women. Such women have the sureness to give themselves to their husband and their children, they have no reserve.

And the whole of a woman, like the whole of the earth, is such as one could sing of it for lifetime upon lifetime. To know other women used to be passing recreation with me. But now the song between Girly and me seems to overflow all measure.

Could it be said that the half of my mind that does not acclaim our wholeness belongs to the matter of death? It is not true that I am in continuous awareness of myself going away, being trimmed down to the ghost and becoming accustomed with being a spirit. Death presents to me tonight in the duty I have to punish Clawback's violations, that terrible rite that is necessary to maintain the world. Each man, emerging from his mother, inherits the world as a gift and a burden, and I am of an age to judge the exact weight of the burden. So, as I am more mindful of joy than ever, I am also mindful of duties, and the shallow laughter has been replaced by a longer and abiding laughter that is in me, but also larger than me. Laughter is a mother, laughter is the air. The sky is made for receiving laughter. And I have always been pleased to be alive in the way I am alive — in these latter days. I am appeased by the idea that I will be sung to death by someone, neighbor or hero, in love and in resentment. Someone will sing me, someone will lethally invoke my name. For all one has friends, it is the flea of malice that ends up finishing us. But singing and laughing as we wait — that is what I relish. I have never sung better, though the songs are sometimes silent. My life is burning up in a flame of praise.

Older men have told me things work this way. The night overflows with their gratitude for day. The heavens are crowded with it and praise is the track, the thread, that connects them into the great heroic lights of the sky.

And in the second half of that night, I am unexpectedly on a track to the heavens.

So, back to earth on that night. No sooner had I felt the icy spikes of fur within which Girly and I lay wrapped than I felt the familiar and not to be mistaken wrench of my soul taking me away, and my spirit slid up the tendrils of the night. It has happened thus a number of times, and is a tendency for which I was chosen. Some men have fits on the earth, and fall to the dirt and writhe in daylight with everyone to see them, perhaps betraying that they are in the power of a sorcerer from another clan or of a Power beyond that struck them but did not remove them into the sky. But my skyward tendency has nothing to do with malicious intentions exercised by some man of high degree, has nothing to do with anyone who might have got hold of a belonging of mine or something cast off, like my waste, and sung harm and fits into it. No, I know as I ascend that this is an utter gift from you, the Hero, meant for me, that it has to do with my dislocated toe, the mark an important visitor put on me, the glory and the onus. But in our furs, I lie dead in Girly's grasp as the Gray Bounder Man calls the living me to the sky.

In heaven I see you, moving amongst stars as a person might amongst trees. I see you the Hero, Gray Bounder Man. It is as if my soul has been up there with you some time and I have just joined it. I have been walking like your brother amongst great lights while the husk of me slept on the Lake shore. Here amongst the thickets of great blaze and dazzle. Here it was in the past, amidst the shining, that I met our Son Unnameable before his birth. He sat in a bowl of curdled light, smiling at me but demanding an exit to the world of lake and heath. That time, returning to earth, I imbued Girly with him and with a great roar of joy planted him there in her kindly belly. I did not know I bred him as meat for the slicer, the great snarler of a beast with its cutting teeth and slicing thumbs.

My first boy, not my Son Unnameable, was killed by a curse that overtook his mouth

71

when he was still young and swelled his head to a dreadful size. Afterwards, our clan marched forth with spears to face the Parrot clan, and we contested them on the ground of war until a necessary measure of blood had been shed. There is a young man of the Parrot clan who still does not walk evenly, and his gait is a tribute to my son, whose spirit I sometimes see in silvery trees on the Nightside of the Lake and whose ghost name is Son Unnameable.

And so you are waiting, Hero, on the edge of a thicket of lustrous trees, wearing the wise smile. I don't know what you are about to tell me. From the history of other men, I know how heavy your pronouncements can sometimes be. Because you see the way of things but get no joy from it, there is certainly joy in you at the notion of things going well for your children. If it were not so, there would be no sense to things. In being born of one's mother, or in the effort, once born, to address the world. And then, in the dying. "Father," I tell you.

You put your arm around my shoulders — or the shoulders of my spirit, which imitate my body precisely without any pain in any joint. You speak to me in the echo and image and language of my body, that is. There's kindness in that.

"Look," you tell me. "Look, my boy. Look." You guide me forward beneath the boughs of stars. I inhale the aromatic radiance of heaven's trees.

"What do you want me to see?" I ask.

"I want you to look sharply on the earth. You should look hard. You have the eyes for it."

We see a woman coming towards us. She flits amongst the forest. Clearly, she is the Hero's wife. She is the lustrous Parrot Woman. She is gravid, round-bellied with the souls of the unborn, and she staggers awhile with her burden and resumes that birdlike, darting, skimming look and sees me with her own acute eyes. I can tell the worried appeal in her eyes is for me and not for her husband. It seems it is in my hands to help her. I sit. I feel a languor come upon me. Then she raises before me her own transparent womb as if it were a gourd, and I could see dream children enclosed. No sooner has she raised it and before I can properly contemplate it, it bursts before her parrot face, and blood obscures it from further sight just as I think I am being given time to study it and weigh its distress. No time is given, though. It is often this way. No time to arrive at wisdom. A number of dead dream children lie in an entangled, sallow, glossy lump amidst spiky grass at my feet.

"You see," says the ancestor Hero with his eternal patience.

"I see," I admit.

I still need time and advice about what it means. But before I have either I am hurled out of the sky and land again in Girly's arms, yelping with the shock. "Stop dreaming!" she tells me. She knows my tendencies. And then she makes a tapping sound and opens her body to comfort me, and though I caress her and avail myself, as is the simple wisdom of things, I cannot forget or wipe away the memory of my journey in the sky and the livid reproach of the dead dream children.

Yet I begin to think I have the answer to the manifestation of Parrot Woman and the burst womb. It was very clearly a warning. Something had *entered.* Yet the only entrance had been that of Baldy and his party. Evil sometimes entered by plain means. But then, of course, I remembered illicit Clawback, the friend of children and the blood violator!

In the morning, after eating warmed grain Girly made, I go to the old man named Clay. He has just acquired a new wife from

74

the same Parrot clan as the Hero's, the ancestor's, own spirit wife. Clay nods and signals me with his air of irritation to sit by his side in front of his firestones. Long ago he took me on a journey and harangued me the whole way, and in part he was meant to rail at me and in part he was made that way. There were also matters of pride involved. But if I resented him then, I no longer do.

I sit with him awhile and let the cleansing smoke from morning fires fill my nostrils, and then I say, "I think you should hold a meeting in the law place. I have had a worrying conversation with our Hero and the Wife."

"And so?" Clay asks, as if the news lies light on him.

"Well, there is disorder. The thing was clear. I think that the punishers may need to be sent out." I say it as if I were not one of the punishers myself. As if I do not have the deformed foot for that task.

Clay knows at once I am not talking from bile, as much as he might like to pretend I am. "Yes, all right," he tells me softly. "I'll gather the fellows." His new young wife is busy at the fire. Her youngest child is pestering her as she cooks Clay's morning grain. That infant reminds me of Clay. *Wayward child, wayward father,* I think.

75

In the waiting time, before the meeting is called, I am reminded by the taste of my meeting with Clay of the journey he and I had made when I was young. It was not to be forgotten easily, a cold journey across shallow, frozen marshes and amongst clans painted up for bitter killings. For the moment, though, we have our own bitterness to reflect on.

The men's law ground is away through the brush, a testing walk for Clay and Sandy and the other men of their age. It is in a different corner of the earth from the place of the old women, which no man would want to enter. Thus Girly, though not quite old, has places and mysteries which are unknown to me, unknown in fact to any man. Her globe of secrets can never be owned by me, but at the height of couplings I reach for it despite myself, as she too reaches in her turn for the secret me I do not myself know.

You will see the forbidding stones as you approach the law ground through the green brush. You will see by these marks that it is forbidden ground except for men of high degree. There are august stones also laid there by the passage of ancestors, and beyond and amongst them, the law ground itself.

It has taken time to get the word out and

to reach the men's law ground, and by that time the sun is high. We are all fully armed with long spears, the kind that are used for ceremonies of blood reconciliation, and for the larger creatures such as the slicer and the huge-hearted, big-bodied dome nose. We have brought shields too, and have slung throwers, wedged prong outwards, against our shoulders and, in front, the returning sticks wedged in the cords around each of our chests.

These councillors, men from the whole people, start a fire, light branches, and stalk around sanctifying the place with smoke while chanting a prayer. All daemons of misrule, all spirits of malice are to depart the place, leaving behind unclouded spirits of wisdom and order. It is an old chant, of course, to which we all respond "Let it be so!" after every enunciation of the plea. We all stand there, four and four, and four and three of us, all we councillors. My old rival and friend Baldy, home just yesterday, is there. "Let it be so!" he sings.

Soon the ground is cleansed by the smoke sufficiently to allow us to sit in council. The old councillor of the Small Lightning clan, Croaker, is too much under a baleful wasting to allow him to come here. He is a loss of wisdom, and so to begin with, we murmur away to the All-Father to smile on our deliberations, and then we cease to do so one by one, the oldest men first, the younger ones like me and the returned Baldy carrying on the plea, acknowledging we need it more, being further from embarking on our last journey, as far as we know.

All this became a matter for Council to sit about, since I did not wish to act on my solitary interpretation. The meeting was called and at last we were all seated, and Clay began to explain that I had beseeched him most earnestly for the meeting following a revelation on my sky journey. And then he asked me to speak.

"My friends," I said, "while traveling in the star forests I was met by Gray Bounder Man and his face was stricken. Parrot Woman came from the trees. Let me say, I have only glimpsed her once before. Whenever I see Gray Bounder Man he is sure, he is serene. But now he looked harried or saddened, like a normal man, and his wife walked towards me with a terrible grieving in her face, and she held up her womb. It was the womb of all women, I was sure, not just of one clan but of all peoples. To be brief, it burst in front of me, and its children washed up dead at my feet. It was a warning, I knew that. It was a warning about

78

disorder . . ."

Clay made a throaty sound. Grieving and authoritative. "It was a warning all right," he declared. "It was a warning we must not be slow about rooting out disorder."

Two of the councillors repeated that as if to themselves. "Rooting out all disorder."

"It seems you have been slow," Baldy said, almost as a suggestion. "From what I saw on my return."

He looked at me then, assessing me and not condemning. I could see he was not at peace, had not been since his return yesterday. But he knew it was my duty to name the name and be done with it.

I said, "Our brother Clawback has violated that woman, the one from the Earless Lizard clan. Her blood's forbidden to him. He's a stupid creature. And I believe Parrot Woman told me last night that in poisoning that womb, he is poisoning all wombs."

There was terrible and utter agreement around the ground we sat on, and I could not help but grieve for Clawback.

Clay said to me calmly, "You had better get started on all that. It is the narrow bone for him. There's no other cure."

The other councillors agreed.

"You and Stark," said Clay. And then asked it as a question. "Shade and Stark?"

There were sounds of immediate sad assent from those lovely old men.

Clay said, with an edge of doubt in his voice, "You are sure it is all as simple as that idiot Clawback. Were Gray Bounder Man and his Wife talking of something worse? You mentioned many children bursting from the womb . . ."

An old councillor called Bandy said, "No, he's the criminal of the moment, he's the one on the ancestors' minds. What a fool! But a violator, fool or not!" And he talked on further, in tones you would expect from a lawman.

Stark was there, on the far side of the ground from me. A very slim man my age. He did not speak. Like me, he had the dislocated toe of our caste. It was not for either of us to speak.

Clay cast his eyes in my direction. I could see he was tired and touchy. "You should go at once," he said, and one of the councillors groaned agreement. "Then we can soon wake to a clean day."

And then after all the grunts of the older councillors as they hauled themselves upwards to make their way home, Baldy stopped by me. "I must speak to you soon. I must do so . . ."

"Yes," I said.

He paused, as if thinking he should do so now, but he was mumbling with exhaustion. He had put a hand, and a great deal of his weight with it, on my shoulder. "Take your sleep," I advised him. "You're right. I do not sleep enough." He grinned crookedly, made a decision, and walked away under a high sun.

SURFING WITH JACK

I am going to have a meeting with the professor of gastroenterology whose name is Colin Brown. He's the top bloke, says Dr. Gleason. And I'm seeing him in two days. He's not going to let my wayward cells proliferate by seeing me later than that.

I remain in a calm mood and plan a letter to the prime minister about Learned. I'm not expecting a great prognosis because, in my generation's imagination, Jack the Dancer has always been his own prognosis. Death.

In the meantime, life does not await the diagnosis. You discover at such a time that the entire world operates on the assumption that no one is ever dying. It *must* do so. When I complain to Cath about the unstinting tide of online correspondence, she says, "Send all your emails to me." And I know she will do them more competently than I, since for some reason Cath knows how to say the sort of no that people actually accept. No because everything is changed and bets are off and any undertaking of being delighted to launch Cranbrook School's film club's festival of student documentaries is now madness.

I go to my computer and send Cath a number of my invitations to deal with. I open a file ready to write a letter to the prime minister. He's not such a bad fellow — by vision an old-fashioned conservative who believes in keeping the punters prosperous by giving them a stake in the equation. But he's a captive of right-wing brutes in his party who still believe in serving the market Moloch as an almost theological duty. But give him this — or so I hoped — give him a vision, give him Monsieur Learned and the chance for him to take his own vision to the three sets of elders . . . Well, he might yet make a leader of himself. For no one in his position, no one with a revenue stream, has ever taken a passionate vision of his *own* to the elders.

I get as far as putting the prime minister's address in the letter. After that I sit and my hands begin ridiculously to tremble. That's never happened before. I want to see Cath as acutely as I want to take my next breath. When I leave my office again, I see, over a few intervening rooftops, the harbor beyond the glass. Then, in front of me, Cath sits at her own little desk in the living room, and her unconscious generosity being an aphrodisiac, I'm moved by more desire than I have recently had the chance to experience, and the images of black lingerie and unloosed breasts come to mind and do not leave the supposed sexual Sahara of my groin unaffected.

Before Cath bends to answering the first email she raises a hand and runs it down my forearm, cosseting me. It is much easier now than when we were thirty. Then we had all the juice but poor knowledge of the other. Grievances as well as hungers inhabited the embrace. Alas, alas! Grievances which by eighty have either driven you apart, or killed you, or been absorbed. How often the breathless ardor of those days, which seemed based on a more gravid and cosmic need as vast as the sky and not unconnected to the earth's furious core, was, in the way of lovers, interspersed with a gasping rancor.

I can tell Cath is herself a bit awed today. Even though the omens of this have been there in the vanishing years and her husband's follies, I don't think she's prepared to be a widow. We have failed to believe in

84

the weight of our own years, and to prepare ourselves.

Cath has always had such competence. She was a very fine and exacting editor. How often did she drop the kids at school before coming to the sound suite I rented in North Sydney to induce order in the too-much I had exuberantly filmed. She also did the production schedules of a number of my films, which I shot to an extent by making things up on the spot, seeing what came along, and taking a stab at how much money was left after I got the footage I wanted. I chose to do things in that way — it was my *thing*. Extempore. People thought my method-less method was remarkable and even wrote learned articles on it, elevating what might have been a character flaw into a theory. And I could let myself go because in the editing Cath always took the care I had no temperamental gift for. Mind you, I always had a clear sense of narrative, both before I started and, in a more nuanced way, when we'd finished, and I was able to convey the narrative, and Cath was typically loyal to my intention.

Yet even when she was a visitor to a shooting location, I felt she had a stronger sense of the practicalities that were in play than I ever had. I had, after all, shamelessly left the details of our life to her. As I got older, I became cavalier about waking up and thinking about who I had to see that day. She had it all written down. She was, fairly or not and without apparent rancor, my diary.

But then . . . I know many men who say their wives were happy to serve the flame, the career. I sometimes tell Cath I am guilty of repressing her career, or subsuming it into mine. She tells me not to be ridiculous, but she says it with a particular flavor, not as if it isn't true, but as if it's a proposition she does not choose to examine — the dear old Pandora's box itself. I have certainly given our daughters lectures on the matter of subservience, woman to man. But I am not utterly sure I do so from a position of innocence.

People told me I was a good grandfather, in part for being the joker. But I am aware my record with my daughters is, in my memory, more ambiguous. I was already in my thirties when our first daughter, Colley, was born. In our house in West Ryde, with its big backyard, Cath and I envisaged a playground for our children, where each of their movements would be intimately studied by us, the enchanted witnesses in the garden. In those days the father was considered superfluous in the whole drama and pain of the birth. He was told to compose himself in the waiting room and read old *Time* magazines. But because Cath knew some of the nurses, I was allowed in to see Colley the instant after she was born. Improbably small, those few seconds after birth, the creases of the struggle on her forehead, the smears of her passage on her body, Colley was already a mixture of wariness and energy, both of which qualities would mark her in the future. For a number of seconds, she would not begin to breathe. She had a placidity, an air of making a considered Libran decision — it was, after all, a morning in October. She was deciding whether to retreat back under the blanket of time, or to go forward onto its surface. She seemed to know either had its pitfalls.

In those seconds she did not seem blue or short of breath. A doctor approached with a hypodermic as big as her leg and injected something, and she decided, with apparent good humor, that now she would make her first claim on life. And so it came. The first cry of an estimable woman.

A year later, the vigorous, alert Gracie was born, and I saw her after a prompt passage into the world she seemed unbewildered by. That is, more like her mother. Like Colley, Gracie chose early morning to be born — both were daughters of the dawn.

Oh, what a work is man/woman. For example, the child grows in its solitary cell — some poem I read, yes, Judith Wright, called the child in the womb the eyeless laborer in the dark. Its sole discourse with its mother's heart, which imbues it with rhythm. And then, it emerges as a social animal, ready for a meeting, a party, a seminar. Particularly Gracie, born with opinions writhing in her.

In any case, just as our deaths are each, at the ultimate moment, the only death in the universe, so every birth is the first. The father of Mitochondrial Eve's first child could not have looked on an infant fresh from the blue with the wonder I brought to both occasions.

With Colley, a wariness Gracie would not exhibit. Even at two and three years of age. Elizabeth and the Queen of Scots; Bette Davis and Joan Crawford. And like my quiet mother and vocal father, it may be that the bite of the quieter one, Colley, was subtler and more enduring than that of the tumultuous, daring Gracie.

But it's not the damage they did each

other that worried me.

There was at one stage a great conflict between Cath and me over the term "brusque"!

Because of the delicacy with which my mother conducted the life of the Apple household, knowing that my father was capable of great verbal passion, we Apples were a polite family — sometimes to the point Cath would come to condemn as emotional dishonesty. By contrast, Cath's family, the McKelveys, insulted each other routinely and robustly and in ways I sometimes thought extreme and harsh and wounding. When Cath began verbally disciplining our daughters, there was conflict between us. I felt I had the same sensibility as Colley — and partway that of Gracie too. But when Cath was tired and furious at mayhem in the kitchen or living area, she could turn ferocious and bark instructions in the McKelvey manner. If I was home and, of course, playing at being the jolly giant, I would see the girls recoil, would see their eyes bruise. And when I raised the matter one day, using that silly and inadequate term "brusque," Cath chose to see in the nicety of the adjective evidence of the Apple family's fear of conflict and their mealymouthed, neurotic politeness.

I see now that we were both right — the McKelveys too reckless with abuse, the Apples crafting everything they said to avoid the risk of affront. At this distance of time it is obvious that Cath did moderate her "brusqueness," just as I moderated my fear of terror. And yet there was another aspect of the Apple family's ethos that wasn't as tame as fear of brusqueness, and in some ways was more ruthless than the McKelveys' brand of easy-come, easy-go fury. For we did not forgive. My father taught me that forgiveness should be denied unto the third and fourth generation. And in my middle years, still not utterly reconciled and when tempted by the urbanity of this or that woman, I remembered, or chose to remember, my daughters' bruised eyes.

Both Colley and Gracie claim to have forgotten it all: my erratic rages, Cath's, our arguments.

My reluctance to forgive is so far gone now, but perhaps I hung on to it, willfully, a stored-up reason for ultimate betrayal.

I sometimes ask myself whether, had Cath not yelled at our kids with passion, she could have displayed her profound enthusiasm for beating Jack the Dancer, and his ambitions for my organs. People are, after all, a package. And I am now more puzzled by the package I am than by Cath.

Now, together, we went to see the gastroenterologist, Professor Brown. He took me by surprise, as many young doctors do now. Instead of a professional gravitas — the irreproachable carapace of a well-cut neutral suit and a tie with some medical association's or college's restrained logo — Professor Brown was tie-less, ageless, healthy, and at peace with earth and sea.

There was something in me that resisted these younger, unpretentious specialists. Did I want a sun-addled democrat with a shock of rich hair negotiating with Jack the Dancer on my behalf? Or did I want a God-the-Father imitator of august mien, whose severity and inscrutability were so absolute that you felt you were in the hands of heaven? In my childhood, great-aunts and -uncles died without doubt, were buried without second guesses or grievances, under old doctors — the young ones were in the army for World War II — whose capacity for impersonating God was probably much better than their surgery.

In any case, I was to have the surfer kid. We shook hands and all sat down, whereupon Dr. Brown became earnest in that new sort of way, with a far more egalitarian manner than that of the old doctors. He had the report and X-rays from my recent endoscopy to go on, along with an MRI I'd undergone the day after Dr. Gleason had broken the news. He explained the terms he flung about, and encouraged me not to leave the office with any unanswered questions.

This young man, distinguished but humble about it, but without any demigod ambitions, explained that there had been until recently only simple and grievous options or outcomes for people in my situation. If the cancer had metastasized, or spread, the esophagus would need to be cut out. If the whole of the esophagus needed to be excised, the stomach was then connected up directly with the throat. The victim's stomach, as I understood it, *my* stomach, was then in my chest for the rest of my life.

As well as taking out all or part of the esophagus, the surgeon during a total or partial esophagostomy took out any lymph nodes that might contain cancer cells. Apparently, unknown to me, lymph nodes encircled the esophagus. They too had been doing their humble dark work since my infancy. Now I heard about them as a line of vulnerability, the support trenches that the enemy wanted to overrun. For they would tell whether I needed therapy before the slap-up surgery.

"And scars?" asked Cath, who did not want to see me bear heavy ones.

"I used to go the transhiatal route." Brown smiled as if he were discussing methods to ride a surfboard, regular or goofy foot. "But even now, the cutting is substantial. I won't pretend otherwise."

Cath, nodding, began to weep. I reached for her and hugged and hushed her. It was so poignant she did not want me dead or marred that I struggled myself with tears.

"But that may not be necessary," he hurried to say, because these days there *was* a third option, which started out with a smaller procedure involving mirrors and lasers, and a surgeon who could remove the carcinoma from the mucosa itself and leave the structure intact and even cauterize the Barrett's syndrome with radio frequency and tell us if it had spread. That was step one, he told us. I mentioned I had read on the Internet that if the tumors were in Stage III or IV the prognosis was pretty dismal.

"No need to order the flowers yet," he assured me. "It's good that you can eat normally and don't have many swallowing problems yet. So let's see what we find."

He wanted to send me to a colleague who

could assess the state of my cancer with her esophageal cameras — she too would do it within a couple of days as a matter of urgency. She had a way with those new cameras, he said, and with her radio-frequency wand. I would need a general anesthetic. This, he said, could well be the answer for me. Though no one knew.

Then he said in a "hey-dude-it's-only-death!" manner, "You won an Academy Award, Mr. Apple?"

"A long time ago," I replied with the apparent indifference even a documentary maker should show towards a lottery like the Oscars. "A feature documentary on Vietnam."

Cath said nothing. She knew how uneasy I was over the death of Andy.

"Maybe you could bring it in one day," he said. For no one had a doctorate when it came to the movies. Everyone was a peasant. "The Oscar, I mean. Perhaps you could let me fondle it awhile."

It was as if death was not the fourth member of our discourse. But of course, I didn't quite believe that myself. That was another theory of mine: that there was a chemical resistance to belief of death in us; that even in the midst of cataclysm we are convinced of survival; or at least that even in ghastly terror our money and hope is on it.

If we were truly convinced of death, we would do nothing in life except intersperse our despair at the ferocious weight of time we would serve in our death with brief spasms of sex and alcohol. And yet, though we had not here a lasting city, we insisted on paving its streets as if we did, and we were (hence the kindness of Cath's work) outraged when even the dying failed to answer their emails promptly.

I was pleased that for now, though the world was old and the universe without heart, in that clean surgery office amongst glossy bas-relief images of the esophagus, Cath was seduced into believing that death held no mortgage on her own man.

When we returned to chatting about my tumors, it was as if they were some fungus attacking the sclerophyll forests.

At home again — I insisted on driving — I believed it time to write to the prime minister with new energy and persuasiveness.

The HON Roger Milland
Prime Minister
Australia

Re: The Learned Lakes World Heritage Site: The Chance for a Great World Heritage Site.

Dear Prime Minister,
Learned Man, a set of bones waiting on a bench at an Australian Museum depository for disposal and return to his native Learned Lakes' area north of Balranald, is 42,000 years old. Learned Woman is a set of remains nearly as old. They represent the two oldest human ritual burials we possess evidence of on earth. These enormously ancient members of the species *Homo sapiens,* our species, were also members of a community which inhabited the lunette of Lake Learned between 60,000 years Before the Present Era . . .

I had written all this so many times, with so little effect, to so many politicians. The rhetorical flourishes and the pattern of sentences were all familiar. I had a feeling that in another time they might have an impact but that in the current political world, where the issue of the economy and worship of the market overrode all other issues, they did not compel, they did not cut ice.

Despite the day, I had failed to make a new, compelling language. I could not therefore create a revelation in my addressee, or evoke a new urgency. I saved the file.

THE SINNER UNNAMEABLE

Stark and I were left at the men's law ground. It was getting dark by now. I took a handful of dust to douse the fire.

"No," said Stark. "We need some light to find the shoes."

That brought it to me, the realness of the punishment we'd been ordered to inflict and could not avoid inflicting.

"Stupid prick," I said wistfully. "Clawback. Aren't there women enough?"

"Yes, there are women enough," said Stark, already searching for resolve, since he was the one who had to actually kill Clawback. I was to hold the violator, like an enemy and a brother, while the duty was done.

"Let's fetch the shoes," I told him. I remembered where they were kept on the low ridge behind, amongst the cone bushes glittering by the last light of the fire. There where the earless lizard had left her eggs before defying the All-Father, who turned them to stone.

Stark was the one who got there first, though. "You remember these," he asked me, according to the ritual. "How they give us flight?"

"I remember them," I said, giving the normal response.

The shoes were hidden there, in that nest of boulders, in the place I left them after our last task. I had dug them in deep in a crevice.

I joined Stark, and together we dug down to the fur-wrapped parcel and drew two pairs of shoes out. Stark unwrapped the skins and removed the equipment inside, which he arranged neatly before us. The strange shoes for him and me to contemplate. Because we were required to assess them. The bone canister was there too, the shinbone of a long-gone, ancient councillor. It served as a cask, and when I raised and shook it, two long slivers of red bounder shinbone fell out of the shin-cask onto the unwrapped skin. Each had hair attached to the end, the hair of a heroic man, with a gum the blood trees exuded.

But first it was my duty to raise the two needles of bone from the shin-cask as we sang death into them. Stark then went a little aside, shitted, and drew both thin bones through his fresh shit.

"That's necessary only if a death from ailing is intended. Whereas we will lower a sliver from his neck into his heart," I argued, a little annoyed at the delay.

"Well," Stark said. "It can't do much harm to make sure of things."

The two slivers of bounder bone, nearly as long as my forearm, stank a little now as, reassuring the Gray Bounder Man and the All-Father, I reinserted them in the old shin-cask and wrapped it again in the dusty furs.

"The shoes," Stark insisted again.

I contemplated the two pairs of shoes, revealing them fully with a few more unfoldings of the furs. Feathers from the great walking bird bound solid by the blood and hair and incantations of initiated men. We did not know how they were made — it was a secret of a certain family. We did not understand the mystery of how they traversed the earth for men tasked as we were. Though made of such flimsy matter — feathers, hair, and blood — they never fell apart. Between the two pairs stood a large wad of thornbud pulp, thickened with ash to make it chewable. In the shoes and with the help of the thornbud pulp, we could fly.

We could *really* fly. Speed and enhanced wisdom — that's what lay before Stark and me.

Each of us carried a pair of shoes, wrapped in hide, on the belt we wore at chest level. I carried the wrapped shinbone in my hands, but Stark had the thornbud pulp in a netting pouch, as was his right as the chief actor.

It was a cold afternoon by the time we reassumed our furs and went off down into the flatland again, which the early moon came up on soon, and silvered. We waited, but not long enough for Clawback to visit the girl from the Earless Lizard clan. We put on our shoes. Then we skirted the town quickly, leaving no, or else only unreadable, footprints on the ground, flying above the crusty earth and amongst the cone trees without being sighted or greeted or desired. Our song called for everyone except the miscreant to be set towards a profound slumber, to be absent in soul from our passage.

Only poor Clawback himself was the one to be roused, alerted, alarmed by our skirting the huts. We felt ourselves the echo of his urgency, and the haste of his taking to flight was like a shift of moonlight. He was away, we were now sure. He was governed by fear and there would be no unholy desire in him. He had running to do.

We loped as yet to let him get into country far from any witness. Our track was amongst blue bushes and under the tall branches of spearleaf trees. We skimmed the earth in our shoes of air, hair, blood, and feathers, our tracks unseeable by the inhabitants of earth. Seen only by the expectant Heroes.

When we were young, and due to become men, Stark and I had each been abandoned by our elders at different times, and for long periods, far away and without directions. In my case, they left me by a crooked tree in the firewood country. This was towards the Nightside. Until my induction into manhood we had never been there, nor was it noted or praised in any song we had heard, and so it was off the map of our childhoods. It was the land of nowhere, where brush was sparsely set in ground of black, moldy earth and yellow, icy clay. It was clearly land designed to be prized by no man. There was the stonewood tree and, spaced like the wraiths they were, two others of that kind, which said to us that they were the hard presences of an unyielding region. Here there were no women to find grain, no one else to make fire, no old man to sniff out the cavities of water or to point to the humpbacked movement of bounders on the horizon. The bushes were not the bushes of our accustomed tubers, the ones women dug up to grace our meat.

Nor, I could tell at once, were the spirits of this earth known to me. Once I was there, I could not remember having been brought. It seemed I had been stupefied with gum and spirited by my elders, my betters, the knowers of the earth and of my crass, untaught condition. As well, the light in that place seemed soiled, unfit for enterprise and endeavor and enlightenment and any access of wisdom. That light hung on my eyes heavily, like an ache, yet I was supposed to bestir myself and put myself in the way of whatever mysteries and challenges this place, this fallen earth, could present to me. Implanted in my mind too was that I would be here for a moon's phase or longer, until the old men chose to come back for me. And for all those days and nights I would not be permitted to return home, even if I knew the way, or to surrender myself up — my elders and betters expected me to be more robust of head and heart and soul than that. When they came back to rescue me, they expected to see new wisdom in me, and not a longing for the usual world in my eyes. They expected to see that I had grown stronger off this haunted and un-nourishing place.

I wore white pigment all the time, so that I was alert to ill will and ghosts and managed to look prohibitive. In terms of keeping myself alive, I lived two days off a sinewy and flavorless old lizard. I baked sour, thin tubers on the fire. I speared a lean bounder of the kind we would not bother with at the Lake country. It seemed apparent to me that the bounders sent their aged males into this country to die.

I spread smoke around my resting place at night so that I sat in what I hoped was a protected circle. But spirits with black souls harangued me all night, prattling to each other as I tried to sleep. They knew me well — I heard them recounting sentiments of mine that I kept secret from everyone else. They had the complete log of all my foolishness as a child, and they ran through it without relenting all night. I felt my body changing under their haranguing. I felt my own sinews stretch and creak. The voice of one spirit I got quite used to. Its voice was in the yellow sky but in my head as well, and it was not excluded by the smoking of my space around the old stonewood tree.

"Who put you here?" the voice would ask.

It was a man's voice, older than mine, though not as old as the initiators.

"It was the old men and they know what they're doing," I told it. But in all those comfortless days, I wondered if they did know.

"You were just born with a mucked-up foot, that's all. They made the wrong judgment on you. Now they're getting you ready for things you aren't fit for. You shouldn't be here. You're a lost child in this place."

"We'll see," I answered.

"It is a terrible thing to be judged as being ready for talents that are above anything you can manage," this voice told me. "You have been judged as being one thing, but you're another thing, a plainer thing. Do you want to fly? Do you want to curse the criminal and stop his breath with a poisoned bone? There is plain hunting, the ordinary duty of plain men who can dwell on the surface of the earth, and lie at night with their wives, and are never jerked up all at once amongst the stars. That's the proper life for man. That is certainly enough for you. You don't want to be here, with me chattering in your ear."

The thing is that this voice questioned me every hour of the day, leaving off only if I went to look for water and somewhat during my hunt and my shitting.

Once I felled a lush, plump hen with a throwing stick — good fortune on my part. It was a rare gift, and my companion voice said at that stage, "All right, I'll let you eat it. That's only fair."

With nightfall then, the voices and their hubbub increased, until I thought that I might become as mad as old Lightning, who was famed for never recovering his real mind from his own experience of being made a man. The ghost voices of the wasteland had followed him back into his life by the Lake. So I knew the ghost voice was lying. I would either come out of this wasteland as myself, or else as a broken image of myself. There were no pleasant, middle choices such as the ghost offered me.

But over bitter days I did grow thin and light-headed with sleeplessness from countering his arguments and those of other tempters.

Amongst these others, above all, was a woman of startling darkness of eye and gourd breasts who slouched beyond the little circle I had cleansed with smoke. She commented on my manliness, which was still healing after the cutting rites, and which could not be touched in case the most excruciating, bitter seed gushed out of it and poisoned the earth. Yet she was awfully languid, this woman, a terrible and desirable taunter. I could have raged on top of her like a whimpering child-man. I could have accepted the apportioned pain and the easy ecstasy. For all those nights upon nights I wanted her, and she spoke to me ceaselessly it seemed. Despite the distraction, I might fall asleep for a little time, but her voice would insinuate itself again before a tenth part of the night was gone. I would see her move temptingly beyond the reach of the failing fire, separating her thighs with her hands, leaning back into the night to allow me to see her sweet parts, though in her case I knew them to be the gateway to madness. Not that that seemed to matter much. I was willing to lose my mind and all its judgment, all the judgment the elders had perceived in me to this point, all the judgment I was meant to acquire.

"The old men who put you here — they lie between young legs tonight. Yet they magicked you here, to this cold place. They say they'll take you back, but why would they want you to be close to the young girls that are in their gift? Why would they want you near the ones that were betrothed to them before birth, that they give away like adornments? Why would they want you back when they require all the young women for their own warmth?"

And with that she stroked her inner thigh to let me know she was there and could be touched and had warmth and possessed, for a ghost, a terrible substance.

It would have been easy at noontide to reject her, and to disbelieve her version of things at night, if one had slept under furs in a comfortable habitation within the ambit of fire warmth. But without sleep, warmth, the conversation of living, daily creatures, without an earth of robust beasts, without men and women striding the line between the dunes and the Lake, and with a throbbing, healing man-plant agonizing for her and for its own sake between my thighs, it was easy to yield then, and give oneself up forever to those yellow claypans and this bitter, gorgeous ghost woman. Had I given her my seed, it would have spilt out of the sliced seam of my man-root and tainted the earth further as undue seed does. If I had entered her, I would have ended up forever in a middle place between the harshness of that punishing country and the wished-for fuller life of return to the people. I would not then know whether I was man or spirit, alive or dead. I would be caught howling in between clouds of a false heaven and the surface of an uninhabitable earth. That is, I would turn mad.

THE HARVEST OF EYES

In the early to mid-1960s, I acquired a belated university degree in modern history. My earlier youth, after high school, had been spent as an insurance clerk, earning money for rent and film stock, and hanging around the Sydney Film Society, where I showed my occasional weekend-made documentaries. In any case, not long after obtaining my degree, I set out for the Northern Territory with my slightly younger university friend, Andy, and his tall girlfriend, Denise, a handy stills photographer.

Andy and I were barely cameramen but thought of ourselves as documentary makers. We had been bowled over by the New Wave films. We had watched all the classic documentaries, but had been most taken with Dziga Vertov's *Man with a Movie Camera,* and that other great study of a day in the life of a city, Jean Rouch and Edgar Morin's *Chronicle of a Summer.* We were

110

trying to be Rouch and Morin and remain friends. Andy had an Arriflex 16 he had bought with an inheritance. I had a portable Ariel camera like the French filmmakers themselves. So Andy and I did a deal that we would make cinema verité together, shooting with our separate and distinctive cameras and styles. Roughly, he would shoot the broader and more authoritative footage, and I would shoot intimately and even let things wobble and blur, and then we'd edit it up, the best of both. It worked so well at first that we thought we were geniuses. And we promised each other we could make important documentaries in half the time and with twice the creativity of other film-makers.

We were looking for a significant story to film, and — other than Vietnam, the war we disapproved of, yet hoped to visit — one of the most significant of all for the urban young was a strike by Aboriginal stockmen. These stockmen had worked at a cattle station run by the huge Vestey Brothers conglomerate on the tussock grass of the vast floodplain of the infrequently flooded Victoria River. It was very remote country where, one day, Vincent Lingiari, a soft-spoken Aboriginal drover of the local Gurindji tribe or language group, had sat beneath a desert oak in his big hat and declared not only discontent over low and token wages, but that the country he sat on was his Gurindji people's land. The idea was so outrageous that it was even heard in the coastal cities.

Into that flat country southwest of Katherine we drove our ridiculously fragile van with not enough spare tires, not enough jerry cans of fuel or water — adequate only in our supply of hemp, of which Andy in particular was an aficionado. We traveled on the red-dirt Buntine Highway and the God of Idiots protected us from ourselves.

The Aboriginal people had walked away from the Vestey Brothers homestead to protest their disgraceful working conditions, and followed the fence line northwest to the Victoria River, which was dry at that season. In spacious country of desert oaks and natural pasture, they had set up a camp. It was both a protest and a claim.

There, stumbling in like downriver crocodile fodder, we found them. We filmed the nuggety leader, Lingiari, a restrained, silkenly spoken prophet. With him was well-known novelist and communist Frank Hardy, and he and Lingiari spoke intensely. But Lingiari owned his own soul.

Conservative folk would later say, "Those

city commos stirred 'em up," as if Lingiari lacked the wit to come to his own conclusions, or didn't know when his people had been treated like dogs.

Two well-equipped medical vans were there too, along with a youngish eye doctor. This man, who had an unscarred, part-combative, part-humorous face, would take up a powerful place in my life, but we took minimal notice of him at the time. He was named Ted Castwell. He was looking into the eyes of the Gurindji people with ophthalmoscopes and phoropters and tonometers — an exercise that only peripherally interested our cameras. Indeed, we did not understand fully what he was doing, or why. We were there for the politics, not for the scandal of Aboriginal desert blindness. Much later I would become aware that his care of eyes was as political as the Gurindji walkout itself.

"Giz a look at your eyes, luv," Castwell would say. Or "mate," if it was a male. This question he addressed, in the days I first heard it, to Aboriginals of a number of indigenous nations, and later it was a command or request he directed to Nepalese, South Africans, Palestinians, Ethiopians, Eritreans, Vietnamese, South Pacific Islanders, Indians, Pakistanis, Afghans. It was

113

normally followed by the cry, "Oh Jesus, that doesn't look too bloody good, does it?" Castwell would then pull down and up on the eyelids, lower and upper. He had an international reputation as an ophthalmologist, but he dressed, as a friend said, in about $5 worth of clothing — the sort of stuff you might wear on a construction site where a sewage pipe rupture was an imminent possibility.

I didn't pay as much attention to Castwell as he would demand of me later. Instead, Andy and I focused on filming the striking Aboriginal families, the faces of a historic resistance. We felt honored to be there, and part expected them to find out we were not that experienced as cinematographers and order us away.

In those days I had an eye on the casually beautiful Denise! But at least I behaved myself there, as I did with the two young nurses who worked with the crusty Castwell. I was lonely by night, under the piquant multitudes of stars, as Denise and my amiable sidekick, Andy, took mutual comfort in the riverbed.

Meanwhile, the dignified anthracite-black male Aboriginal elder spoke to us about the walk-off. "My name is Vincent Lingiari. I come from Daguragu up there, Wattie Creek country. I got all the stories of that country." He had gone on to turn the walk-off from a mere industrial issue into a title claim for his country.

It would always be our footage of Lingiari and his friend Donald Nangiari that was shown whenever Aboriginal people made a land claim. Because Lingiari's was the first such claim voiced, and we hapless children, Andy and Denise and I, were fortunate to be there to film it.

"I been thinking this always been Gurindji country," said Lingiari. "We been longer time here than that Lord Vestey mob."

Indeed Lingiari had collaborated with Frank Hardy to erect a sign at his camp, and it said "Gurindji — Mining Lease and Cattle Station." That seems a mild claim on the world now, but it was large for Lingiari and confirmed his pride in his land. For one thing it was the first time he'd seen his people's name in script!

Ted Castwell went on doing his daily eye work, but we considered him superfluous to our footage. For now it was the politics of the walk-off, and Lingiari's humble yet unprecedented call to be given back his country, that attracted us. The footage we shot gave me my career, and Andy one too, as long as it lasted. Denise was already a professional.

FEATHER-SHOED CORRECTORS

So Stark and I knew that only Clawback, exempted from the sleeping spell, had heard us coming. Our footfalls thudded in his heart, but he had time for a few more instants of alarm. All that was how things were expected to go. We knew now that his wife and children were in the hut, stricken with sleep, but he would not ever be there again. It always happened this way. The criminal led the feather-shoed correctors out into the country beyond. He was running to seek shelter amongst foreign people but would achieve nothing but lonely ground.

Stark and I were slow-paced at first, finding Clawback's tracks amongst the multitude of others coming and going on accustomed paths near the Lake. Stark took the wad of thornbud and ash and broke a piece for himself and one for me. After chewing it we could read, twice as fast as

before, the tracks of Clawback's flight showing up amongst the others like an increasingly clear path to the Nightside, whereas
only the Heroes, the ancestors, the makers
of the earth, could have read Stark's and
mine. Soon Clawback's tracks were utterly
on their own amongst the tracks of small
nocturnal beasts, heading down towards the
Great Snake River, which we knew to be
the normal boundary of our daily concerns.
It was a river vast enough to make the
miscreant think he would be safe beyond it,
that the land beyond was his haven. In that
country beyond, which we had heard described chiefly in song, even we might have
doubted our powers. But half the criminals
went that way. The Morningside brought
you to steep hills, the Nightside into drier
country. Generally we, the punishers, flew
after them and caught them on our side of
things, and exacted the sad and necessary
adjustment of punishment on familiar
ground. But it seemed to those who sought
to flee that the river was good to flee towards, and there were many tree-logged
backwaters and marshes, enough to confuse
a chaser and hide the escaper's tracks. And
enough to confuse the escaper too, for that
matter.

The truth was that if Clawback came to

the river and crossed it, he would need to negotiate further passage with the elders over in that country. And some old woman, liking Clawback's line of humor and frame and ignorant of his crimes, might take him in and make a husband of him, a gift fallen to her from another place. Meanwhile, in our country, dead fish would be cast up from the Lake, and children would leave their mothers' wombs before they were ready. Stark and I knew, thus, that Clawback had to be caught.

At times while we ran we sang the song for a stretch of country, for in some cases we had not been in these parts so often and needed the song to remind us where we were. The Lake usually kept its people close to it, and even hunting squads did not need to go too far afield, certainly not as far afield as we would go tonight. The bounty our ancestors had made for us at the Lake caused us to be strangers to many parts that were not so far away, parts occupied by a family if at all, or by a clan in good seasons. Stark and I both knew the song for the sky as well. We saw the darkness of the heart of the great path of stars. That darkness was the great Dark Bird, who hung above as a judge.

Chewing thorngum as night deepened, we

were empowered to see Clawback's tracks shine beyond a moonstruck stream, and amongst the trees around backwaters. We were not detained when his footprint disappeared — we saw it radiate on the other side of water or claypan. Not only were we incapable of exhaustion, but we knew that Clawback was subject to it. We knew, in fact, that it was in Clawback's nature not to be too exacting a prey. He was too much of a joker, a popular man, a man made for skipping around campfires with children and one eye on the women. The jokes that seemed to be for children were, in fact, directed to their mothers, their sisters, their generous aunts who would sometimes expand their bodies to accommodate a humorous fellow. And now all that had happened, to a fault, with the Earless Lizard girl.

Amongst the ghost trees around the backwaters, silver gliders flew above our heads with a small, piercing shriek of joy that sparked Stark and myself onwards. We had seen the way Clawback's tracks were now slewing, and knew that he must sleep soon. His traces showed that he had no animus against us pursuers, as we had no animus towards him. He knew he must be stopped for his own sake, and for the sake of the rest of us. But we understood that it is impossible for a normal man to sit still and wait for such an ending, though some had done so in the past, when they were too weak to move further. And Clawback might be cunning in his hiding place, and so delay us into another day, another night.

We drank water from our water skins, ate thorngum, and continued without a meal through the darkness.

There was a backwater that had once been a reach of the river and had made its own hill during old, old floods, and that was where Clawback had chosen to rest. The day was breaking on our sunwards shoulders when we saw him spurt from rocks and saplings atop the hill and lope away towards the river, still distant though it was. We paused then, and took the time to drink, and then we were away again, skimming the ground beyond the trees of the backwater, bounding amongst the gray bushes, sure in our stride. It was clear dawn with the earth drenched in a frost we had not felt so much during the night. Our shoes remained compact on our feet, which were not influenced by edged stones or gravel or icicles. Clawback's footprints now showed up black on a silvery terrain. As Stark and I ran, the earth seemed to move us further out into the daylight, stirring itself to run beneath our feet, dragging what was behind us into light.

The morning wind came up from beyond the river and could be felt if we chose to. According to the rules of light and distance we could see a far-off dome of rocks beyond the river, glimmering as if it promised a short journey to those who might desire to go there, whereas it would take the first half of the day and some hours more to reach that place. Mother and Son Rocks — flung by a mother and her second son at the vile Cockatoo Woman who had tried but failed to create hatred between them. We could be sure Clawback had his eye on that, that it drew him even if he had no chance of getting that far. For the marks of his passage showed up as dark criminal welts, shallow but legible. He could not erase them, in the way ours were disguised or erased by our extraordinary feathered shoes.

We saw his footprints once more skirting a backwater and its world of trees and rich water, frogs, lizards, the furred creatures of the trees and the sheltering bounders beyond, and then in a space amongst bluebush and within reach of the mercy of fallen branches, we came upon a family who had started a fire and were cooking their morning meal of grain and a flitch of point-nosed tailer. With them were an old man and a very weak old woman. The old man chewed the meat for her before passing it to her mouth. She who had been his beauty and his companion for long seasons. She had nearly gone from the earth now, and her feet were shriveled. But it should not be forgotten that young men returning from their trial may have once been grateful to be taken into the compass of her arms.

The younger woman of the group carried an infant in a sling made of a small bounder's skin, and the young man bent to the fire and called to two children who were dodging about at play. And near the fire slept Clawback, better at jokes than at flight. Certainly we flew, Stark and I, birds all at once, into the branches of a tree. We observed the family but were not ourselves observed.

But even asleep Clawback saw us strange adorned birds there, and he woke and jumped to his feet and called to the old man, who turned to him. "They're there!" Clawback cried out in our tongue, which this outlier family must have also shared, because they looked as he urged them to, but saw nothing. He grabbed his short hunting spear and his water gourd and was away, leaving one of his fur garments behind. We descended from the low tree; we were no more than an arm span from the earth, and were in stride as soon as our feet hit the dust, leaving it unmarked. Clawback was pitiful, running while we flew, lurching when we were direct. He was clownish in his attempts at escape. I began to weep for him then.

On the alien ground I had endured as a test when I was young, the ground the ghost woman told me I had been abandoned on, I ate sin-meat with my sore jaw, from which my elders had taken my two lower fangs with a stone chisel. I spent an entire moon and days more there, expecting my elders to liberate me. One morning I saw them coming at last out of the sun, their faces painted white and yellow. Some of them trod carefully, having painful knees and cramped feet, but knowledge and mercy flashed about their heads and I wept to see them. The air was empty of all spiteful voices now, vacant of the ghost woman and chiding spirits. When they got to me, they covered my eyes with clay, gave me thorngum to chew, and led me away. It was half a day or more we walked, or so I believed, the clay drying and dragging at my eyes, but I was as happy as I had ever been in life.

"You did well," a number of them sang or murmured. All along whatever road we were on, they sang. It was as if they too were relieved, as one is, by the coming of a kindly day and the repeating of seasons. The earth sang its song to them and so they repeated it back.

I asked an old man named Whisper, "Did you all keep watch on the border of the badland to make sure nothing but old meat reached me there?"

He laughed with a keen amusement, as if no other young man, reborn, had asked him that question. "I am a man who likes my campfire," he said, "and the company of friends and my wife. Do you think I and men like me had the need to wait out there? Just to stop good food coming your way?"

"But did you sing the country so that no young animals approached me?"

"It has always been a country where the beasts send their old and cursed to die. Surely you are convinced of that?"

"Yes, I can tell you I'm sure of it," I said, and this time I joined his laughter, for it was merriment and sorcery, and dying as a boy and rising as a man, and it had all been accomplished. Then someone sang, almost absentmindedly, of the coming Lake, and of the shield lizard who had made it shallow, for he had lost his power to swim, and grew a shield on his back to thwart his enemies. He was announcing we were near home, and near the deeper lake, the Nightside Lake that all creatures, including our Lake people, favored.

I could already hear women shrilling, for they had seen us coming. It was at the top of the dunes that, singing a song in praise of sight, they met me and dragged the clumps of clay from my eyes and gave me some water to wash them. And the first thing I saw with new eyes were women milling and smiling. My mother was not amongst them, nor my aunt or sister. They had been ushered away from the shoreline to allow the other women to perceive me. My sore plant swelled, for it was as if one woman would come from the mass of them and favor me. They all cawed like crows over that, finding it hilarious. Picking up stones, they hurled them at me in mockery of my stiffness, stinging my flanks. The more I stung the more my plant rose. Manhood begins with the mockery and the love of women's laughter. With women seeing at once and all together your great weakness, your lightning and your wound.

The hardest-flung stones came from the hands of a number of women, older but not aged, one of them notable for her long tubular breasts and fine plump stretch of belly gleaming with bounder fat. Her name was Ash, wife of Glancer. The more she hurt me the more my itch for her enlarged. She moved forward now, a clod of earth in her hand, but she did not throw it. She began to dance before me. Women trilled in a sharper tone and then stopped all in the same instant. They turned and walked away, conversing in a normal manner, and were gone. Ash danced in a style not unlike that of the ghost woman, as arousing but with a different heart within it. While the ghost woman intended to take my soul, Ash wished merely to reward me, twisting before me and grasping both her inner thighs and somehow causing them to tremble in unison. The amused chatter of the old men vanished behind me. They were gone too.

Ash and I were alone in the bowl of earth. She trod round me in a circle, chirping like a knowing bird.

"I'm a man," I insisted to her. In fact she made me feel like all men. "I am now all the men there have been since the start of the story."

Ash increased the volume of her trilling,

as if she could deal with and take the surrender of all those men. She slapped her inner thighs. She claimed in answer to my boast, "If you are the man of men, my cunt is the cunt of cunts." And I felt dragged to it as by the force of kindly spirits, muscular ones. She was now in a time of her own, a woman without husband, a woman open to the approach of a lover. She loosened the fur that hung down her back and flung it to the ground. She pointed. There was going to be a change in me. I would be taught and rendered down and given my final shape. She advanced then, still dancing, little puffs of pink and yellow dust thrown up by the energy of her feet. Raising one hand to distract my gaze, she reached to my plant with the other. She made a sudden soft mewl, a promise that she would not be rough with it. Then she took it in with the smallest effort and dragged me towards her and fell down and took me into her spacious, long-lipped mouth, and I felt her healing saliva and her gentle teeth. Here was my reward already for ignoring the ghost woman. I sang now, but nothing sensible. After she had healed my plant, demanding now and then that I not succumb yet and give her my sap too early, she eased herself backwards onto the fur and that great passage of hers was mine to go into. How we toiled. For all the men she had ever volunteered to welcome, I lurched and arched, bounded and trembled, bellowed and gave myself. In shorter time than I had been lost and found in the wasteland, I riotously gave all away to Ash, but then rose again to her as if not yet fully comforted.

"Ah," she said, "I am a fortunate woman." Then she laughed, tickled with herself and, I could tell, willing to warrant my membership in the league of men.

OSCARS

The Academy Award for Best Documentary came my way as a result of the film Andy and I made about the walk-off of Aboriginal stockmen and their families. It wasn't the walk-off documentary that actually won the Academy Award, but it was the documentary on the strength of which we were able to go to Vietnam, where we further traveled by US helicopter to Phuoc Tuy Province and the Australian camp and fire base to film *Shakespeare in Nui Dat.*

Before we left for Vietnam, the Australian and British television networks who'd commissioned the film had insisted Andy and I clean up our partnership and have at least a letter of agreement concerning advances and residuals and, in the remote possibility that one of us was killed or injured, the disposition of rights over footage shot by the unfortunate one.

We thought we knew what we were filming, but going out that day with Andy for routine patrol footage and nifty shots of light through the foliage of rubber trees, we would soon encounter what Vietnam and its insurgents did not usually deliver: an old-fashioned, unambiguous action, a version of the Battle of the Little Big Horn or Rorke's Drift, redcoats holding off the Zulus! It would be an action that, taking place without any choice on the part of me or Andy, could be seen as a feat of honor of the kind the public did not generally associate with Vietnam, however much they wished it.

On the strength of that action, on the accident of my being there, and on the basis of witnessing mangling and the reduction of men to bundles of clothing, I would in the end be rewarded with an Oscar. Our government had by then half repented of the war and decided to cut down on the number of decorations awarded for Vietnamese actions. As a result, few of the soldiers, the survivors and the dead, were ever honored.

I have lived so long since that day, and my accidental and richly rewarding fame was that precisely . . . accidental! It was built on all that young flesh, that multitude of gifts and desires quenched in the skirmish/battle and dismissed from the earth too early.

There was a moment, therefore, when Dr.

Gleason gave me the initial pronouncement of Jack the Dancer, that I thought, *Here's justice, Shelby, and not a moment too soon.*

In the 1940s, '50s, and '60s there'd been a long sleep for the film business in Australia, except for American films of course. The distributors were all American-owned. But in the 1970s there was a gesture of survival in the Australian film industry starting with a film eccentrically named *The Coonamble Bush Shakespeare Prize.* Its formula involved rock musicians in bush towns competing in country pubs to stage the best updated versions of three scenes from Shakespeare — a mad scene from *Hamlet,* the assassination of Julius Caesar, and an Away-with-the-Fairies love scene involving Queen Titania and Bottom from *A Midsummer Night's Dream.* The lead parts were all taken by Australian rockers and the country loved it — Shakespeare brought down to Australian demotic, and Australian romance elevated to Shakespearean weight and moment.

Now the cast was on tour in Vietnam, performing scenes and songs from the film for the Diggers in the big Australian camp at Nui Dat. Andy and I had arrived at the Australian base by Iroquois helicopter three days before. By then we had already filmed two shows the Australians, unfamiliar with international cachet, had staged for the Americans at Bien Hoa, and an extempore show they had put on amongst the spices in the long, impossibly humid aisles of the Saigon markets. So I had plenty of footage of the performance, but needed the eager faces of the Australian regulars and, as I liked to think of the conscripts, the innocents.

The film Andy and I had planned was designed to be subversive of the Vietnam project the Americans and their allies were pursuing, and we were all nuance as we arrived amongst the bunkers and weapon pits of Nui Dat. Soon nuance would be driven out.

Nui Dat was a serious-sized camp with a Vietnamese village in the midst of it. Most of the Australians lived in sandbagged huts or house-like canvas tents, and every man had his own weapon pit in the event of an attack. Patrols went out beyond the perimeter every day — for that reason, there were at least two concerts, and Andy and I had already shot the initial one. There was a nice sense of tension added to the first day's excursion by the fact that the previous day's patrol out in the rubber plantations had been briefly shelled by mortars and had driven some Viet Cong off, causing some of the insurgents to abandon the base plates of their weapons. The captured base plates, brought back to camp, served as props adequate to show the war was real, and Andy and I took hungry footage of them.

Overnight, some mortar rounds had been directed at the camp itself, landing in an area some distance from us, and there'd been the thunder of recoilless rifle rounds in reply. There were reports of North Vietnamese Army units in the area — a more serious proposition than the Viet Cong on its own. But if so, this fact did not seem to cause massive concern amongst the Australians; indeed it was seen as not much more than the "amateurish gestures" of the late-night Viet Cong who had left their base plates. Not that they had sounded "amateurish" to Andy, me, and the rest of our group, but a briefing officer used the term in speaking to us. It was frightening enough and exciting enough for us — those crumps and thuds had been potential death. But Andy, I, and the others were the gifted children of the Flower Power Age, one we expected to survive, as Andy and I had survived the arid, stony Buntine Highway.

I cannot deny that Andy and I were playing with Vietnam, and did not know how stupid that was. And we were febrile, up early on the morning after the base plates were found, and making a nuisance of ourselves in the battalion headquarters. There was a company due to go out on patrol towards the southeast, to relieve the company that had already been sent out there to hunt down the source of the minor fury unleashed on the camp overnight. Everyone seemed calm about us going out with the infantry company patrol.

We had breakfast with the Shakespeare people, who were wan and tired but up for another performance that day. I told them we might be going out with the infantry company. But the added benefit was that we would be able to hear them out there in the rubber trees, as their music and good humor reverberated through the plantations of Nui Dat. This would be wonderfully strange, and it would be bloody subtle, and not like anything that had been filmed about this war. Diggers going on patrol, and in the background the comforting sounds of Shakespeare as transmuted by Australian rockers. "Ophelia, you got me / Feelin' the blues / I ain't the man for you / And that's hardly news . . ."

Naturally, I felt that morning that all the

135

elements of art were coming together for us. The idea that the North Vietnamese Army might have its own intentions caused me no doubt. In fact, a tall Australian major, the company commander, met up with us and seemed almost tolerant of our artistic intentions. We were issued field rations and ordered to stick with his signaler — behind him, that meant. "You know you're missing out on the concert?" he said.

We filmed the company commander speaking to his platoon commanders — young men who seemed too busy to extend suspicion or contempt to Andy or me. Soon enough we were led out into the numbing glare of day and the thin shade of rubber plantations, advancing in the rear of the company signaler, exercising the same caution as the infantry up ahead, though not as competently. And I remember thinking with some national pride, *These boys are good.* The boys of southwest Victoria and western New South Wales, the boys of the central vacancy of Western Australia and of Far North Queensland, the boys of Pommy and German migrants in South Australia, conscripts and Australian regulars. They went forward, if carefully.

It was hot to the point it took one's breath. Patrolling south, two platoons ahead to right and left, and one in reserve screening our pretensions, we felt very alive and very much at one with the young warriors. And from the camp still came the sound of rock Shakespeare — a promise that we would be going back soon, with a bit of fill-in footage, and that this withering tramp in boots that sloshed with our sweat would operate as a nice counterpoint, together with a few other patrols we'd done earlier in our Vietnam stint. And when we went back to camp again tomorrow morning, Andy and I would fly out in an Iroquois to Tan Son Nhut Air Base in Saigon, and after a few days take an uncomfortable Hercules back to air-conditioned Bangkok.

We were creeping forward to the place where the base plates had been found the day before, and at last in sepia heat the soldiers ahead came upon weapon pits where they found a shell casing from the recoilless weapons that had interrupted our sleep the night before. We continued on, following a track amidst the rubber plantation, and when the track split one platoon was sent down the north branch and one along the south, while we waited with the headquarters platoon.

After a while Andy and I sought permission to go forward from the company headquarters' position and film the faces of some of the advancing infantry. The major agreed and sent us up under the care of an NCO, and as we went forward under advice to bloody hurry up from our escort, we had the extra small frisson of meeting the other company, the one sent out in the small hours, now returning and rendezvousing with ours amongst the trees. The two companies of men spread out in the long grass like school chums, chatting while their officers conferred and their scouts were ahead somewhere keeping watch. It was great footage and I played merry hell with my portable, after which Andy and I conferred happily, liking what we had. I even unscrupulously took footage of a young soldier vomiting with heat exhaustion. When he was finished, orders were called and the other company disappeared towards camp and concert.

We crossed a quiet road through the rubber plantation, two platoons still forward on parallel tracks, one in reserve, then Andy and me. At some stage I looked at my watch and saw it was after three in the afternoon. I saved and relished my thirst for another forty minutes or so. But before I could reach for my canteen, there were a few bursts of gunfire, and then massed fire sounded in the trees ahead.

I heard one of the headquarters platoon around us cry, "What in the fuck are they doing there?" Indeed, unlike all other military signs of the enemy we had encountered until now, this noise, in its demand for our total attention, did not seem temporary or merely insurgent. How did those young men in front of us know how to respond coherently when all I wanted to do was drop on my stomach and hug my knees up under me as a means of becoming smaller, and ask myself how so much unplanned and chaotic reality had intruded into our documentary? There was a continuous thump-thump in my spine. I briefly recalled what my father had said about North Africa: while you were being shelled in the open, it was impossible to believe you would live.

It seemed to me the nameless men who were loading the shells that exploded ahead were using my fluttering body as a registering device. And the sound of automatic weapons had joined in, not there one second, massively there the next. All terrible in scale, a sound in its own right, independent of who was making it. I knew from zapping and thumping sounds near me that a soldier was wounded or dying. I saw Andy on his stomach but deploying his Arri camera levelly and with care, panning without panic. Whoever had been wounded was at the limit of my periphery and beyond Andy, but the damage was implicit in the very scale of things.

That afternoon I was shooting on a new Baillieu lightweight camera, like a true French filmmaker. It was hard to handle in this circumstance because of its long lens mechanism. Following Andy's example, however, I turned and sat up a little and shot footage of the company commander and the wireless operator conferring over the fact that the wireless antenna had been shot through. In this torrential fire, nothing was too thin to be shot through.

Ahead of us I saw a young, well-barbered soldier buckle and fall on the far side of a rubber tree, and on the flank a rush of unfamiliar figures dark amongst the trunks, and under someone's orders. So there was an enemy. The "enemy." What a shock! His pith helmet and dark khaki clothes and the humanness of his movement. He was both strange and yet like a revelation, a brother whose existence you never expected to have proven, whose ever-familiar, ever-alien features you never expected to adapt your life to. And his movements were careful. He was one with me in not wanting to die.

Brave Andy was capturing it all, around the trunk of a rubber tree, in a careful superhuman pan, barely interrupted by the violent vibrations of the earth. Again, I felt I had to do the same out of pure industrial equity. I was so dazed that I could not explain to myself what was happening. But somewhere in the back of my panicking brain I was confident Andy could suggest what narrative to impose on the footage later. I believed somehow we would find the story for the images after getting the images for the story.

I could hear the headquarters radio close by. A young lieutenant commanding the platoon on the southern track was reporting to the major that there were at least two companies, if not a battalion, pressing forward to his direct front. I heard that squawking statement between mortar rounds. Soon, mortar rounds began to fall only a little way off to our left, and the major ordered us all to move away, which Andy began to do with the soldiers around him, and I then did too, in wooden imitation. With the sharp and high-velocity thudding and hissing amidst the grass, I simply chose not to define what it was. Newly settled by a more southerly rubber tree, I watched Andy change film while lying on his back. I did the same when my camera warned me, and could manage it chiefly because I had seen Andy do it already. Then the major called the base for artillery support, and those rounds began to fall with new and even more massive detonation ahead of us. FFE, they called it apparently. Fire for Effect. The effect was that the jolts of this prodigious if friendly fire drove the casing of my camera painfully into my cheekbone.

I'll tell Andy about this ridiculous episode when things are quiet, I promised myself. Someone in all this noise and shuddering could be heard occasionally talking calmly to the artillery, so they could adjust the arc of their trajectory.

Communications were lost again, and then again, and again and again restored. Amazing that men had the time to arrange this amidst the tumult. The major ordered the platoon a little ahead of us to move forward to take pressure off the one to the south. Andy and I filmed them going forward and saw some fall over in alarming compliance with the fire from ahead. I did not use the word "enemy" in my mind. I simply saw men scythed down by a natural force. My imagination still refused to extend itself to the concept that this was the work of a foe, despite what I had seen of the careful soldiers in their sweat-darkened flimsy uniforms and pith helmets. Some of our men who'd continued struggling forward now came back to join us. I filmed two carrying a damaged third. Thus the wounded were brought back, gravely altered and bloodied, through our line. And when I saw them placed on the ground behind us and then one of those tending them slapped to the ground by some projectile or other, I knew we were all but surrounded by spiteful forces.

And as if the heavens wanted to own up, it began to rain, and all around the drops were so large and heavy that they raised a little mist of mud, a brown speckling of the film I was shooting. It rose and threatened to obscure the filmable world. The rainfall was astounding, like another dimension, with no apparent consciousness of ever planning to stop. Somehow I saw and filmed a dead face with rain in its visionless eyes. It was a young lieutenant nearby. Twenty-three, it would turn out. Even younger than me. And there was nothing there, in the vacated face. I filmed him as if to save myself from being infected by his nullity.

I saw smoke grenades nearby seething in

the rain and a soldier reaching up to receive a case of ammunition from a low-hovering Huey chopper that I had not even noticed was over us, such was the combined racket. The major was yelling into the radio for APC, which, it would turn out, as they groaned up towards us through the trees by the last light of day, were armored personnel carriers. Then there was the wail of fighters overhead, but they dropped nothing into the murk for fear of napalming their own.

The rain ceased, though it seemed the bruised air ached for it to start again. I saw a tousle of clothes beside me nestling the Arriflex and a bag with film containers marked with sticking plaster and pen by Andy. There was a bloody puncture in Andy's khaki at the hump of his shoulder and I asked him if he was all right. But he had left the world of polite inquiry. Late in the day's firing, a splinter of mortar casing had entered his shoulder near his neck. Andy had apparently died softly and without any complaint at this intrusion, and without my noticing. The casing had traveled down the length of his body and exited by his left buttock. That was worse, I saw. The exit wound.

■ ■ ■ ■

It turned out we had been attacked by a full regiment of the North Vietnamese Army, a regiment of provincial and irregular Viet Cong, and a third battalion of North Vietnamese in support. Without knowing what else to do, Andy and I had shot the only footage of an old-fashioned heroic standoff.

I watched as Andy was collected up by the medical corps, and I got aboard an APC with him and his gear as he was taken off for the trip to the refrigerated morgue. I was appalled, of course, but saved from grief because I could not believe it had happened. I believed Andy would be with me at breakfast.

An intelligence officer spoke to me and I must have answered him, though I can't remember anything he asked me. Nor did I know what to do next. I was shown to a room appropriate to an officer and given a bottle of bourbon for my comfort. I did not like it for it seemed sickly sweet beside scotch and its comfort was ersatz. I could not stand, I could not sit, and any normal exercise of living seemed excessive or irrelevant or an act of pretense. I thought how stupid I had been not to countenance death, which had been so authoritative in the rubber trees.

Within a day I had all this footage, and nothing to do but take it to the US lab in Bien Hoa. I still thought, now and again, *I'll talk to Andy when they let me and ask him for his ideas.*

I crazily thought, *It was that fucking letter of agreement they made us sign that killed him.*

And what culpability of mine had prevented me from seeing something so momentous happen to him — the moment when the bit of steel entered him?

The combination of rock and Shakespeare, and of the mayhem that killed young men, and Andy, made *Shakespeare in Nui Dat* a feature-length success. Critics mentioned the mud mist as a filmic phenomenon of which Andy and I had taken advantage, an image of the sundry obfuscations under which war was mediated to the public. A symbol. It was particularly effective in Andy's footage, and I must say that Andy's material collaboration was crucial. And, at least in theory, what greater claim could be made for a documentary than that a man had died making it?

Even American hawks loved *Shakespeare*

in Nui Dat because it showed what noble allies they had. To doves, it represented the comprehensive tragedy of Vietnam and the young sacrificed for imperial dreams. All of them found the Australian rock performers charming and a counterpoint to conflict, etc., etc. I asked the Academy would they give Andy an award posthumously to go with mine, but they said that sadly he hadn't had the chance to edit and produce the documentary. I still, on balance, took mine, and was not forgiven for some years by that wing of opinion interested in punishment and even by some reasonable enough people. As the years passed I paid the sum of $10,000 to Andy's estate, that is to his family, for rights to Andy's footage. It was a substantial enough figure for me to have to take a mortgage at the time, though it seemed negligible after inflation took winged foot.

Andy had reasonably been waiting all this time for my body to turn on me. He had been very patient as I had continued to devour the world through a series of lenses. And now that I was going towards him, I could not argue it was unjust. It was time.

And if I had been so ashamed of my good fortune in encountering the Viet Cong in that rubber tree plantation, and of the collateral damage to Andy, there was much I did do that I need not have done. I need not have dressed in an Armani suit and gone with young Cath, whom I had met when I employed her to edit the film and who inevitably felt ambiguous about the circus atmospherics of the Dorothy Chandler Pavilion, which we reached by limousine. I need not have accepted an Oscar. Twenty-four young dead, of whom thirteen had been conscripted, barely reproached me as I advanced on the stage under a wall of applause from people who chiefly wished proceedings to move on to the big items of the evening — feature films and their stars.

When I heard my name called, I made it to the stage and there appropriately began to dedicate the Oscar to those who had perished amidst the rubber trees, including my friend Andy. My tears became a minor story in themselves. They were authentic but derived from shock as well as grief. The artillery of renown had thundered down upon me. Yet how piteous that Andy wasn't there to be so thundered down upon! I wept because his death seemed so gratuitous and thus remediable, as if a little effort of grief would bring him back. Then I made some remarks through my tears about my government and the Americans consigning conscripts to fatal encounters. And finally I said with sudden insight, "Andy died within the sound of a rock concert, as if peace did not know what it was anymore, and nor did war."

Andy, who had perished from a barb into the meat by his collarbone. I doubt anyone would have been able to get Andy into a dinner suit to go to the Academy Awards. He was what they called "authentic." He abhorred such indignities as dressing up like a pox doctor's clerk. It was as if he had died to avoid doing something he would have rather died than do.

And the battle at Nui Dat was not just a tragedy for Andy and the young Australian conscripts and regulars. It was a tragedy too for nameless hundreds of North Vietnamese regulars, who should be remembered somewhere, if these things are not to achieve total absurdity.

But I got an Academy Award. And with it, a sort of license to point my camera at the world for a lifetime.

MENDING THE WORLD

In Clawback's track we flew amongst the many stretches of cone bushes to the south. The frost had melted. Nectar-eating birds paused in their probing of fronds to observe us. We were composed. We knew now we would have him by dusk at the latest, so half the task was done. We were content to follow his path on the yellow earth of the country.

By late afternoon, beneath purple-streaked clouds, Clawback began to falter. He did not have certainty, he lacked flight, and though we could see him chewing, his wad of thorngum had lost its power to protect and speed and numb him. A remarkable river bird flew by as if to mark a limit, and then a white ghost tree, magically tall in grassland, presented itself in the same spirit. I thought, *He will be run down and executed before we reach that tree.* I surged ahead with Stark, since that was our duty, singing,

"I am fast down on you to mend the world."
I saw Clawback look back and my tears went his way. Poor man. Poor clown. Poor violator. Soon after, he stopped, turned, hands dangling.

He threw his short spear to the ground and called, "Forget me, Shade!"

"Am I Shade?" I called back, still running, with distances of running coiled in my limbs.

He stood at the end of a spear-throw's length, as close as that, and pleaded, "Forgive me, both of you. Stark, forgive me."

Stark did not answer him.

"I'll go to another country and apply for manhood with other people," he offered us. "No one will be hurt anymore. If I had known . . ."

But he *had* known. Stark and I, having been tempted in the wilderness by luscious phantom women, and withstood them as well . . . could not listen to or let ourselves be distracted by Clawback's cheap prick penitence.

He flung his shield and throwing stick in our direction, just out of hopelessness. He would not reach the river. That was settled. But seeing we could not be persuaded, he did run on then. The sun was falling and throbbed between two bands of purple

151

cloud. It lit his shoulder.

If it had not been such a serious chase, we would have let ourselves think that we had won it. But this was too important an effort to be savored in that way. Stark said to me, flatly, "We'll really get him now."

I caught Clawback in a golden stretch of sweet bush. I cast my spear and thrower aside since I did not wish to fall on them. I flew at his shoulders and he crumpled beneath me.

He howled. I held him by the upper body so that he lay against my chest, and sweated and writhed. I could smell him, his urine and shit. He smelled like a boy. His strength equipped him only to writhe at the end. From the cord around my chest, I pulled the bone with the bounder shinbone slivers in it.

"There it is," I called to Stark.

To Clawback I cried, "This is kind. Don't struggle."

"But the ancestor is angry with me," Clawback complained. "I wanted to go somewhere where he would come to forgive me."

"He'll forgive you soon," I promised, kissing Clawback's head. "You'll go walking in forests of stars with him."

"I know what you're trying to say," said

Clawback, peevish now. "I don't want to hear that sort of thing. That you're going to finish me." And he began to struggle again, though he had no strength for it.

Kneeling before him, Stark had now opened the cavity of the human leg bone, and drawn out the long needle of bounder shin. "You have to die because of your crimes against blood," Stark said. "Shade and I have no hatred of you. Here we're not even ourselves. It's the order of things and that's it."

I clamped Clawback's body in my arms and legs with all the strength I had, which was adequate to prevent him moving. He was again in the state of a child, and I restrained and caressed him as I would a child.

Stark appeared above him. "I wiped this bone in my shit," he said, displaying the long sliver of bounder shinbone.

"I'm weak with women," said Clawback, thrashing his head back and forth.

"That doesn't matter," I cried out to pacify him. "It doesn't matter now whether you were weak or strong."

I nodded to Stark. Clawback was nearly still. Stark plunged the sliver into Clawback's heart-side collarbone. Down it went with barely a hiss. Clawback was amazed by what he was feeling, and I said, "It will find your heart . . ."

But it already had. After all that energy of escape, Clawback trembled and was utterly still. Stark withdrew the plunging sliver. It was barely red. The wound on Clawback's collarbone might have been a scratch. There was a flap of skin there that Stark closed. A passerby would have considered him struck dead by gods.

Stark said, "Well, we can go back now to normal things."

I hurled Clawback away from me. I wanted no commerce with his ghost. Then I stood and took the sliver of bounder bone from Stark's hand and returned it to the casing. I picked up the gear I had dropped.

Clawback would be left to the birds and the ants and the large striped hound.

BRIGHT STAR

It was perhaps ten years after I had first met him in the Northern Territory that I encountered the eye doctor Ted Castwell once more. It was at a party in Sydney, and he took me seriously enough to be brusque with me.

He addressed me in these terms: "You thought I was out there in the desert that time doing charity work. Nice Dr. Castwell. But not so. Two hundred years of us and they're blind. Two hundred years of mission clinics and they're blind. I dare you, now you're a big shot, to go out west with me, out to Bourke and beyond the Darling River. Because, Shelby, I'm actually a revolutionary. I am working to a plan. The plan is to wipe out cataract blindness and fix the causes of glaucoma and trachoma amongst the first Australians. And to give themselves the means to do it. You see, it makes no sense to me being just another bloody potterer."

I have to say that as well as being gruff he had an easy, contradictory charm, and thus he argued further, "Now, it's all right getting het up about some fellow who died forty thousand years ago. But these are his descendants, and they're hostages to blindness. D'you reckon they deserve a bit of your attention?"

This was not so long after I had met Peter Jorgensen and made my first film on Learned Man. Shown on Australian and British television, in part through the voice of Jorgensen, the documentary argued that the modern descendants of Learned Man deserved to be treated with national respect as the true owners of the continent of Australia.

Ted gave a little aggressive praise to the film, but concluded that some jokers were more interested in the remote past than present injustice. My contribution was to say that a well-made documentary was the best way to take public opinion by storm, rather than a drip-feed of news items. Ted said, "All right, then let's make a bloody film!"

He and I set off from Sydney without his saying explicitly that I was to document what he was up to, bringing my authority as

156

an Academy Award winner to the task. God knows he never fully approved of me, and I was hungry for his good opinion. Why, I can't explain. But everyone seemed to want an accolade from him.

Sometimes on the country roads, just to show that he was more than equal to the task presented by remote Australia's eyes, he would leave the four-wheel-drives and run in the brilliant ocher clouds of dust behind them. He was tall but chunky, and powerful in the upper body. He did not run to show off. A militant lack of pretense seemed bred in the bone. Yet he combined this with a passion for John Keats, whose poems he could recite in couplets in his aggressive proletarian accent.

"Bright star," he would have breath to declaim at the end of a five-mile jog, "would I were steadfast as thou art . . ." There would be a beer in his hand as he continued. A nurse had put it there, and her name was Danny Cullerton, a dark-haired beauty who bravely had her eyes on Ted and was up to his level of strength.

Not in lone splendor hung aloft the night,
And watching, with eternal lids apart,
Like Nature's patient, sleepless Eremite,
The moving waters at their priestlike task

Of pure ablution round earth's human
shores . . .

Despite the Keats, at evening campfires
beneath the lights of an entire explosive sky
in western New South Wales, where you
could see the universe hurtling away on its
out-gust, what was undeniable was
Castwell's authentic fury at the clumsy
earth, too many of whose children were
blinded.

For out there in the desert there were
Aboriginals so afflicted by eye diseases that
they tried to tear their agonized eyelashes
out by the roots, and went on suffering a
gravelly blindness, their eyes full of abrasion
and muck. Their disease was called sandy
blight. The $5 name for it was trachoma. It
was a condition spread by sharing the one
standpipe and tap with a hundred other folk.

It made him testy with people, not least
me, since he saw me as fussy about technical matters — light, sound, shooting reverses
— and tired of me asking him to repeat
crucial statements. My strength was that at
heart I didn't give a damn for his judgmen-
tal mien. I took it as one takes weather on
the shoulders. So in our way we got along.

While we sat drinking whisky one evening
after the nurses and others had taken to

their swags in the outer velvet dark, he said, "You make a bit of a show of being a polite man, don't you?"

"I hope it's not a show," I told him.

"I thought you'd bloody well say that. But you must be pretty ruthless deep down. I'm ruthless too. I'm using you to shame people. But you needn't pretend to be so bloody polite. You're not fooling us."

"I save my impoliteness for the commentary," I warned him. "And the editing."

"Can you, boy-oh?"

"Do you talk to other ophthalmologists like you talk to us?" I asked him.

"Some," he admitted. "Only the bastards that are worth bloody saving."

I would continue to seek out men like Ted Castwell all my life. Sages of the tribe. Castwell and Jorgensen. Their certitude was a balm, though I found them bracing too. It was a tonic to be measured and, if necessary, judged by them. Cath did not understand this in the least. It seemed crazy to her to queue up for chastisement. And reasonably enough, since she knew I did not relish her own chastisements. But also, any respect they retained for me had been through the furnace of our collaborations, and so was tempered metal, unadulterated.

"Well," murmured Ted, "at least you're

good at your job."

I was honored, nonetheless, to shoot footage for him. He spoke to the sufferers with a jovial, tradesman-like patter as if he'd come to fix the toilet — not that there were any plumbed toilets on the cattle stations or reservations beyond the Darling River. That was part of the trouble. That all helped the trachoma along.

"You see, they believe there's a curse on their eyes. And you know who the bloody curse is? It's us. We forced them off their land and made 'em live in shitholes in the bush without sanitation, and reduced them to a crappy diet."

"Why do you think none of us have trachoma?" he continued. "Go back to Europe four hundred years ago and you would have seen it. But go back four hundred years in Australia and if you'd been a whitefella here you wouldn't have seen it at all amongst the indigenous. Because then they weren't disinherited, and being nomads they left their shit behind them and their religion was all to do with keeping campsites and water pure. We took away their freedom of movement and used their water to leach mines and gave them the freedom to contract trachoma. This is a disease of disadvantage," growled Castwell. "The more disadvantage, the more bloody trachoma."

I directed the filming of his work at camp after camp in the country around Bourke and the strangely lovely but harsh hinterland of Wilcannia. Since I had not paid attention to what Castwell had been doing at Wattie Creek those years before, I was shocked to see Aboriginal kids sit up in a chair and show the full, excruciating, swollen-eyed condition named trachoma.

"We need clinics all over Australia to defeat this," Ted growled. "And run by the people in the area, not by city cunts."

The trachoma, the cataract sufferers, neglected out in bush camps, all needed surgery. "Where am I to get the resources? The authority? Well, your film will help. It better be bloody good."

The handsome dark-eyed Danny, who was the other fearless member of the party, was an ophthalmic nurse from an unreconstituted Irish-Australian bush family — they were the sort of people who traveled from the boat into the bush, bought and stole livestock, and exhibited unchanged attitudes and virtues from the 1840s to the 1970s. Cancer had killed Ted's first wife three years before. And what a woman was this Danny! What a tigress, as Cath was! And Danny shone with his certainties and her own.

We laughed, we cheered, we cherished him. Was he a bully? Was he an abrasive prophet? He delivered. I became more renowned just for filming him.

"We can't fix this one operation at a time. That's what fucking missionaries do. We're not bloody missionaries. We've got to fix the system."

After we left the arid but weirdly beautiful country around Bourke, we returned to Sydney — me to the editing suite with Cath, and Ted to his crusade. He appeared one night on the ABC and brought the news of an unjust blindness to a nation's people in a way they hadn't heard it before. A conservative minister for Aboriginal affairs on the show with him was mocked and harried and exposed as ignorant and institutionally callous. Ted shamed the nation with his proposition that not only had we disinherited Aboriginals, we had blinded them. And just as I took insults and chastisement from him, so did the public, who loved him. Because Ted had this capacity to love us enough to expect better things from us.

After my documentary came out, with its withering footage, the respect for Ted and what he was doing was enhanced, and the whole country was ready to be harassed by him into decency or, to put it more in Ted's terms, justice and efficacy. And all this somehow suffused with an air of kindness, hard to convey simply in what he said. The arguments continued, with politicians shifting blame but not able to deny the disgrace. For Ted Castwell had emerged as the man whose terse revelations could not be denied.

Ted's obsession with not being seen as "bloody missionaries" was a topic he returned to frequently. In Ted's worldview, to be a missionary was to dip down into the pool of misery, succoring a case here or there but not giving the oppressed the tools to eliminate misery. And thus he demanded Aboriginal eye clinics be run by Aboriginals in the remoter, blinder bush.

"If we keep doing it the old way, with us calling the shots, we'll never be anything except a bloody visitation. A bolt from the bloody blue. *They*'ve had enough of that."

As for politicians, "Look up what E. E. Cummings said of them!" Ted urged us.

NOTHING IS USUAL

We left the now Unnameable Sinner's body and traveled for the rest of the light, and found a plump little runner and fed on its fat tail. Then we slept deeply, waking in early morning. The world felt different. We did not eat any thorngum but ran home swiftly, easily.

Near the great ring of dunes by the Lake, we came upon a woman howling and cutting herself with sharpened stone. Her bared breasts were sodden with blood. This was not good to see.

When she saw Stark and me, she ceased all mourning and self-cutting and regarded us in a way that, now we were simply men coming home, stopped us where we stood.

"My daughter has drowned herself in the Lake," she said.

Stark raised his hand between us and the woman, telling me, "This is the mother of the Sinner's woman."

The woman raised her stone knife to full stretch and brought it down onto her hip. Fortunately it was not flint and did not gash deeply.

"My poor daughter has drowned herself in the Lake!" she screamed.

The shame and her daughter's extreme act had driven the mother out here to gash herself. She gashed her side with an edge of quartz. Her blood fell to the bluish earth. "My daughter," she railed at us as if her daughter's crime were our fault.

Acts of self-destruction were uncommon. But the rarest and most frowned on was drowning oneself. To use the Lake for that purpose was considered a form of overarching selfishness. It said, "The death I take from the lake is of more meaning than the life everyone else takes from it."

"How do you know she drowned herself by her own will?" I challenged the mother.

"She told her friend she would, and now she has," raged the woman. "Her lover has gone."

"This happened yesterday, mother," Stark asserted. Before the problem had been dealt with, that is.

"It happened this morning," she told us.

So this was an evil business. How could we tell her, as if boasting, "We have ended the curse"? Her daughter had caught the echo of the Sinner's death and had killed herself with it. Stupid girl!

"The world is poisoned," she said. To us, who had just unpoisoned the world!

Without the influence of thorngum, the weariness of my journey entered my limbs. I was just a man now. I wanted my shelter and my wife. We continued on past the woman, who barely saw us. Her flanks ran glossy from the wounds she had given herself.

Back at the men's law ground, we took off and redeposited the feather-and-blood shoes. They had lasted the pursuit and the return. Now we cleaned the weapon of correction, and deposited the wad of thorngum. Going home, we were usual men again, though tentative at news of the girl's self-destruction. Such a thing had never happened to me before: a girl killing herself with Lake water as if to dilute what we punishers had justly done to her lover.

In the village by the Lake in the late afternoon light, people were watchful. Because the Earless Lizard girl had used the Lake to contest the justice of our killing of the Sinner, people expected to be restless, with questionable spirits streaking through their night.

Girly told me the women had found the place her family had put the body and sang over it and burned fires. "This is a time," said Girly, who both knew and did not know of my duties as punisher, "when nothing is usual."

Girly and I clung to each other that chill night, as if there might be an unexpected gap in the darkness, and we must prevent each other from being spirited through it. I was not at ease with the girl's astounding act and nor was Girly or anyone else. As we found each other and a socket of warmth in the freezing dark, she asked me, "Have you dreamed a girl child for me?"

"No," I confessed. But I had seen a great orb of loss in Parrot Woman's hands.

"Good," Girly said. She considered herself past bearing in any case. She had a grown daughter.

"So you had some warning after all?" I asked.

"The mother of the stupid girl came to the grave and told us there would be no girl child born alive."

"How did the girl get such power?" I asked. "A child who decides to choke herself to death on Lake water. A child who thinks she loved a clown?"

Girly said nothing and seemed willing to

be reassured. I think that beneath our disapproval of the girl we were thinking of her bravery and love. That she would try to poison the Lake with her contempt and reproach.

Girly yawned and said dreamily, "Yet it may be something bigger than just this drowning girl."

I felt a nudge in the air. Our Sinner Unnameable, who'd had a name a day ago, was questing his way through the shadows and testing out his humor in the world of spirits, and no doubt by now knew more of what was wrong with us than did I.

LAKE LEARNED
AND THE CARNIFEX

As I awaited results and medical options for my esophageal tumors, I was overcome by an urge to go out to Lake Learned again. I suggested the long drive to Cath, and she agreed with certainty that it was what we should do. My reasons were less clear, but I did realize that Lake Learned had been a sort of birthplace to me, where Mr. Learned appeared in his afterlife, and where I might undergo a similar revival.

Though it is dry and vast now, the country is beautiful in its own way, with its saltbush and bluebush tufts looking sharp and vivid under rare rain clouds. We drove in on the one still-open dirt road, for this is red clay country, made famous for bogging in the folk songs and poetry of the nineteenth century, and in these days closed by traffic authorities during risky times. We skidded in from the west, from the direction of the Darling River, on this wide track set amongst the mallee trees and the native cypresses, and arrived at the lodge to find ourselves the only guests.

Going to the visitors' center, a modest enough low-slung structure, we were faced with the melancholy old mallee-wood Lake Learned shearing shed, so sharp-etched in this light. We were the only ones there that day, and the loneliness made us edgy, as if we were trespassing.

The visitors' center, normally staffed by members of the tribes of the area, was empty, but unlocked for anyone willing to turn up. When we passed a screen in the entryway, an excerpt from my first documentary came on: Learned Man was discussed and his bones shown and his height of 170 centimeters mentioned along with the ochering of his body, and his osteoarthritis of the shoulder. "We think of uncles having osteoarthritis," said Jorgensen. "There's something human conveyed when Paleolithic man has it. As if Learned Man is the uncle of us all."

And so there in that great landscape, empty except for plenteous ghosts and zoological wonder, the visitors' center sprung alive and the lights went on automatically at the appearance of two octogenarians, in a dry lake bottom with saltbush and

bluebush, and bush tomato and bush ba-
nana and all the other antipodean goodies.
Learned Man and shattered young Learned
Woman must have eaten these with the fish
taken from the bright lake which, though
now empty and occupied by silver-blue
foliage and mallee trees hissing and shifting
in the wind, just like lake water itself under
the steely sky, suggested the lake outside
was as it had been in Learned Man's day.
On such an atmospheric day too, *Megala-
nia,* great lizard, was credibly out there as
in Learned Man's day, returned razor-
toothed amongst the foliage, devouring
small marsupials. He could almost be heard!
We knew the center well, but given that
the lights had bothered to turn on for us,
and did so as we progressed from room to
room, we felt we should pay attention. We
looked with new eyes at the collections of
stone tools taken from around the lake, and
of sharp quartz that must have been brought
in from other places or traded for.
More than the drudgery or knapping and
shaping of tools, I was attracted to repro-
ductions of the megafauna that had occupied the earth as it was experienced by
Learned Man and his community. If you're
going to have a life-sized model of any
member of these vanished beasts, you would

171

have a life-sized model of a *Diprotodon*. And the visitors' center did have one, and I was soon gawping at it. It was a hippo-sized wombat, though with a curiously shaped long nose, and represented two tons or more of protein on the hoof. Its extinction was said by experts to have something to do with Learned Man's arthritis. Perhaps the old man had acquired the damage to his shoulder hunting the *Diprotodon,* running on great trunks of legs, towards the point where it could no longer make a claim on a future. What a feast the felling of one of these must have been!

The megafauna item that gave me a delicious and childlike thrill was the marsupial lion. A creature with a terrible prehensile and opposable claw on each of its front legs, a beast with no descendants in this landscape anymore except in our darkest dreams, its DNA implanted on our phantasms. And what was it? Not a lion. It was a bear by some lights, it was a huge cat by others, and in fact, its like has not been seen since the last died out here, ailing in some fastness of rocks or panting by some billabong, some thirty millennia past. Its hunger for meat vanished from the landscape. They called it *Thylacoleo* when they found its bones. The pouch lion. For it was marsupial and grew its young to maturity in its pouch. It had all the ferocity the giant kangaroos, pouched folk themselves, lacked. *Thylacoleo carnifex,* the *carnifex* being the name of the public executioner in ancient Rome. Quite a title then — the executioner pouch lion. It had molars in its cheeks like blades. Scientists have created computer models of its jawbones and skeletal structure and claim that while a modern big cat will take up to fifteen minutes to suffocate its prey, the marsupial lion killed in a minute by crushing the windpipe and ripping the spinal cord, and slashing the carotid and the jugular with its great thumbs. Yet it begot its children as did the most amiable kangaroo — each as a mere worm which made its way to a pouch, in which it acquired nourishment and burgeoned towards maturity.

Cath and I moved outside, finding ourselves beneath dense steely clouds, not so common in this country, semiarid since the last ice age. We decided to walk north to an old pastoral lease and homestead. You can't say that the European settlers didn't give all they could to the dreaming of sheep and cattle, for they persisted a century and a half here with the consolation of intermittent rain. Cath and I were now the most dangerous creatures to be seen, and the red and gray kangaroos who inhabited that basin knew by their steady inspection that we were perilous to them. On seeing us, a sturdy kangaroo infant took to its mother's pouch, its legs protruding comically, like a child who believes that because its eyes are closed it cannot be seen. A magnificent muscular male stood amidst the gray shrubs to stare at us, its female partner remaining hunched and grazing on the leaves. This huge male gazed at me so levelly, with the most unquestioning but serene authority, that I could see at once why in the Aboriginal cosmos the kangaroos stood for an ancient, marsupial-faced ancestor and fount of guidance.

We passed by an old sheep station water tank, a red scar in the gray-blue. We held hands and rejoiced in each other's company as we had not necessarily done when young and bemused by each other's closeness, now relishing it! When young I had wondered why the aged were capable of such affection, and I attributed it to soft-headedness. But death is close and touches are precious, and the beloved remains beautiful even to the aged swain. This had been delightful to discover.

The hero ancestor kangaroo amidst the

saltbush saw us go. There was pity in his eyes. I was sure of it. There was pity.

■ ■ ■ ■

II
THE BOOK OF WARS

■ ■ ■ ■

TED AND TESFAI

By the early 1980s, Ted Castwell had made the nation believe that his task of initiating Aboriginal eye health was ordained and not to be resisted. Around this time he told me he'd met an impressive East African man who had come to him with eye trouble — a corneal degeneration of both eyes, in fact. The East African, whose name was Tesfai, said that in the Red Sea area his eye disease was called "Dahlak blindness." Ted told him that it looked exactly like the sandy blight the Aboriginals suffered from and asked Tesfai about the unfamiliar name he'd used. Tesfai said that the disease was named in this case after the Red Sea's stony Dahlak Islands, whose bright light on barren white stone struck men blind, and not only there but in Ethiopia and Eritrea.

"Where in the bloody hell is Eritrea?" Ted asked Tesfai, who told him it was on the rhino horn–shaped coast of East Africa.

By asking the question, though, Ted had engaged himself on an inevitable journey. For he never asked a question without ingesting the answer thoroughly, as if in his own flesh. Ted's radical apostolate of the eye applied itself, now, to Eritrea.

Tesfai was a freedom fighter, or according to the Ethiopian ambassador in Canberra, "a bandit." His rebel movement had sent him to Australia, where there was a handful of politicians who knew where the bloody hell Eritrea was.

Tesfai and Ted became mates. And thus I met the Eritrean, a tall young man with curly hair, wide eyes, and delicate features. He was an intellectual of Coptic-Christian background from the Ethiopian-Eritrean Highlands.

Tesfai explained to me that his country had been fighting against Ethiopian tyranny for a quarter of a century. His task — on behalf of the Eritrean People's Liberation Front — was to negotiate with the Australian government and NGOs for relief food and medicine by building contacts here. After seeking help for his own corneal degeneration, then, Tesfai began to turn an Australian rebel named Ted into an East African one, with results for all of us who knew either Ted himself or Tesfai. For to be within Ted Castwell's ambience was to be subject to his enthusiasms. There were no excuses for apathy in Ted's world, and — remarkably — he did not seek excuses for himself.

"Look," he told me on the phone, "this is a rebel front, okay? But it controls a swath of the country. And no eye doctor. We could bring one of their doctors to Australia to do ophthalmology, and we could also put in place a new scheme, the sort of thing we can't do here, but can do there."

I gave an enthusiastic answer, but he went on as if I still needed convincing. "Your old friend, Learned Man — he's a star, yes. But look at the map. This place is at the north end of the Rift Valley. And his mother and yours come from there. Mitochondrial Eve. I mean, that's one thing that should interest you?"

Such shiny concepts interested me, of course. I was not sure of the extent to which they interested him. For he was a man in perpetual and urgent wrestle with the present. But he did like poor tubercular Keats. That was a clue to something that accommodated the history as well as the eyes of humans.

Emperor Haile Selassie of Ethiopia had

come down punitively on the Eritreans, canceling their parliament and proscribing their language. Massacres were carried out by the Ethiopians in Eritrean villages, and urban atrocities began in the Eritrean cities of Asmara and Massawa. Tesfai, who'd had a decent education, became a mountain rebel in a country of inadequate water, shared washcloths, food tainted by the hands of those whose eyes ran with discharge. He had as well a very good chance of being hit by automatic or artillery fire by the army of Ethiopia's emperor, which then became the army of the emperor's killer, Mengistu Haile Mariam.

As well as being a guerrilla and ambusher, Tesfai became a safe-keeper and distributor of the Ethiopian army food stocks the rebels captured. He negotiated with the nomads, the people of the camel, so that they would transport food, and issued them with payment from the Eritrean People's Liberation Front. This food that had belonged to the Ethiopian regime reached rebel distribution points in the shadow of the mountains, or in the dry country stretching west to the Sudan.

Tesfai was soon removed from combat peril and sent to work on a primitive but well-organized aid network. If the Eritreans, in the time of the emperor's famine in the 1970s, had waited on the mercy of others, they would have died. The rebels were attractive because they were such a valiant group with an ideology of brotherhood between highland Christian and lowland Muslim, and because they had begun a war, ultimately unwinnable, against the traditional practice of genital mutilation of girls during childhood. Thus they attracted friends from progressive countries, not least the Norwegians, the Danes, and the Swedes, who found them Mercedes trucks to help move relief from other directions, southwards from the Sudan into the rebel areas. And Australia, in a rare year of spaciousness, took an interest in Eritrea as well. There were a few senators who had spoken in favor of Eritrean independence, or at least of a compassionate settling of the war, in the federal parliament, and that was enough to cause the shadowy head of the Eritrean People's Liberation Front and Tesfai's boss, Issayas, to send Tesfai to study and to raise Eritrean relief in the Antipodes, a long way from East Africa.

Tesfai was a different kind of persuader than Ted. He exercised a measured and even monotone mode of persuasion and captured the ear of certain influential politicians.

Throughout the early eighties, Tesfai was able to finesse the transport of Australian surplus wheat and canned tuna and high-protein biscuits to Eritrea. "Wastage" was an accepted part of all relief efforts, yet operating from a depot in Port Sudan into rebel Eritrea they had the lowest wastage of any relief organization in the world.

But what Tesfai offered Ted Castwell was, in the rebel quarters of Eritrea, a harvest of eyes with no eye doctor, and a field for his plan to train Eritrean medical groups to go out and treat cataract blindness in the furthest settlements. The Eritrean rebels offered Ted not only a republic of eyes but one within which disabling niceties would not restrain the good work, the initiation of eye teams going about their business in drought and flood, and in war and hoped-for peace.

So Ted, now the spouse of splendid Danny, settled in a large house near Centennial Park and paterfamilias of a young family, decided he must find time within his professorial, clinical, and surgical regime to travel to Eritrea, which was so innocent of ophthalmologists.

When I asked him how he was going to get there, he said it was all set up — Cairo, Khartoum in the Republic of the Sudan, and thereafter, well . . . trucks would be involved. The Eritreans would get him into the rebel areas, and that's where he would begin operating on every corneal grief and cataract blindness. He intended to take a supply of intraocular lenses and go there by truck to assess things, and be back out within a month with enough data to base a program on.

This proposition on its own was astonishing. He was a professor of ophthalmology to begin with. He had students to deal with. He had people awaiting operations. He would attend to them and then be off. Travel in Eritrea was unpredictable, and yet he was determined to go.

He would come back from his journey and reconnaissance an Eritrean partisan, and fervent with plans for a decisive attack on eye disease in the Horn of Africa and nothing less than the world.

THE VILE EYE

Stark and I needed normally to make no report to any old men. They usually took it as undoubted that we had found our quarry and inserted the bone. But the old man Dart came, bowlegged, down to my hut and stood in the sweet morning smoke and seemed to be looking to me for reassurance now. For he was the uncle of the girl who had drowned herself in the Lake.

"Yes," I assured him. And, once more, "Yes."

"Yes?" he wanted to know again.

"Certainly. Yes." All had been restored.

"Then what sorcery is this amongst us?"

"What sorcery do you mean?"

"The despair of women?" he said.

"I can't account for that," I confessed, not quite knowing what he was talking about.

He proposed a further meeting at the men's law ground at a time he would tell me. I could sense his alarm, which was unusual for him, as if for once he expected no result to be reached.

That day we watched a hunting party returning with a bounder haunch and a fat lizard. Women brought cod, threaded on twine, up from the Lake even though the girl had sullied it with her death. On the weaving ground my daughter worked with the older weavers. The reeds were best here, in the country of lakes, and when we went out there on the Nightside to trade for ocher, and off to the Morningside for flint, our nets were seen by the women of these distant places as far preferable to anything they made in their own country.

So the earth was still pretending its bounty. But I was the one who saw a fog of uselessness falling over these lovely endeavors. So did Dart. He waddled off but seemed to leave behind the shadow of his confused authority. I went to praise the day's hunting party, but Baldy reached me before I had a chance, and he too had the same air of concern.

"I must tell you about my journey," he told me. "I have not till now had the chance."

I agreed that was to be regretted.

"Let's go along the shore," he suggested, looking round like a man who believes even his thoughts might be visible to others.

We walked barefooted on the cold crust of the morning shore. The earth was a warm body beneath our feet. That was still true: sun and earth. Baldy told me that while on his journey he'd encountered the first Upper Waters mountain people, who had been amiable, and that his party had participated in the binding ceremonies with these serious-minded people. Thus both people confessed what dominated and united them. Some of the people spoke our language just as Baldy spoke Mountainside. Some of us had known their language since the beginning — not all of us, but the learners like Baldy — it was why he had been given the leadership of the journeying party.

So he had gone, and soon after the first contact with a hunting party, some of the Upper Waters people had offered Baldy's party two worked stones with intricate markings for use in our own ritual regarding the venerated spotted slicer, the most feared of presences and the most just; one very common in their mountains, less common to the Lake people, but, of course, one intimate to me. The slicer whose meat not one clan ate! Whose meat, that is, in the entire world was forbidden.

It had been normal trade after the ceremonies. Our yellow ocher and nets. Baldy also offered our emblems of Short-Faced Bounder to ease the Upper Waters people's way into our Hero's presence, which they knew they needed to reach. By means of similar stones given to us, we had always enlarged our own dream travels.

One of the members of Baldy's far-ranging party had, however, beaten one of the Upper Waters boys in a fight over a claim to so humble a thing as a burrow hopper. Both men had claimed the right to the tasty little creature, our man on the grounds that his stick had killed it, the other man on the grounds that it was on mountain land. The business had ended in blows, the fight favoring our man excessively. Baldy had made the appropriate extra gifts for that, more of the famous net bags wrought by my daughter and the other women. These bags were precious to them because they were raging river people and had no association with the calmness of lakes and the way their banks favored weaving grounds. The Upper Waters elders easily accepted all this. Their seers saw no ill will in Baldy and his party. It was all pleasant, the brotherly feasting.

But, being in other people's country, Baldy knew he must travel beyond that half-known and scarcely understood land and its people and be guided towards the lesser-known picture of the region, of the kind owned by the older men. He hoped to be given insight into their chief rites and on such a basis trade our own stone and wood emblems of holiness for theirs, in full brotherly understanding. These Upper Waters people were also, half of them, associated with the great Dome Nose, and they had over time shared some of the outer secrets of their rituals with us. There were beautiful hills where they lived, notable mountains of dense stone, and we had always cherished their dense stone emblems as helping our entry into regions amongst stars. It was by such trades between people located at a distance from each other that the world of mysteries was kept in balance. It was a sort of divine wrestling.

But there, at the foot of blue mountains, Baldy had spent time in the settlement of the Dome Nose half of the Upper Waters people, and disturbing news was brought to him by their eldest holy man very soon after he arrived, while he was still tired. The holy man was a little wisp of a fellow named Cawl. Baldy told me he was one of those men who gave you the wonderful impression that he had never done a thoughtless or ill-chosen thing in his life.

Cawl said to Baldy, "I've been waiting for you. I saw you coming in a dream. I saw you and the others hunting a red bounder. I can tell your features from that dream."

Baldy did not doubt any of this. Such a small sliver of a man but with huge authority. As he sat down by a fire with Baldy, many of the Dome Nose people watched on. Whatever they knew about what Cawl was telling Baldy, they seemed to know it was of moment for them.

"You will have my young wife for warmth tonight," Cawl announced, "but you must not touch her because your body will not count. Instead, you'll meet our ancestor tonight in your dream self. He's been waiting to see you. But you must understand that as you traveled you were under a cloud of your own ancestors. Now you're under him. He's the great cloud above you now."

All this, the promise of a dream journey, sounded reasonable to Baldy though he would have preferred a normal night, one of profound sleep after, of course, accepting the graciousness of the young wife. But as so often, urgent business was involved.

When Cawl had finished speaking, Baldy was given a meal. A particular grain cake the Dome Nose women made impressed him. Cawl's young wife came and sat by

191

him. Unlike her elderly husband, she lacked much grasp of our Lake people's language.

"You've been to the Rainside," Baldy asked her in her language. "Over the tops of mountains?"

"I've been to the Rainside, yes," she told him distinctly, trying to make it easy for him and giving him the briefest but most jolly smile.

"What did you see there?" he asked her carefully.

She put a hand on his wrist and gave a smile as if it was in consolation for what she was about to tell him. But then all she said was, "There were great ferns there. As big as the dome nose."

Unlike us, the Upper Waters people never hunted the dome nose, nor did they eat it, though it was a giant of a plant-eater with vast meat on its bones. It was easy to corner but dangerous to hunt, chiefly because of its power to charge and, above all, to fall on one of the party. Baldy was quite taken with the girl, and discovered that her name in her language was a word to do with the predawn. But he knew that for now her limits were those of keeping him warm. Pleasure would distract and was almost too trivial an accompaniment to his coming audience with Dome Nose Man. Baldy drank from a calabash of water mixed with the bitter honey gathered from the larger and more ferocious bees, with thorngum mixed in. Quite a drink. But he could not let it ease him too much. Then he opened his cloak and the young wife sat on his thigh, and they shared the warmth of their blood. But she knew too that providing Baldy with warmth was the limit of what would be happening that night. He was drowsy when she went ahead to their hut. A man of high integrity, he did not indulge in any further advances to the young woman. He turned his back on her and slept.

Baldy would later believe that during his sleep with the young wife some manipulation of his head and neck had taken place, some procedure carried out by eminent men of the group he had found himself amongst. Their presence, not the presence of the young wife, preoccupied his dream self. In that dream he said to them, "I would not have objected had you told me it was going to happen." But then, the old man had told him something was to happen, and so it was apparent to him that some adjustment of the spirit-self must occur which Baldy, being a man of another country and other emblems, would not understand. Even while half-awake, he was appropriately humble as they shaped him for his spirit journey.

And then, falling asleep, he had the experience of speeding along a skein of light to the serious-minded world in the sky. He walked in thickets of stars as did I when taken up. He bounced off their great bulbs of light. He walked humbly, without any resistance of the muscles, and in that spirit accepted the forces that operated on him, his body just a wand, buffeted in the strange air of the Allplace.

But even then it was these Upper Waters people's Allplace, not the one he had sometimes already penetrated while rising up the sinews of light to our own high places. Here there were different gods. And so he found the Dome Nose Man, a man not his own Hero but divine just the same, sitting crosslegged by a fire like any ordinary fellow. His massive upper body had an undeniable realness. He had very friendly eyes, Baldy remembered. Manly and companionable.

"Ah," Dome Nose Man said to Baldy, "you have come at the right time."

Baldy could not understand why it was the right time, but the meaning of it would become clearer, he was sure, so he said nothing. He sat.

Dome Nose Man said, "Your ancestors

agreed with me that we would share the curses of the earth between our children. So we have borne a curse on our women, which we have endured in the normal way, with mourning and suspicion on the part of the ignorant. But it is time it passed us by now. It is your people's turn to endure it, and I must pass it to you so that you carry it back to your country . . ."

Baldy said, "Forgive me, Father, but you want me to take a curse back to the Lake people with me?"

"Yes, that's the way it has to happen," Dome Nose Man replied. "You can deal with it, and ease it through your people by the right behavior and the obedient rituals. Some of your women and girl children will die. There may be times, my dear traveler, when you come to believe that all the women bearing girl children will perish. But you must trust in your own prayers and rites," Dome Nose Man continued. "You will come through this, and one day a man, a traveler to your country as you have been a traveler here, will come to you and you will pass it on to him. And he will take it to his people. If this curse were not shared around, there would be no women. There would be no girl children anywhere. We would perish, people after people after

195

people. Do you understand that?"

Baldy felt he could be a questioner with this kind-eyed God in the face of such a hard offer. "You want me to take back to my people a stone that will kill women in childbirth?"

"Yes. Do you want the people here in my country to die out, and then the curse would still be on the earth and would travel to you in any case, and travel on and on? The girl who was at your side now . . . She was brought to you so that you would see her face and share warmth with her. Do you not want to take the curse away from her?"

How accurate the elder and the God had been in limiting Baldy's choices, and in showing him that superb woman, who in a good world would be abundant and live long. And the Hero did not lie. How warmly Baldy wished the Great Creature was lying, as men lied in discourse with each other. But the nature of this sky journey itself proved what must be done.

"But why do I of all men get burdened with this news, this curse that traveled the earth?" Baldy asked in a breathless manner. How could he willingly take such a broad curse back to his people?

He understood though, and it now made sense to him, that in the workings of the earth there was always a measure of grief inflicted by alien sorcerers and alien presences, the whole weight of which could not be permitted to fall on one people. That could not be argued with. He realized now that the overriding curses of the world would need to be shared for fear that they would do away with all living beings. And then who would there be to honor the ancestors, the makers and Heroes? Who would there be to keep the earth in order? Who would there be to sing the songs of creation, to reenact and empower the renewing of things, to keep the water flowing at the base of the rock?

"I will bring you it." Dome Nose Man sighed and rose from the fire amongst the stars, leaving Baldy by its blaze. The departed Hero thudded his way amongst the forests of heaven, and cracking branches could be heard as he traveled, just as an earthly dome nose might.

Taut with dread, Baldy could not suppress a childish hope that he would take a long time to return with the embodiment of the curse, in whatever visible form it might possess. But it was not long before the Dome Nose Man could be heard on his way back to his fire.

Baldy rose as the Hero, the Earthmaker,

approached and took a handful of some material from beneath the amplitude of skins around his massive upper body. He offered his clenched hand to Baldy, who could not help but extend his palm to receive whatever dreadful thing it was. It was a stone the size of a waterfowl's egg which weighed on Baldy's hand because of its density — he believed he had to take special care not to drop it — and it emitted a low malign whine.

"Look at it," the Ancient Dome Nose hero of the Upper Waters people urged Baldy.

Baldy resisted but knew he had to obey. And when he looked, Baldy did not like what he saw. It was a cold spectacle and it caused a sensation of ice in his blood.

"You will not like it either," Baldy promised me after he'd recounted his first meeting with it. It was like a great dense eye, but clouded, like the eye of a blind madman, denied sight but stricken with color. For it also flashed with boastful, thick color. "You'll see," he promised me.

Listening to him, I felt reluctant to meet it. Baldy admitted that on his first day of return he had hidden the stone amongst us, its weight and its color wrapped in furs to protect us from some of its harm, as Dome Nose Man had suggested he should do.

Baldy said that when he got home from his journey, he did not take notice of the wrestling or the feast or of his wife. He knew he must place the stone amongst the holiest emblems at the Short-Faced Bounder clan. They would combat it or cramp its ill will, and might smother its influence in the end.

Baldy was tormented by this stone and its wish to spread damage amongst us, and the sad business of a Hero and a God commanding us to take a turn of its evil.

"Why must I see the thing?" I asked, though gently because I did not want to make little of Baldy's anguish.

"Because he told me, the Hero, it would be too much for me to bear. That I must share it with a wise man. Otherwise I would be crushed by its single weight. The weight of what it would do."

At first I thought, *Don't pick me. There's plenty of wisdom around the Lakes.*

But he had selected me and that was it.

"I will rouse you and take you to it tonight," Baldy told me. "Then we'll both know the way it looks. We can uplift each other until a messenger comes to take the thing off us."

And so, of course, I agreed.

Girly asked no questions when I painted my flesh and face in slits of white to enable

199

me to flit through shadows and be as invisible in darkness to spirits as the white-barked trees. Nor did she address herself to me when she walked to rest in our hut and amongst the furs. Until recently we had thought we might at some time create a boy child to replace our Son Unnameable, who in one beastly stroke had been robbed of his proper organs. But there would be none of the sportiveness of reviving and remaking ghosts tonight. Girly knew without being told, and we lay separate until Baldy chirped outside my hut and I was awake with instant dread of facing that curse embedded in stone.

With skin cloaks on our shoulders but our chests bare, Baldy and I loped off under a sliver of moon and a sky of looming, spinning stars. Though elders, we were both still young enough to make distance easy going. We got to the rocks that sheltered the Short-Faced Spring, the spring lying safe beneath the soil and the base of the standing stones, its fullness protected from being diminished by the avid sun. We were not so very far from where Stark and I had secreted the feather shoes and implements of punishment.

Baldy let me get my breath. We both needed breath for this. "Oh, why did they give us this shit?" Baldy asked hoarsely. He began groaning out a chant invoking someone with heavenly power to stand between us and the evil stone, between us and the vile eye.

He circled in on the Morningside rocks of the spring, and went around the site three times, closer and closer in, and turning the last time, he knew he could not delay too long. So he reached down amongst the rocks with the face of a man whose duty it is to extract a plump adder, coming up with a lump of something wrapped in bounder felt. "I have put the most powerful tokens with it," said Baldy.

As he unwrapped the things, I saw the ancient embodiment of spirits compacted into wood by powers beyond us, but left with us for our protection. These wooden and stone pieces that were as long as a man's arm. He knelt down by me as he unwrapped the felt, and paused and retrieved one of the amulets, and paused again and then continued.

"This is the poison," he told me. "Look at it for yourself, my friend."

I too knelt down amongst the tokens and saw the baleful rainbow of the stone, death in the yellow, a curse in the thick, clotted blue. It could not be doubted that this intense stone was lethal.

"Does our Bounder Hero know of this?" I asked him.

Breathing noisily and unhappily, Baldy said, "It is as if our ancestor has broken the line to earth. I can't reach him. I have no hope of reaching him while I have this stone weighing on my memory and under my care."

I could sense that I was the one Baldy hoped would reach the ancestor, that I was the one suited best to be given the burden of this lump of malign color.

"Have you told the other old men, then?" I asked.

More breathing, then Baldy replied, "I wondered if they might want the bearer of such a stone punished? And I would be pleased to be punished to avoid what is coming. But it won't do any good. In all, my friend, I don't know what to do. I am hoping that you can tell me, or else find a way to save us."

This stone had a way with time — it dazed a person, and brought all the past forward and made the present far off.

When Ted Castwell invited me to travel with him to Eritrea to make a film on his eye project there, he seemed, as ever, like a man in a hurry. In fact, though I did not know it, he was suffering from renal cancer. His only protection, a friend would later say, was that like most gods he did not believe in his own death. But of course he did, and he brought with him huger plans and hopes than I had ever expected.

We traveled in from Khartoum by way of Port Sudan and the oasis of Kubaraka with a young Eritrean doctor Ted had trained in Sydney and who had received his letters as an ophthalmologist from the Australian and New Zealand College. His name was Freselam, though Ted called him Fram. The three of us occupied a vehicle in one of Tesfai's food convoys of green trucks, and thus crossed the dry river that marked the border, embarking on twelve dark hours of mad jolting. I would later wonder, when we knew Ted had been sicker than he looked, at the vigor of the ailing man who let himself be hurled about in the hard-edged interior when he could have been at home at the side of Danny with his children — as a more timid sufferer might.

One thing Ted had made clear to me was that, amongst other things, he wanted to assess what was called a laminar flow sterilization plant the Eritreans had built in the side of a mountain in Orotta, the place we were making for. In the plant they made their own surgical fluids for intravenous use, but, Ted said, since they had built the plant, they could manufacture eye lenses there too.

"Bloody astounding," he said of this and other instances of Eritrean cleverness.

I knew he had been talking to eye doctors the world over, from East London in South Africa to Nepal to Ho Chi Minh City, seeking allies willing to implement his antiblindness program, though still in the spirit of not being a "bloody missionary," of letting the locals take over and adapt the plan. He had plans to build lens factories to be run by Indians in India, and southern Africans in South Africa, and by Vietnamese and Nepalese and East Africans in their respective countries. Thus he could defeat cataract blindness in the entire world.

The Eritreans had not won the war yet, and Asmara, the mountain capital and site of the envisioned lens factory, had not yet been captured. But Ted was never daunted by that sort of consideration.

The thunderous impact of the stony road up into the Eritrean Highlands allowed Ted and me little time for conversation, and I saw how he closed his eyes and made his face neutral, in classic meditation mode, and breathed his way tranquilly through it all. "People say I'm a bloody Marxist," he had complained to me on one of the legs of our journey here, the long one from Singapore to Cairo. "But if they knew anything, they'd know I'm an anarcho-syndicalist. But let me tell you, the flame of anarcho-syndicalism burns bloody faint in Australia."

I was tempted to say that anarcho-syndicalism burned pretty faint everywhere, with most people hard put to define what it was. In a period in my early twenties when I'd briefly desired a young leftist university tutor, I had found it exciting to hang around the Socialist pubs, where people loved or hated each other on the basis of being Trotskyists or Stalinists. I was fascinated that both these camps shared a special aversion for anarcho-syndicalists, who were apparently dubious about all states and even a supposed "workers' state" like Russia. Why the factions bothered turning up in the same pubs as each other is a question I still can't understand, but I did hear men and women described with viperous hatred as "syndicalist bastards!"

Over time, though, I began to see that an anarchist skepticism about the orthodox state and its officials drew Ted to this rebel movement in the Horn of Africa, a rebel movement which had the marks of cooperativeness to it, the possibility of a new form of state, and generals whose victories were frequent but rarely celebrated in the noxious manner of the West, which we had learned, to our peril, from the Romans. This nascent state, insofar as the rebel movement was one, omitted the marks of triumphalism and self-importance. The operations of Eritrean Relief, compared to the competitiveness and sometimes the shiftiness of other aid organizations, appealed to Ted for the same reason. They seemed innocent of arrogant governance and driven by results achieved without bureaucratic clutter. So the laminar flow sterilization plant dug into the sides of mountains at Orotta beckoned Ted as a sort of syndicalist moral wonderland. And he was motivated to collaborate with the Eritrean rebels to break the nexus by which powerful Western states and their corporations supplied what was necessary for continued life at the price they chose. The Eritreans would, he hoped, change the balance of the world by making lenses for their fellow Africans. The man with me on the violent plains and inclines of Eritrea harbored a potent plan to puncture the tires of established order. And now, just when he'd found a place worth leaving the side of Danny for, here was Jack the bloody Dancer to put a limit to things. This increased the energy with which he pursued the plans.

Because I did not understand all this at the time, our conversations remained superficial. He told me significant things I did not have the equipment to hear. Yet, at least in the film I made, Ted the ideologue is more than visible. I filmed him operating in the caves of Orotta, and then greeting in the morning those whose sight he had restored. He would take off the dressings from their eyes and savor their immediate smiles. "Aren't you lucky to have a handsome bugger like me to look at, first up?" If you wanted quick customer satisfaction, ophthalmology was the answer, for it could vanquish so much blindness so promptly.

■ ■ ■ ■

We reached Orotta in the first mauve light of day and went into the camouflaged stone guesthouse, half-dug into the hillside and of the same texture as it, and drank lots of black tea. Ted looked fine, of good color, ready to work, full of conversation with Freselam, discussing the meetings they had planned for the afternoon with those who administered the hospital which lay indiscernible at the bottom of the slope, on the valley floor.

After a breakfast of bitter *injera* and canned tuna was carried in by our guides, I suggested to Ted, "I could shoot a conversation between yourself and Dr. Freselam discussing what you mean to raise with the Eritreans this afternoon."

Without a trace of exhaustion in his face, Ted winked at Freselam and said, "We're in Hollywood now, Fram."

"The purpose of the journey is threefold," he said functionally when I set up the conversation. "Or maybe fourfold if you count my selfishness. This place, and these people, are like a new home to me, but that's a narcissistic purpose." He cocked his head to assess this statement. "But the three

208

main purposes are . . ."

And then he showed his credentials as a university teacher by laying them out. "Firstly, it's a chance to operate here in Orotta with Dr. Freselam, who is a recently qualified ophthalmologist. I think he is a very important man for the future of this country, where eye disease and eye trauma are pervasive. Secondly, as I'm always saying, we're not bloody missionaries and the occasional visit by a great white father of eye medicine barely makes a dent in the blindness figures of African countries, and doesn't do enough to guarantee what I consider a human right — the right to see. So Fram and I want to discuss with our hosts the idea of setting up teams of nurses and aides who can work in the villages that still exist and combat cataract blindness wherever they find people in the bush. The operation is straightforward in its way — it has to be done properly, but intelligent squads can do it under Fram's administration."

I swung the lens towards Fram's lustrous, perfect eyes.

"And the question then arises," Ted continued, "where do they get the intraocular lenses from? These teams in the field? Well, of course we have to donate them for now.

And that brings me to the third purpose. Fram . . . Dr. Freselam . . . and I want to propose that we establish our lens factory here in Eritrea — even in Orotta, if necessary. These people have the spirit of innovation in them, and they have a laminar flow sterilization plant right here in Orotta. We could put the lens manufacturing phase on the front of that, and the Eritreans themselves could run the whole shebang. The time could come when they are exporting lenses throughout Africa and Asia that cost a fraction of what the rip-off lenses in the West cost."

He paused, his eyes on the middle distance as if his grand plan were visible in the air. "I'm glad I saw this place. I always knew it *had* to exist," he said.

Too rattled about by the long truck journey to sleep well, I was awake again in a few hours and went out into the dappled shade of the stone veranda. Here, within a little while, I saw something remarkable in the form of an Antonov bomber appearing at the clear apex of the sky. Someone had told us that they flew high now, not wanting to be killed in a losing war. And as if to show why that was so, the entire desolate valley sent forth anti-aircraft shells from guns, and the sky beneath the bomber's wings was filled with intense, broad black smudges. The bomber arched its way into a bank and hauled off southwards again, having seen as much as it deserved to of Orotta.

From where I stood, just a little way southeast, in the direction of the Red Sea, was the Rift Valley. During a recent call Peter Jorgensen had excitedly reiterated to me the fact that the mother of us all had lived there, the newly discovered and named Mitochondrial Eve, whose bean-shaped mitochondria apparently lay at the core of all our cells, including Ted's, Freselam's, mine, the gunners' cells, and those of the edgy Ethiopian aircrew. It was Eve who had initiated in her own womb the string of daughters, all women now alive, Cath, Danny, Margaret Thatcher, Audrey Hepburn, et al. And now that so many of her daughters strode the earth, the reign of her human chemistry was assured, even though that of other women she had lived amongst sometime between 100,000 and 200,000 years before had died out. What were those women like — kinder, more rational, or crueler, less succoring? That her home valley was now the scene of a war between her children . . . well, however banally, seemed cruel. All mothers want their issue to get

211

along. All mothers have a uterine yearning for peace. But their children are quickly sundered from each other by mere concepts such as nation, ideology, culture. Indeed, you could not think of these ordinary contradictions without suffering a kind of vertigo.

Learned Man is her Australian son. As am I.

The meeting that afternoon had been held in the guesthouse with the male head doctor of Orotta and a sturdy middle-aged woman director of nursing. The head doctor was a calm man. He did not come to the party with the ramified awareness of codes and budgetary inhibitions and regulations which marked the Western bureaucrat's confrontations with Ted. The proposition for a mobile cataract team had obviously been received well in advance in this doctor's head, and he presented Ted and Fram with a map indicating the area of operation of each proposed group. It became apparent from the man's enthusiasm that he saw the plan not only as a medical tour de force but as a means of attracting people in the Ethiopian occupied zone around Asmara and Massawa to join their comrades in the north and enjoy the benefits of assured vision.

212

That night — with *injera,* spaghetti, and tea to speed us — we descended amongst the rocks and the thorn trees to the hospital. Ted and Fram were robed and gloved for the theater as I did my best to wipe down my camera with disinfectant swabs and robed up like them, filming the surgery from 6 p.m. until after midnight. Dozens of Eritreans had come to Orotta on the strength of the news of Ted and Fram's presence. The two surgeons operated on twin theater tables, chiefly on cataracts. Some of the operations that Ted performed and I filmed involved traumatic injuries of the eye caused by shrapnel and other shell fragments, in civilians who had been bombed or in soldiers shelled far down the escarpment, while pressing against the ports of the Red Sea coast.

In the ensuing days, Ted and Fram addressed the teams the Eritreans had chosen for the surgical cataract tasks. They provided instruction in the classrooms of the Orotta schools, after which Ted astonished me by operating each night without apparent exhaustion. At last, Orotta cataract surgery was performed by the nurses of the squad, supervised by Ted and Fram, and everyone seemed happy with the results.

One night after surgery Ted and I sat

drinking tea in mutual languor on the terrace of the guesthouse. I heard him sigh. Out of nowhere he was into a recitation — I presumed Keats.

> Here are the craggy stones beneath my
> feet, —
> Thus much I know that, a poor witless elf,
> I tread on them, — that all my eye doth
> meet
> Is mist and crag, not only on this height,
> But in the world of thought and mental
> might!

"Well done," I said, because it was, and its ambiguities reflected those of the hour.

"Do you happen to have heard of this thing, the human revolution?" he asked.

"1917," I replied hopefully.

"No, that's not it. It's fifty, sixty thousand years back." He leaned closer and fixed me with his exhausted eyes. "They say some random burst of DNA in the brains of humans took place. And out of it came language and culture. And religion and ideology. And Keats." And Learned Man. Language and culture. The coating of ocher and the funeral plaints they sang for him.

"I've heard of it," I told him. "Peter Jorgensen said something . . ."

"Yes, a grand moment. Eh, Sonny Jim?"

"The best," I told him.

"But it could happen again. Anytime. In fact, it will happen, for sure, if we survive. A burst of DNA, and we would wake up wiser, finer, less contradictory. More unified in our humanity. Less tribal. Less warlike."

I agreed with him that this would be a fine development.

"Well," he said, "don't think me bloody mad. But it could be happening here. A calm wisdom. No one will settle this war, but the Eritreans are fighters, not haters. They have religion, a lot of them, but it doesn't divide them. They have bugger-all resources, but they make their own IV fluids and antibiotics, and they built that sterilization plant out of nothing. They're against female circumcision. They run the least corrupt aid system." He yawned. "Now, I know you think I'm bloody mad."

"No," I said. "I'm fascinated."

"We'll never know for sure. Not in our lifetime. But maybe your film will be evidence of it, Shel! And by the time our kids are our age, if the splendor has lasted . . . they'll bloody know it and it'll happen to them too. If I was a Catholic like Danny, that's what I'd pray for."

At dusk a few days later, we left Orotta in

two trucks for a place out in the west, towards the Sudanese border. There were Ted and Fram and me and two cataract teams. At one in the morning we arrived at the appointed place, a dry riverbed. Here, in withering heat, we shook out our air mattresses and bedrolls in the darkness. Mosquitoes descended and bit us with abandon, and though I tried to wear a hat with mosquito netting, I found that it was far too suffocating. As we settled down, we were aware of others asleep in the dark river, on the cooled sand of the watercourse. I was awakened at first light by the sound of pounding. Around us the nomads had already risen and were pulverizing coffee beans in the wooden mortars that seemed to be part of the personal gear of every inhabitant of the Horn.

Within a half hour everyone had abandoned the riverbed since, apart from the issue of bombers, what had been deliciously cool at dawn had already become a furnace. Ted and I were amongst the last to withdraw to the trees under the sting of the heat, and there we found a food dump, with young Eritreans of Tesfai's organization in charge, and a hut in which Ted and Fram supervised nurses as they put lenses into the eyes of Hadarab men and women. As I filmed, I was struck by the composure of the patients, the comfortable smiles they wore as they entered the tent where, after all, someone was going to cut into their eyes. I mentioned this to Fram during a pause in the work. "They do not get nervous like Western people," he told me. "They need no preoperative treatment."

When the operating was over, the surgical team seemed to vanish, and Fram told me they were visiting friends nearby, as if this forest were full of cadres of old chums from the rebel medical corps.

That night we went back up into the cooler Highlands again, reaching the guesthouse in the small hours. There had been a lot of excited speech in the truck — the Eritreans had fought their way down the terraces of the Rift Valley and across coastal plains and along the railway viaducts, to threaten the port of Massawa, occupied by Mengistu's troops. An ancient town, the Italians had filled Massawa with their architecture as they had supposedly filled Asmara.

It turned out that the Eritreans had made a nifty attack on Massawa, outflanking it by land and sea, raging down the coast in motorboats — showing all the Eritrean inventiveness we took for granted.

After taking the brief comfort of a slug of gin, we took to our beds.

I was woken at about 7 a.m. by loud voices, specifically Ted's. Getting up, I went to see what was driving him to such a volume and found him haranguing — or to the ignorant it would seem so — Ghebrehewit, our guide.

"But didn't they think of waking me and checking with me?" Ted fumed, to which Ghebrehewit mumbled apologetically.

Ted saw me arrive but kept his gaze — and frustration — focused on our guide. "You know how much it cost to train that little bastard? And not in money, in time above all! In expertise!"

Ghebrehewit gave an unabashed shrug, very Italianate, as if there'd been some exchange of habits of gesture between the old colonial masters and the Eritreans.

"And we're in the middle of training the cataract squads," Ted protested, casting his eyes up to whatever gods anarcho-syndicalists had. "Bugger me! I didn't think the little prick would do this."

Now he turned to me. "That little shit Fram has cleared out to Massawa. He left me a note, but he knew I wouldn't let him go if he'd woken me."

"There are casualties there," said Ghebrehewit in doleful apology.

"Two of his young mates from the hospital here called by in the small hours and they all cleared out in the truck. To operate on battle casualties!" Ted shouted at me. "That prick Mengistu is going to bomb Massawa, you can bet! And there, in the midst of it, is our Fram, as likely to be killed as any other bastard. This country's single eye doctor! Due to run the programs and the lens manufacturing!"

Ted looked hollow-faced. I understand it now. He was dying. And if Fram was killed, when would another anarcho-syndicalist come along and train another Fram to replace him?

Ghebrehewit murmured, "He told me to say he would be back Thursday night, even if he has to steal a truck to get here."

But to Ted it just wasn't good enough.

At breakfast, which consisted only of black tea for Ted that morning, I tried to console him. "Look, Ted, consider it from Fram's point of view. The Eritreans have been through murder and bombing and shit for a quarter of a century. And throughout it they dream of two places — Asmara, the capital, and Massawa, their key to the Red Sea. And now they believe they're going to take Massawa. Of course Fram would accept an invitation to go down there. He shouldn't have, but it's understandable he would."

Ted shook his head and said in sorrow rather than fury, "I'd expect you to say something stupid like that. As if Fram's an adolescent. He is a man of fucking thirty-two. *Thirty-two!*" The number was supposed to rout me. "Don't you put this in your bloody film!"

Over the next three days Ted went on giving his classes to the cataract squads, operating most of those nights as well. His anger at Fram seemed to energize him. When we got back to the guesthouse after midnight on Thursday, we saw a truck in one of the camouflaged bays, a wreck of a thing with a scorched back door and bullet holes along its length. We walked inside the guesthouse, where Fram was drinking tea at the table.

"Did you get bloody shot at?" Ted asked.

"No, Ted," said Fram carefully, laying down his words like arduously chosen cards. "They just gave me that old wreck to get home in."

"To get home," Ted said, and made a dubious sound with his teeth. "How bloody dare you, Fram."

Fram lowered his head with some dignity, but inviting his punishment.

"Just in dinners we fed you, you little prick! Just in the dinners we fed you, Danny and me, you had no bloody right!"

Fram nodded, acknowledging the argument.

"As for irreplaceable knowledge . . . You have it but it's not for your own sake, it's for the *plan*. It's even for more than Eritrea. It's for the world. And you dare bugger off with it and risk being killed in Massawa!"

After Ted walked out of the room, presumably to collapse now that his anger was vented, Fram raised his head and greeted me with a nod, saying, "He is right in his view. But perhaps I was right in mine. Will you tell Ted I am very repentant?"

"What was it like?" I asked.

"You know," he said, "shrapnel is merciless."

I was grateful I didn't quite know how merciless it was.

The documentary concerning Ted and Freselam in Eritrea did not contain Ted's fascinating suspicion that the Eritreans might be the first version of a new kind of human. It concerned human blindness, but also the blindness of the world to the war raging in Eritrea, still largely unreported. World leaders did not step forward to end the conflict. They had their reasons, which we were powerless against. But it worked adequately in terms of marshaling support for Ted's plans for cataract teams and lens factories.

Ted would make two further journeys to Eritrea, but then his decline became more severe. At his house in Sydney crowds of visitors gathered — old Marxists, boxers, footballers, and other patients, along with Nepalese doctors he had made plans with, Vietnamese surgeons, Aboriginals he had treated, and a few senators who had a passion for Eritrea. They represented his global project. So did the prime minister and the leader of the opposition, from whom he demanded "no-bullshit" promises that whoever won the next election would establish a lens facility in Eritrea to be run by Fram and the Eritreans.

One bright winter morning, before seeing the Eritreans win their struggle, Ted died. A journalist rang me to tell me and I choked on tears of disbelief.

SAVING THE OCHER PEOPLE

It was hard for me to face that long ago —
under the direction of an elder, Clay — I
had helped other people quite casually — at
least, that was how I thought of it, even if I
had been deprived of blood in the cause. It
was about the time the woman who would
become my first wife had begun to enchant
me by her quiet means. For the right woman
the ways of meekness can be as alluring as
the ways of display, loudness, teasing,
flaunting, and mockery. If at that stage I
thought about journeys, it was a journey
towards Morningside, where, amongst
peaks, stood great crystal snakes of ice with
faces taller than trees. One could imagine
the wonder of being in such places. But after
my trial in the wasteland, I was happy to
stay at the center of the dreamed-forth
earth. The country of the Lake. I knew that
in the country up sunwards there were
people who found, amidst their fields of

clay, the most intense stones, almost too dense to be worked into useful knives or devices. We did not envy these people, however. Nor did we envy the Nightsiders, who had their marshes and forests and variety of ochers but no great fields of kindly water as we possessed.

One morning of particular frost, that elder of unceremonious words, Clay, found me by the fire of my Vanished Mother, who still breathed and fussed over me then and doubted if there was one amongst the young women fit for me. Clay was polite to her in a way unfamiliar to me. He asked could he speak to me, her son, briefly.

When I gathered my skins about me and joined him some paces away from my mother's fire, he looked at me full-on and scratched the corners of his mouth as if he had no idea of what to do with me.

"I met my ancestor," he told me. "I traveled . . ." He made a bowl of his hand and then raised it briefly, nearly negligently, skywards. His Hero was Earless Lizard. "He told me that the people in the Ocher country, the Nightsiders, live in a state of warfare and murder. I did not know that. My feeling well might be, 'Let them.' But the Hero has a better soul than mine and thus is the Hero. I said, 'These aren't my people.' It took some cheek on my part to say that. But I did, being a sensible man. And he said, 'Many of them are mine.' "

As Clay looked at me intently, I thought resentfully, *If they have nothing to do with you, they certainly have nothing to do with me.* I thought he was intending to ask me to accompany him there, that the Hero had asked him to make peace in that country.

But the news was worse than that. "The Hero named you," said Clay as if disgusted. "You are needed, since a young man like you was murdered at the base of their wars." He looked meaningfully at me.

"I am not that young man," I told him.

"I know that," he rushed to tell me. "But according to the Hero you have that in you that will console them for the man."

"How do you know that?"

"The Hero told me," he declared with a measure of distaste for having to explain things to me.

I shook my head in defiance at Clay and his air of disapproval.

Clay said, "Don't worry. I questioned his choice of you. 'Him?' I said. 'That empty boy?' But the Hero said, 'That's the way of it. Him.' "

I was frightened by someone as reticent and scornful as Clay telling me his Hero knew of me, and that I could somehow pacify people I had never met. But to confirm my fears, Clay said, "You have to come with me encased in white clay to make peace over there in the marshes and forests of the Ocher country."

The idea of traveling with Clay as my sole companion did not appeal to me.

"You can encase yourself in white when we reach the clay pit at the early marshes," he told me, as if this were a powerful motive for me to consent. "Because they will see you coming even if we don't see them."

He spread his hands and said, "It's what the Hero wants."

I had no choice, since I knew Clay would not of his own will have chosen me as a man to travel with and a figure of peace amongst these far-off people.

There have been many journeys in my life on the earth, but this was a plain if not a harsh one. We moved out into the flat country beyond the Lakes. Clay was a poor fellow traveler for me and did not try to hide his amazement that his Hero had named me and that his task, as an eminent man, was simply to deliver me to some people his Hero had an interest in. There was no long talk by our campfire at night. Instead Clay would examine the flames as if he had once been capable of reading them but had now reached the sour conclusion he knew nothing. He uttered no best wishes for sleep when we rolled ourselves in our skins.

The earth on our path presented grassland and low stony ridges for two days. On the second of these a great but far-from-clever dome nose traveled some distance off but in our direction, as if influenced by our passage. We lost her amongst a reach of marsh grasses she seemed to relish. We could see she nurtured a young one in her pouch. Thus, even if we'd had time to hunt, she was forbidden to us.

Clay would sometimes say, remembering his conversation with his Hero, "I told him, you can't mean that big lump. But he said, 'Him. Yes. He's the one.' And I said, 'But he has no marks of cleverness.' And he said, 'Just the same. Him.' "

I did not have the authority to lose my temper. Instead I just murmured, "I'm as surprised as you."

" 'That one,' the Hero told me," Clay reiterated, as if wanting to press his amazement with other invisible wise presences in the broad night.

We rose on the third morning while it was dark, and wrapped our feet in skins and ran across a wide icy marsh, sometimes breaking the surface. We had run a great way before day broke, and we reached a stony rise beneath red mountains. Ahead of us was a country of trees, which sometimes revealed patches of grassland thick enough to hide entirely what was ahead in a country whose intentions could not readily be seen. We found a white seam of ocher, and Clay told me to take off my skins and cover my scalp, my plant, my back — the latter exercise he helped me in. I was to be all white. I was to let the sun dry the ocher on me and was not permitted to scratch it where it itched me. I was unsure how long I would wear this clay skin and wondered if I would ever be permitted to take it off. In the meantime I wore no skins. Pure white and naked.

Later in the day Clay and I came to a little brown hill of stones on this plain, and I could see women, mothers, grandmothers, looking at us over the small ridge above. They seemed timid and twittered in their form of speech. In our country, where people lived sensible lives, I might have been a figure of amusement in this white clay, a naked curiosity, but to the people beyond I seemed astonishing and something to be puzzled out. In a clearing further on, with a suddenness that horrified me, we came

228

across two dead bodies gory and decorated in brownish ocher. They had that deep unmoving of the dead. They had been stripped of their skins and weapons and were sadly naked. One of them had many spear wounds in his chest and stomach, and lay within a circle of his own squandered blood. This broad patch of dark red made me wary, since I did not know what influence it still contained. The other Brown Ocher man, his chest lined with mourning scars he had inflicted in grief for others, had a broken, bloody skull, and some of the matter inside it had been exposed with a blow from a stonewood club.

Smelling smoke from somewhere, we skirted these corpses and the shadow of their influence and saw a party of five men in yellow ocher at the far side of the open space. They had a fire going to protect them from the dead men and to celebrate the victory they'd had over them. They began to stand as we drew closer and I saw the influence we had upon them, these the winners in the recent conflict. They stared and spoke tersely to us. They had all been comfortably arrayed by the fire, settling themselves to what had happened. Now, for whatever reason, we were all unsettled, them and us.

I heard Clay's breathing. He had nothing

mocking to say. He too seemed bewildered.

As one of these Yellow Ocher men advanced on me, as if to temper the fellow's behavior, Clay began singing something about this country, a song he had learned at some stage and with which he now armed himself. The man who advanced on me was some years older than me but still much younger than Clay. He was sturdy and his ribs were outlined with yellow ocher and half his face was a mask of yellow. He came forward slowly but with an air of intending to make some judgment on me, head to foot — to test me out in some way. I looked to Clay for a word of comfort, but he went on singing his song as if he were content that it would save him. I could sense I was not a part of his song, and neither its power nor its meaning shaded me from the eyes of this terrible yellow creature.

The friends and fellow killers of the man who approached me called to him in a language that carried a glint of meaning for me, was somewhat like ours at the core but not enough for me to understand. How would the extra skin of ocher I wore protect me from the stonewood club or the spear he carried, a long one with its single glistening head of bounder bone, not as ornate as some of those by the fire which he had carried into the recent fight. This was a spear for impaling, for a sharp passage through the meat of the body. He addressed me loudly, but I showed him by a gesture of my white hands that I did not know if it was something he wanted me to reply to. There was one other harsh statement from him, though whether addressed to his companions or me or one of his Heroes I could not have said. He repeated himself, his eyes enraged. I spread my hands. I felt stupid, and Clay was still consumed by his song and was giving me no help.

The Yellow Ocher man ranged to one side then drew his spear back and drove it straight through the ham of my leg so that it entered the outside of the leg and went right through and emerged again, below my penis, and — continuing on — inflicted a shallow wound in the inside of my other leg. The instant it slithered into me so smoothly I knew that I must endure it and not buckle under the scalding wound. Everything he had said suggested by tone that the worst thing would be for me to fall over. He looked at me as if assessing how I had absorbed his spear.

I felt the desire to loosen up my waking mind as he withdrew the spear. I fought the desire to be numb and made sure I remained on my feet, and a gush of blood ran down the whiteness of both my inner and outer leg. Sensing what I was required to do, I stuck my thumb in the wound of my outer leg, as before my eyes the earth spun and then settled.

There was now applause from the men by the fire, and from the man who had driven his spear through me and extracted it. He briefly inspected the threads of my blood and began to chirrup as joyously as a child and came forward and embraced me closely. The other men by the fire were on their way too, clapping hands, raising arms, crying greetings.

Clay stopped singing and said to me, "That is your brother."

The pain was so intense that I said in my irritation, "He's not my brother."

"Greet him," Clay ordered me, "because today he is."

The men of the Yellow Clay were all around me, letting my blood stain them, embracing me by the shoulders and even pulling my hair. I was helped towards the fire and permitted to sit as one of them wrapped skin around my wound, and it was clear that I could acknowledge the wound now and gasp with pain if I chose. They returned to the men they had killed then and sang songs to soothe their spirits and wrapped them in their skins to preserve them for collection by their relatives. And then we all set out, my brother for the day helping me along in view of the damage he had done me, the wound for which he felt no remorse. One of the party had run ahead, and as we drew near a little upland I saw fires burning and the hearths of people and, on a neighboring blunt, low hill, the entirety of the other warring group, the Brown Ocher men. Both aggrieved parties hunted each other not here, by their firesides or their home grounds, but in the forests and the plains, and up and down and around other hills than these ones.

People from those home sites came running to greet me. I now began to understand that at the same time I was and was not the young man whose death had begun this spate of killing, and that the Earless Lizard Hero had wanted it to end now, and somehow my appearance had signaled an end to all the bloodshed. And the part of me that was Shade, the me who had been harried into this journey by the elder, Clay, half-crazed from the wound, felt both close to and very distant from this scene of greeting and rejoicing. I was the returned man whose name I did not even know but whose soul was somehow in me. And so I was caressed by aunts and a mother, and I spoke in my own language which seemed to delight them, for I had traveled after all into death and back again, and they seemed to think it was normal that my words should be skewed. My brother was weeping and shouting and receiving congratulations. There were people of Yellow and Brown Ocher crowding in around me, for my appearance had allayed the war and meant there would be no more wounds. If the families of the two dead men Clay and I had come upon earlier were grieving and wailing and punishing themselves, I did not see them.

Accompanied by her noisy aunts, a young woman was pushed forward. I noticed her colored headband first, and its woven-in feathers from the great-footed birds. She raised her face and gave me a long-lipped smile and I saw she was very beautiful. They could see I was stunned by her, and laughed and cheered.

"Your wife, you idiot!" Clay hissed at me.

The beautiful young woman opened the skins that protected her from the cold and took me in against her breasts. My wound sang in a sort of joyous complaint and there was more rejoicing and howls and animal noises and laughter.

I was given some thorngum to chew because of the wound and made warm with skins and forgot pain and my particular whiteness as I sat with my — his — young wife and saw dancing and heard song and was fed bounder haunch seasoned with leaves. The air of the place, the thorngum, and the woman in the headband delighted me. Her eyes were startling and the way they moved was also striking. They skittered like a bird, but when they settled they filled up with a meaning that, even if I could not understand it, was visible to me as an entire joy. I was ardent for her, and at last, when the feast ended, she led me to her hut and I found myself holding her, wonderfully strange as she was. Outside, the night creaked with cold, and the grass and the marshes froze and the silence of the air was relieved only by the sound of the last conversations and short protests by restless babies. She wiped the white clay from my face and rediscovered the features of her husband there. I wasted myself away recklessly over and over to this splendid young widow. I gave the second sign of a man returned from death. In the clearing I had proven I could bleed, and now I proved that I could couple with a woman. And that shown, I fell asleep, blood-warm, enclasped.

Clay woke me in blackness. "We have to go," he hissed at me as if I should have known it without being told.

I saw the truth. She would see my being there as a visit, a kindly event, a sign that I — he — was fully a man of both that other world and of this, that no more blood need be paid to make sure that he had reached the sky, and was of such power and content-ment there that he had somehow acquired the power for one merciful, peacemaking return. I was a party to a divine deceit.

Somehow I extricated myself from the man's young wife without waking her, leav-ing her sleeping on like a child.

Once outside, Clay and I headed Morn-ingside.

"You'll need to get that ocher off," he grumbled, as if I had put it on out of child-ish vanity.

This adventure in an unknown place filled me for a time with rancor against Clay, the man I could not tempt into friendly ex-changes. But now I wonder if it was not a part of manhood, to be made to survive journeys in which one was a tool of the Heroes. To which one was driven by the scathing tongues of our elders.

And the wound? I never felt it. It never

dragged at my leg, and but for the scars it made, I would have believed it a dream.

WELCOMING THE CAMEL

Even before Ted's death, I had returned to
Eritrea to make another documentary, this
time about the war and the sort of society
the Eritreans seemed to be forming. It had
been commissioned and fully funded as an
Australian and British coproduction. The
film company was supplying a crew and
equipment. My relationship with the cameraman was to be somewhat similar to the
one I'd had with Andy long before: I would
shoot my own footage, and so would he,
though I was director of the overall film.

Drawn by Ted and my stories, along with
Ted's barely scientific suspicion that the Eritreans might be reacting to a surge in the
human brain, Cath wanted to come to
Eritrea with me. By that stage Ted had traveled to Eritrea once more to visit Freselam
and the teams and make plans for the lens
facility. Cath and I measured up the perils,
including the risks of orphaning our daugh-

ters. We consulted them. And then — rightly or wrongly, and with their blessing, and faith in Eritrean protection — we went. Underneath our motives lay the Ted-implanted suspicion we might be visiting something transcendent, a shift in the human tale. The bold surmise! Was I amongst the new humans here?

The ongoing war revealed itself in Orotta in the bloodless faces of young boys and girls taken down or partially dismembered by a variety of weaponry including 88-millimeter guns. In the women who gave premature birth from shock during extreme bombardments, and their slivers of babies who might or might not become viable. In the amputees and those whose faces were slashed off. In the somnolent malaria sufferers, and the smiling orphans without any arms or legs. In the unexploded cluster bombs Mengistu denied using.

After leaving Orotta, we made for the newly captured town of Afabet, which was further than a person could have got when I first came to Eritrea at Ted's urging. On the way our truck broke down near what had been the frontline town of Nacfa, where every house was ruined and tumbled by bombing and artillery. We spent two nights in this town, living in a deep bunker, sharing its rear sleeping chamber with the camera crew. Stacey, the cameraman, was at the far end; Cath nearest the door; the rest of us in between. Lying behind Cath's head was a pile of cluster bomb fragments that Cath had collected with the intention of taking them home to give to a particular senator who could, in turn, show them to Mengistu's foreign minister when that official visited Canberra. They seemed emblematic of Cath's resolve, in this chamber where none of us could get to sleep after discussing the journey thus far, the shock of it, all the medical skills of Orotta.

Cath and I had the capacity, as if to seal our suspicions about events, for a deeper discourse, the comfort of caresses. But we could not engage in them in the crowded bunker, given that the camera crew was around us, and our Eritrean minders, drivers, soldiers on the move were occupying the front chamber.

The second night, however, I suggested to Cath that we might meet outside on the ridgeline behind the bunker. Inside the door one could get water in a basin from a standpipe, and I would wash there and then go out into the night. Cath was to follow and if asked by anyone — our Eritrean minders, for example — she would say she

was going out for night air. Such a pronouncement would guarantee none of the
Eritrean gentlemen of the bunker would go
outside, and would yield up as a courtesy to
Cath the entire East African night. If they
noticed that this coincided with my absence,
as far as I was concerned they were entitled
to draw their conclusions. I trusted the crew
and our escorts not to sneer. They were not
callow adolescents.

Cath met me. The air was silken but the
question was, what ground would accommodate us in these granite mountains? Hard
earth had, however, been Adam's bed, and I
was willing for it to be mine.

We kissed at the crater lip, but this
couldn't be our place, for it was used as a
cloaca by everyone, and only the turd-
desiccating sun saved it from being odious.
I suggested the ridge. We rose up hand in
hand, stopping now and then to kiss and
brush our hands across each other. When
we got to the top, I unbuttoned her shirt
while she unbuttoned mine and I held her
breasts. On top of this ridge in the highlands
we were merely half-clean and yet desired
each other's rankness. And it was accomplished painlessly, the descent to the bed of
rubble, for the soft surfaces of the beloved
were enough to make the universe itself soft.

We were far advanced on our congress or consolation when an extraordinary intervention occurred. Over Cath's shoulder I saw a huge, fawn, moonlit leg bear into sight, and became aware that a camel had blundered up beside us, *our* place, and begun eating the flowers on the cactus that grew along the ridge. I saw the prehensile, cunning lips avoid the thorns and capture the blossoms. By now Cath had seen this arrival, this third party in our selected space. We paused and weighed up our new neighbor. Of course, there was laughter, but tears as well. And amazement, as if the presence of the camel cast a meaning we could not fathom over the event. In the Garden of Eden the serpent had cast a shadow, and I instinctively wondered what a camel's shadow might mean.

After we'd paused in our caresses, it became apparent that whatever we did to get rid of it, including the throwing of a stone by the bare-breasted Cath, we would not impact the camel's appetite for nearby cactus flowers. On the one hand the beast was very much present, but on the other the cactus flowers blotted out its attention to all other matters in the universe. And so in that huge beast's presence, beneath the shadow of its great haunches and knee knuckles, hearing its persistent snuffling and chewing, we continued with our grand commerce. Only when we were done, triumphant at our success on that stony earth, and saw that the camel was still harvesting the flowers in his casual, subtle manner, did we understand the absurdity of the scene.

I will be taking the memory of that camel with me into the dark. And when Cath goes, no one will be left to use the phrase we garnered from the experience. Welcoming the camel.

We were buoyant for the ride to Afabet at midnight. The Eritreans, the people on whom the world had turned its back, had fought at Afabet the biggest battle since El Alamein in World War II, and driven their enemy back seventy kilometers; seventy kilometers closer to the end of the war the world would not settle.

We were to be the first outsiders to go to the newly captured town. As we traveled, hard and lovely mountains flanked us and a stony river intervened, noisy with the reverberation of river boulders on the chassis. It was the merest stain of dawn when after three hours our trucks, rolling across the stony plain amongst the highland trees, came to the first houses and overrun trenches of Afabet. Daniel, our guide, shouted over the sound of the harsh road, "Four Russians killed here. *Four!*" According to what the rebels said, the Russians always got away. Not this time. Four Russians were the index of the sudden victory, as were the ten thousand hapless Ethiopian boys who had died here for Mengistu's regime. "And one of the Ethiopian generals — he escapes from here all the way to Asmara to explain the defeat, and Mengistu kills him. Execution. *Finito!*"

The Eritreans had endured a terrible human toll — more than two thousand dead, and ignored by the press of the world. That such a slaughter had occurred during a three-day battle did not rate as big a mention as a small plane crash in Europe or the Americas. Well, we would make our documentary and put a dent in that massed ignorance.

When we reached what had been the general's residence, Daniel said, "There is an American-style stand-up toilet in there. You can relieve yourself in the American way."

But when we went in to look for it, snapping on our flashlights and then finding out that the electricity was still connected in the house, and next turning lights on, we saw a conventional Western toilet, its bowl clearly shattered by sledgehammers and its seat attached by an artful nest of barbed wire to its lower porcelain, so that it could not be used. It resembled, in its strange broken symmetries and deftness, some whimsical but elusive piece of art installation. The high school–age conscripts from three divisions of Mengistu's army had been dying in unutterable anguish as engineers fulfilled the orders of the commander, one Getaneh Haile, and went to work to make a nest of barbed wire for the toilet. The general, having urinated, had then gone to fight his way out to the Ethiopian garrison at Keren in a small convoy of armored cars, and on to the capital, where he had been executed. But he had denied the Eritrean People's Liberation Front and its friends the use of this wonder of plumbing. We walked around the artifact and laughed in hacking disbelief. That this was on his mind!

What did this say of Ted's hopeful surmise that something magnificent was about to happen to human brains? That the colonel was able to shrink his attention from the military catastrophe to this bit of porcelain mocked the idea and declared we were deeply implanted in folly and unreason. In our laughter was an awe at the scale of his stupidity. I would dream of the camel and the ridiculous colonel. And of slaughter.

After we left the Ethiopian highlands, back in Port Sudan we found there was no transport out of the city, for Air Sudan was on strike, and road movement to Khartoum was frozen. Sudanese soldiers were massed around every roadblock in and out of the city to keep the citizenry and any aliens within the limits. So, we were back amongst the fallen, the human race as it was accustomed to be. And it was still the month of Ramadan as well. In the West, people at Christmas put off thinking and reacting in favor of gift-giving and sumptuously stocked tables and bars. In the Sudan, they had put off thinking and reacting in favor of the yearly duty of penance. Leaving our Eritrean guesthouse, Stacey and I were dropped into town to visit a man who chartered aircraft. The man told us he could not organize a chartered flight until the day after Ramadan ended in ten days' time. Eid al-Fitr, they called the day of celebration. Planes were at the moment very much in demand because of the Air Sudan strike, and it would cost $4,000 in American dollars — currency or traveler's checks — to get us to Khartoum. I said I was not sure I had that amount — in fact I knew I would have to go back to the guesthouse and count. Credit cards? we offered. No. These things are not working at the moment, he explained. The politics, he told me. Banks had been ordered to suspend business. Perhaps with wisdom greater than mine, he spoke of politics as if it were a weather front. The eternal verities, God and finance, would reassert themselves after the storm of politics.

Back in the Eritrean guesthouse I found we had the required amount. Cath and I went back to the charter office, and a man, tired from doing the night vigils of Ramadan in the mosque, organized our transport.

On the morning of the Eid al-Fitr celebration the streets around the guesthouse were full of children in bright fabrics and giddy in celebration. Amongst them, the charter plane company man approached the guesthouse's gate wearing a brilliant violet *jellabiya* and accepted our combined currency and told us the plane would come from Khartoum for us at nine the following morning.

We reconnoitered the airport that afternoon. Nomads were camped on the edge of the apron and seabirds had made nests on the light posts. Camels stood arse-end to us on the tarmac itself, foraging the cracks for grass.

At nine the next morning we arrived back at the airport, where a detachment of soldiers, with an air of routine rather than of intimidation, held us at the gate outside the terminal. They kept us there until we heard the hallelujah drone in the air above us and saw a Beechcraft make a pass over the airstrip to chase the camels off.

The Beechcraft landed through shimmering air, and in that light it seemed to be a two-dimensional thing that came towards us, though when it landed and the engines were cut a hulking Egyptian pilot descended from the cockpit. I was delighted to see he was wearing a formal blue shirt with epaulettes on the shoulders, and a black tie, all of which spoke to him taking his profession seriously, which I preferred pilots to do. He introduced himself to our small group and told us his name was Falit, and I wrung his hand. "We thought we were going to die of old age in Port Sudan, mate," an earnest Stacey told him. "Pleased to meet you," said Cath, perhaps the only one of us who was not too grateful. Though she was anxious to get back to Sydney and our daughters, she did not, in her sturdiness, consider this an extremity, a crisis.

Everything seemed to be turning up roses by way of this man with the epaulettes, though the aircraft was being filled in the least satisfactory way possible. A line of Sudanese men bore aviation fuel to the plane in watering cans with the nozzles off, the fuel having been taken by stopcock from a storage tank whose electric pump was — in the spirit of this republic — on its last legs.

Refueling thus took forty minutes, during which time we asked our pilot, Falit, questions about what the capital was like now. He looked at our camera gear and said, "Crazy. You won't need that unless you want to get into trouble. The army is everywhere in the capital!"

The task of refueling finally done, I was pleased to see that Falit tested the quality of the fuel in both wing tanks, port and starboard. He slipped a coin to some scrawny nomad kids who wandered up in their dusk-clogged *jellabiyas,* to pay them to patrol the edges of the tarmac and keep the camels away. These were the meatier and more sluggish Lahaween camels, we had been told by an Eritrean. Bad for racing. But they had, whether through meat or milk, seen many families through the drought and famine earlier in the decade, and killing one would give deadly offense and incur a large debt.

The Egyptian pilot showed us how to dispose our luggage in the bins on the fuselage and throughout the plane. He then balanced us to a T, assessing the bulky Stacey before choosing a forward seat for him. When he asked Cath to sit behind him, I kissed her and she could clearly feel my uneasiness, giving me a little punch in the side and saying, "Now, don't be silly." She was right in her suspicions. I hated it when pilots made too much fuss about weight. They seemed to me to be inviting catastrophe.

Falit disposed the rest of the crew and me throughout the plane, and we made the smoothest of ascents out over the Red Sea salt pans. I looked down and saw the young boys with their sticks chasing a camel, then giving up as we disappeared from their world. We were very quickly free of the city and out over the most vivid degree of blue permitted on this planet to the human eye. We then turned and put that impossibly dense azure behind, and now everything below us seemed trackless yellow and brown, and the next great simplicity after the sea was a seamless sky arching from Ethiopia to Egypt and westwards to Chad.

It looked like the earth had resisted the imagination of God or poets, I thought in exhilaration. The basic startling elements! Just one color contrast.

The aircraft was graceful up here. I could hear the soundman and his assistant chatting. "Is Port Sudan the armpit of the universe?" Stacey asked them. "Or is it located a bit further down the spine?"

I looked around, grinning broadly, my gaze settling on the calm pilot, his preflight sweat drying at this altitude, and, to paraphrase W. H. Auden, I felt that this was not a dark, dark day but a bloody fine day indeed.

Thus we rode for an hour, above politics, above the checkpoints and the intimate wounds of the earth.

Then we saw a great mound of dusty air across our way. I did not want to accept what it was. A sandstorm — at an altitude of 10,000 feet. The pilot confirmed it over our headsets. Would sand dowse engines? I wondered, reaching forward and nudging Cath's elbow. Of course, she turned into profile and smiled and seemed sanguine. These were merely the elements of the earth ganging up on her. She could handle that. She showed it with her quick smile.

We were fine while zooming across the

wispy top of the sandstorm. I waited for the pilot to tell us on the intercom that we were going back to Port Sudan, but in the end the news was worse. "Khartoum Airport is socked in," he said. "If we cannot find it, we must go on and try El-Obeid."

El-Obeid, a city in Kordofan, was nearly five hundred kilometers from Khartoum. I seemed to remember that it was so marginal that it needed its water delivered by tanker. We would be stuck there in that dry city in the midst of civic unrest. I made a face at Cath like that of a hanged man. She seemed to consider that a jape.

We sank into the globe of brown dust. The air beyond the window suddenly looked like a gray blancmange. It grew increasingly dark as we dropped down through 7,000 feet, and the sound of dust pinging on the plane's carapace entered the cabin. This was *definitely* dense enough to smother the vents of the engines.

The pilot picked up a towel from the spare seat, and began wiping his face and neck with it and cried, "Call if you see the ground!"

At 5,000 feet — we were all watching his altimeter now — an alarm went off, and red blips appeared on the altimeter screen. I leaned forward and read the symbols and the news. It was telling him the altimeter was off by 250 feet. I wondered if that mattered in a flat capital? It certainly mattered if you didn't quite know which side of that reading was land. As the red symbols flashed, the pilot cried out once more, "Tell me if you see the ground." He dragged his towel over his dome and neck and then simply switched off the altimeter alarm as one distraction too many.

At 2,500 feet I saw between gray wraiths of dust the earth and a flat-topped building. "I see it, I see the earth!" I cried. But then it was gone, subsumed by the dust globe.

The pilot shouted that he would go up to 4,000 feet and make a last try. Yet ascending again he toweled himself like a man who did not expect easy relief. We watched gauge-struck as the altimeter reached 4,000 feet, give or take, of course, 250 feet. Then we eked our way down, a hundred feet at a time, through the miasma. We reached 2,500, and as I called, "A bit lower," Cath turned and smiled at me. She looked serene, indulgent, as if a little amused at the pilot's towel-play.

At 2,200 feet we all roared, "The ground, the ground!" We had seen an undeniable gravel solidity down there, the core of things, the sweet earth. We sank lower and the dimness persisted, but then we broke out of the cloud and saw Khartoum Airport off to the side, all its lights on for our landing. The lights seemed like a gesture of fraternity.

The pilot dropped his towel, done with it, and let himself be wafted into line with the runway and down to the city in the permanent 11 a.m. dusk of its own storm and grim politics. And so we landed, reborn in the shriek of tires, as Cath seemed never to have doubted we would be.

I caressed her. I felt like the elected of the gods. I considered the landing a great mercy, and I did not face the reality that if today's weird landing hadn't finished us, perhaps the next one would do so with enhanced statistical validation. Even that, and the days of going to the airport and standing under sun or dust cloud to wait for a plane that never arrived — until one night it did — could not dent my sense of being amongst the blessed.

And indeed, Jack the Dancer hasn't convinced me yet. The persistence of believing in a plan, a lot, a destiny, a favor . . . what a lucky persistence is that. Doomed, as we know. What grand fortune to have a life in which the delusion of it can be sustained!

The sense that because the gods have been indulgent to you, the Dancer has a struggle on his hands. As illusions go, it will go too. But in the meantime, it is a sweet one.

FEATHERS

When Girly and I began to live together as man and woman, I was awed by the plenty of her body and gracious accompanying spirit, so that all that happened in our exchanges, as much as I was fixed to that short moment by her body, enforced my permanent wonder at her. It was one of the rare times in my life when I considered life serene and beyond contest. And that seemed to be the way the days were set. I remember sunshine and then slanting rain on the lake with the catch of fish already in, and I remember chasing bounders with Girly, and her racing in a great flash of limbs to claim what was fallen. I believe that such events, whose full meaning I could not utter nor sing, would be somehow cut in the air and remain for all men and women to watch and thereby learn from.

Then Girly became distracted. I remember being confused, and then one dawn she told me, "There is a man following me. He's a man related to me."

This was a great difficulty. Blood laws intervened, though that did not always stop it happening.

"But I think," she said, "he's magicking me. I am so irritable now. He follows me, and lets me know his eyes are on me."

I looked out from our hut at sundry times that day and saw the strict line of the dunes, and then, a distinctive head breaking the line. It was a cousin of Girly's in a headband that marked him for the Parrot clan. A man close to middle years, a man with a marriage. Gone lightning-struck all at once. Stricken by enchantment and meaning to enchant his way to her. He was stalking her, visiting every site of her life, even where the women defecated. He tried to witness all her travels.

When I promised Girly I would fight him, she lost all her calm. There was no doubt she was frightened for me because the man, whose name I do not give, was well tried as a fighter, and a danger to take on, the leader of a hunting squad.

And that was the end of all my early contentment. It was not that Girly welcomed his fixed gaze or his sorcery, or was flattered by it. But I had a mean intention to pretend she did. It was then that she suggested we set out on our own, willing to travel together and find and hunt our food. He was a man of cares and his absence from the Lake would, we hoped, cause note, and women would ask his wife about it if he absented himself in our direction. He had the power to make up his own mind about that, but he would need to see our departure in some way, by naked eye or vision.

Girly wanted me to go with her into the country that I believed was the country of her heart. She wanted me to accompany her to the Morningside of the world, a wooded plain that rose amidst flat hills made by the old rivers that enfolded the earth, and made occasional wide lakes favored by waterbirds such as we had by our Lake, yet shallow enough for us to wade across if we chose. Off there, a long way off, were believed to be the hardest and most dense stones. But hunting for them was not a purpose of ours.

The truth is that I resented taking this path not least because I believed it was the direction to the dead earth I had once occupied following my trial as a young man. Nevertheless, I let Girly lead. At every few steps I had an impulse to turn back and go to the Lake and try to kill this enchanted and enchanting older man. Better to be killed in an instant than lose Girly. She was my sky. But then with those same few steps I saw her care fall away, I saw her full youth begin to plump her features again, and she looked at me as if to say, "Here I am, your woman again, saved from alarm." So I sullenly believed I had to keep going. She had chosen to flee with me, I told myself. She had looked to me to provide her with the simple air of my own dedication, when I knew she was under persuasion to succumb to the seducer's song, the song that lay where love and death met each other. She was content to be my woman and I was proud of that, and in that spirit we walked on into the Morningside country.

We traveled for three days in fine country. I saw no wasteland, and without telling Girly, I kept an eye on the country we traversed but saw no natural outline of earth broken by the crown of the man's head. We made perfectly fine shelters from the branches of the writhe tree and within two days of continuous walking and singing — Girly was better informed on this country than me, as it happened — we reached a riverbank amongst all the shafts of deep-rooted river trees. It was a fine, broad river, the work of an ancestor giant of Girly's who had gouged it with a digging stick to commence its life. One of Girly's skills was throwing the nets, and she sat on the bank happily untangling the one she had brought, and took it down into the river till the water was at her thighs. She stood still then, holding the net like a child, a murmur of tune escaping her lips. Then, too fast for me to see it happen, she flung the net and soon we had strong-shouldered black and whisker fish, and biglips, in there. The sleek sides of the fish when Girly brought them up from the water sang to me with a fresh luster, as if I were seeing them for the first time. We cooked them wrapped in the wide branches of the sour tree that go so well with fish.

This was the place to stay for days on end. As long as the seducer did not know we were here and bring his sorcery and poison to the place! And we had not seen him, though I looked when Girly did not look for him, not wanting to meet or be reacquainted with evil. But I did look, and I saw nothing.

Each night we went to our skins in the shelter we had built on the bank. Then, one morning, I found something beyond the firestones we had assembled the day before. It was a bunch of blue and yellow feathers — I do not know if they came from his headdress, but the message lay there: "The woman I want is here, and I have been here to mark the ground." I hid the emblem, but there was trouble as soon as I said we should be moving on, for in Girly's mind we had just discovered a place to stay for as long as the heart chose! I could not tell her the peril had resumed, yet I could not persuade her to move on unless I did. In fact, we had a normal shouting affair, very bitter. I waved the feathers in her face and accused her of giving encouragement to the man, and wanting to show our direction so she could be caught, as in some ways the feathers showed she had been. Where was the sense in all this? There was none. That was what quarrels were for. I believed her innocent of the latest that had happened, but I was angry that the man had found us and felt bound to give a sign, as if I would not deliver Girly up to him and — above all, I hoped — she would not give herself.

So Girly and I did move on, sullen and listless, expecting that he was trailing us. That night, when we lit the evening fire, I angrily erected a barrier of branches around us, upwind, so that our faces could not be observed, and we ate our evening food facing the barrier.

At last Girly put down her strip of small bounder loin and said with a sudden clear head, "We have to separate from each other. If we're separate, he can't track both of us down."

I said of course that was true. "But he'll only track you," I said.

"No," she replied. "I will track him. He will not bring sorcery into my camp. I'll bring it into his."

"Or you will succumb, and run away with him."

"What do you want?" asked Girly. "Do you want me to say I wish to be his woman? Would that make you happy? You've been asking me all day to say it so you can feel just in throwing stones at me. You want to kill me. Oh, you deny it, but ask yourself!"

I would of course have loved to deny it and even felt the urge to deny it with a blow and so prove it was the truth.

"If we both track him, it will frighten him," said Girly. "Don't you touch him or enter his camp. Leave it to me. I will poison his fire."

It was a frequent enough female boast. Even wives threatened to change their men in various ways for the better and thus "poison their fire." Yet she weighed the words more solemnly and as if in her hand, and then said, "Judge me when you see me by the Lake again. I will be there before you, and you'll *know.* I can say now that all he's done is bring misery to me, but when you see me by the Lake, it's then you'll believe me."

When I woke the next morning she was already gone. Her footsteps could not be seen, only the sweep of the branch she'd so clearly carried behind; and then at a majestic tree, that ended. Beyond that, no further prints. When I saw that, I knew I had misjudged her. She was indeed a serious woman, and somehow in this severe time had been given the power of flight. Now I wished she were there so I could take back all my callow, mannish-boyish threats. What was clear was that she must be left to pursue her own plan, since her plan was in earnest. For the whole day I skirted the earth to the Nightside so that I would not tangle up her path by intruding on it. Except for wanting her, I was contented enough on my own track. I fully believed that as once she had been his prey, now he could very well be hers. For she was a clever woman. As long as she did not suffer any damage from him.

On the next morning I started back on a straight line to the Lake, believing I would meet her there and that she would have achieved something. I wanted to tell her I put trust of the highest kind in her.

■ ■ ■ ■

On the third morning, I came across the
river and tall trees with grassland beyond,
and I began to notice clumps of stone on
the open ground which pointed me on a
track to one of the flat-topped hills and,
clearly visible as a black space, a cave in its
flank. I did not doubt that the stones had
been laid either by the man or by Girly,
brought into small heaps by hand. I saw
some tracks too, but whatever they meant I
felt the necessity to follow. As I approached
the cave in the side of that flat hill I saw a
near-naked man lying on a fur by its door. I
did not try to disguise my approach at all
but went straight up. I told myself, *It's not
him, this fellow.* He looks too hapless. But
before I could get close, he scurried up and
most shamefully fled. I waited and then
watched him make a half-crippled return
after some time. I drew closer. It was him,
or else it was a brother of his. He looked up
at me and said, "Beat me to death. I don't
care." And then he almost wept with pain
and turned on all fours and made his way
out of my sight again, and from the intervening rocks between us came the comic sound
of thunderous farting. Somehow Girly had

encountered him and reduced him to this, this mere pipe for shit. He returned to his skin, his lips looking blue, but vanished again almost instantly. "You'll get over this," I told him. I half smiled. "Though it seems severe now."

"You are welcome to her," he said. "She is a poisonous woman. She will kill you when it suits her."

"She is a serious woman," I replied. "She is not to be played with." And most of the time since I have followed that same advice myself.

It was a joy to go on treading my way back towards the Lake.

THE ESKIMO AFFAIR

I was in my late fifties when I shot a documentary for a wealthy man with a particular interest in the indigenes of the Bering Sea. My first film on Learned Man and my two on Eritrea had drawn the attention of this fellow, and it is apparent even to me now that I sought to have other worlds than my normal, suburban one somehow enlighten and enliven me.

The filming was a pleasant enough task despite its slightly doleful focus: the parlous condition of the native peoples of the region. The toxin that contact with the outside world had introduced into their lives. I shot the first half at a number of locations in the Arctic during one northern summer. This second summer Cath was accompanying me to Anchorage, where I was to meet up with a California crew headed by a fellow called Angelo Rugis, who was good enough to be his own director. I'd worked with Angelo and his crew previously and had trust in them. I would shoot my own footage and combine it with theirs — using the same modus operandi Andy and I had devised, and which I'd used ever since.

The other crew was bringing the lighting and other gear. I felt I was getting away with murder, letting others do the heavy work of formal shots and setting up. I had been lucky enough to have persuaded the world into wanting *my* eye.

After staying in a pleasant hotel in Anchorage, we were bused to the airport, where I waited for the plane to Nome talking to Rugis and his crew about our intentions and the style we had attempted to implement in the first film the year before. There would be a fair number of slanting shots of Inuits, Yupiks, Chukchis — taken from below, perhaps, to get the light on the planes of their faces. But full-on too. The angled shot, though, would suit the Arctic places in which, for example, we would see whale jawbones raised as monuments against the sky. Honest visages were important to the person who had commissioned the film, however. A lot of them. Visages shot against the lines of bare terrain. Fraught visages. Visages with dark blooms and the harrowing of alcohol in them. Our man didn't want us to capture the picturesque, though Arctic indigenes *trying* to be picturesque for a living was part of the story and couldn't be avoided.

While Angelo and I were conversing in fairly general terms, I saw a woman wheeling a fine set of hand luggage, and all the angles of her limbs and even the manner of her toting luggage seemed familiar. Suddenly words stuck in my throat. For this was Louisa Wanstap, the avowed love of my later life. This was a woman I'd once, not many years before, declared myself ready to die for. I wondered if she were here to make good on the pledge. When Louisa saw me, she smiled at me as if I were a fondly remembered item in a history. A phase. And she *was* lovely. I thought, *Then I wasn't utterly mad.* Yet I had been. I was embarrassed that she had encountered me only in an overblown location like this, not in a city where we could meet for coffee and I would be able to apologize for my earlier and flawed ardor. And apologizing to her would mean a parallel apology to Cath.

I nodded and smiled sociably as myself. I did not wish to die for her anymore. I had said to her one morning in Denver that I wished I could be associated with her at a cellular level, to be organic to her, and so to laugh, sing, cry, and die with her. The excessiveness of that ardent compliment was the thing that, in remembrance, rankled the worst, apart from having started the affair in the first place. But to say that was to try to excuse the inexcusable. Obviously, I had not been granted cellular identity with her and, despite the lack, was getting on fine.

There was that in our exchange which said, "We'll talk later!"

I wondered how to talk later. The bombast of emotion was gone. Would plain words serve?

This film on the Bering Sea was the suggestion of an executive of an elegant adventure travel company, the man at the head office of the Frederick and Gloucester Travel Company, who had been in correspondence with me now for nearly two years. He didn't want a cruise documentary. He wanted us to see the places we visited, including the Bering Strait and its lack of ice, as a symptom of crisis. Subject to what I chose to do, he wanted the images to speak for themselves. Where possible, without artificial three-point lighting. That would mean interiors would be dim, and that would be fine, he said. I discussed the spirit of the thing with him, the narrative pace, the emphasis on silences between speech. He wanted unpretentious, matter-of-fact narration too.

"I'm no heroic sojourner," I told him. "I'm not Robert Flaherty." Flaherty had been a miner and gold seeker, who in 1922 somehow managed to film, in nearly impossible conditions, the supposed (it's disputed) first documentary — *Nanook of the North.* They also called his style of film, the people who studied film, "salvage ethnography."

All the people at the airport that day were traveling from Anchorage to Nome on Alaska Airlines for one of only three purposes — the first was to travel on our ship, the second was to return home after medical treatment or other business in Anchorage, and the third was to work in the Arctic mines along the east coast of the Bering Strait. It was easy to tell who was who: the Eskimo mamas and their diabetic children were obviously returners, and the mad-eyed tattooed smokers were equally identifiable. It was clear that someone as skillfully made-up and discreetly accessorized as Louisa Wanstap was going on the same ship as us.

I'd been a sinner *and* a lunatic, and was about to be punished. It was an old story

270

but I'd found, when the fever for Louisa had first overtaken me, that it was entirely novel. I was at an age when a man still feels full of skill and potency. He finds though that he has assembled a definite and far from infinite bag of tricks, and that there are no limitless possibilities. He develops an abhorrence for his calm and finite life. He and his wife are busy in all areas of life other than those that serve their love. The wife is depressed by falling hormone levels and fear of falling desirability. What an opportunity for her true lover to be attentive, a consoler, as at altars and other venues we swore we would be. This is the moment of which Camus writes that we must imagine Sisyphus, the rock-roller, happy. Yes, happy! Knowing that all is falling and even absurd, but saved by devotion. I understood none of this then. The drive in me was primitive. And there is a panicked feeling common to many men in my situation that we don't feel we've had, or are going to have, enough sex. We have reached thus the plateau of life: and humankind claims to desire the plateau of security with the same energy that it abominates it. We have a feeling there must be a richness beyond. So we are looking for someone to wreck a life over!

On the plane to Nome, the mountains

crowding out the horizon in impossible numbers, exposing even in these days of Arctic warming improbable bowls and densities of snow on their haunches, I said to Cath, "There's a publicist on board from Ocean Films. You know, the crowd in California. She worked with me on the Four Corner States film."

"Is she that young creature with the fancy bags?" Cath asked.

"Yes. I haven't spoken to her yet. Waved to her at Anchorage."

I felt that the fake casualness of dropping personal pronouns might itself proclaim guilt.

Cath seemed more interested in the immensities of snow below.

The light in Nome was Arctic in its way, at best pearly, part whiteout, part overcast, with air that might at any time turn itself into stinging little pellets of ice. Angelo and his crew and I gathered at the luggage carousel looking out at the daylight, discussing it, how to make a virtue of it, this atmosphere ungenerous with shadows. We would go with it, and with the other options that were sure to present, the bright sunny evenings on isles of tundra.

At the carousel, I saw Louisa across from us talking to a couple of other women.

In a sort of daring, feeling despicably cunning, I said to Cath, "D'you want to say hello to Madame Wanstap?"

"You go. I'll say hello on the ship," Cath replied.

I set out and rounded the carousel. Was there any sense in which this was a renewal of approach? I wondered. Did I want in any way to again toss up into the air my defined and settled-upon life? Even now, as I approached her, and could see the indefinable aptness between her brown hair and the way she wore it, I could see again that she was justifiably worshipful.

Louisa took my approach very leniently. She smiled but did not excuse herself to step aside from her friends as if we had anything private to say. She wore my acquaintance lightly, saying, "Shelby, hello! Don't tell me you're with this film crew."

"Collecting some shots. I've got my own Sony 4K. And then there's the crew."

"So . . . still the king of cinema verité?"

"Still presuming."

"How *are* you?" she asked emphatically, and her two friends turned their attention to looking for their luggage on the conveyor belt.

I mumbled something and then said to her meaningfully, "I hope you're well."

"I sure am," she replied. "I'm married, you know. A production exec at Highgate Films. Nice fellow."

Was she lying about him? The aging boy in me half hoped so.

"Of course, he couldn't come, but I always wanted to see the North," she said with a shrug, which was beguiling, of course, without any effort from her.

"Your wife's here?" she asked, nodding towards Cath.

I briefly wondered if she wanted to get an indication from me as to whether there'd been confessions which, in implicating me, had implicated her?

I lowered my voice. "I don't know when I realized I had to work things out with Cath. But I remember, you were talking about your exec even then. You'd already met him."

"I'm glad it all worked out," she said. "You were so cute. I never believed a word you said, though. I'd love to meet your wife."

As in her first smile in Anchorage, there was no hint of accusation. And yet I had the responsibility now to apologize to her. Because I had seen her amiable soul and her beauty, and had presumed to use it to subvert my own life.

"You are on the ship, aren't you?" she asked.

"Yes," I said. But then residual vanity made me rush to say, "We're not shooting a tourism documentary, though."

"So, no dinnertime pictures of us Americans knocked out by the entrée!" she replied with a laugh. "And no silhouettes of held hands at the stern railing?"

Just then two Inuit bus drivers, a man and a woman, presented themselves at the carousel. The male said in a baritone voice, "Transport for the folk on the *Nunatak* just outside, folks."

When I went back to Cath, the male bus driver already had her suitcase in hand.

In this light from which all vigor had been sapped, Nome looked a dreary former gold-rush town, but the Inuit driver showed its grim saloons along Front Street to us. Passengers photographed each other at the Iditarod finish line, the end of the yearly dog sled race from Anchorage, commemorating a delivery of diphtheria vaccine to the children of Nome in 1925.

Angelo and his crew, and Cath and I, got a lift back to the community center, where we set up lights and installed a sound boom for the dancers who were gathering to welcome our boat. Angelo and I had another talk about what we were after, though I remained preoccupied about having both Cath and Louisa in the one Arctic vessel with me. As I chatted with Angelo, a crowd of Eskimos turned up — boys and girls, hefty prediabetic mothers, old men with walrus-skin drums, Yupik and Inuit. Despite my research, I could barely discern who were Yupik and who were Inuit in the smocks and designs the dancers and singers and drummers wore. I knew the two peoples were related, and that this was Inuit country, so the Yupik must be here for jobs or perhaps schooling. The subtlety of the symbols was lost on us, but not on our cameras. Angelo didn't seem to be afflicted by much consideration or doubt. He seemed, that is, to have the message. He had also seen the footage I'd taken during the previous northern summer.

The walrus-skin drums began to pound. The Yupik and Inuit in their ornamental parkas and mukluks began their dances — drum dances, walrus dances, kayak dances, courtship dances. Long shots, close-ups, close-ups simply of pounding mukluks. In this strange latitude, and its endless Arctic summer evening, under storm clouds, we filmed Eskimos going home on foot or by car from a church parking lot whose puddles were threatening to freeze. I was able to advise Angelo on getting acres of meaning out of the reflective puddles.

Packing up after, we delayed the bus, but at last climbed aboard, apologizing to the other passengers. As we approached the dock next to our ship, the *Nunatak* — which looked to be about eight thousand tons, no egregious cruising vessel but a purposeful one — some squalls began, raking the beaches. There were hovels and lights on in the sand dunes. Beach miners, who washed the gray sands and gravels for gold. There again was the story, the story some film-maker would want to garner. From beside the bus, where we were preparing to identify our luggage, I saw Louisa walk up the gangway of the *Nunatak* in a heavy parka. Cath had left the event earlier than me, and I found her in our excellent cabin. Though I could happily live out of a suitcase, she had dutifully unloaded my underwear and socks into drawers, and she showed me my share of the drawer and closet space.

As the ship pulled away, I looked out of the spacious port and saw a light in one of the onshore hovels. There, I believe, was some soul as transparent as mine. His panning for gold in sea grit would have made

277

utter sense to any woman he had known, and the better she had known him, the more sense it might have made.

The next morning, under a grim Arctic sky which had never got dark, Cath and I ran into Louisa Wanstap outside the dining room. I made the introductions, and soon Cath and Louisa were talking about the Bering Sea and other travel like old friends, Louisa lamenting that she had heard that because of the weather we weren't landing on King Island, which she seemed to think was some apogee of Eskimo-ness.

I heard Cath ask Louisa if she was sitting with anyone for breakfast, and telling her she was welcome to join us. Louisa said she would be very happy to. I floated on this sea of polite language and knew not what it meant or where it would lead — an enriching of acquaintance or of warfare.

From our table in the dining room we saw the abandoned island under the lash of a summer squall, all of its ghost houses full of flitting phantom presences moving on stilts on the cliffside. Despite the visual distractions that had briefly halted conversation, I was pleased when the demographic of the table was complicated by the arrival of Angelo and his crew. And then a bearded man, who hung around the film crew discussing lenses. Louisa seemed to know him, though her raised eyebrows might have suggested she thought him harmlessly quaint. "Leon Silver," said Louisa, "the renowned Shelby Apple."

Louisa had met him on the plane from San Francisco. It turned out that he was a professor of semiotics at Stanford. Cath, who knew what semiotics was, asked him if he was working on Eskimo symbols and their meanings, and he said that though he had done some work on that sort of issue with the Hopi and Navajo, this was pure holiday. We had after a while to excuse ourselves and set up on deck to take our wistful footage of the uninhabited island. It encapsulated, in its way, what we were meant to narrate.

In the wonderfully threatening light the next morning, the ship's crew dropped us off earlier than the other passengers on the landing stage at Little Diomede Island, the last island before Russia. There was plenty to film. At the skiddy landing stage, dogs dining on seal intestines barked us ashore. A husky, tall Eskimo named Warren, in jeans and a puffer jacket, welcomed us. He then guided us through the steep, seemingly crowded town where drying carcasses of fish and seal hung from frames in air of authoritative gray density. Long walrus-skin boats, draped with seal skins, were stored on their frames as well and were photogenic. We talked to women and rowdy kids and reflective men, most with unmarred, ancient Asian features, but little more than pleasantries were exchanged. Pointing at me, Angelo told the eager-eyed kids, "He's not from the Lower States. He's a kangaroo!" After gazing at me, the kids improbably hopped kangaroo-style across the slick slope, the mud and binding rocks of home.

After we asked Warren if we could film him, he asked us to his kitchen for coffee. We crowded in, and were greeted warmly by his wife, a majestic fat woman with a phenomenally flat face, who smiled at us like two-dimensional mercy as she served us coffee. I think, from the little I know, Warren's totem must have been an eagle, for there was an Eagle Beer bar clock on the wall, Philadelphia Eagles place mats on the table.

Out of the window, the outline of Big Diomede — or Ratmanova, as the Russians called their Arctic island. It was tomorrow there. The dateline ran between, through that murky intervening water.

"The Russians took most of the people away to the mainland," said Warren. "They made them send us messages. In my father's days they were always saying, 'Come across to us. Eskimos are allowed to oil machines and to drive them here, and date white women.' "

One could make a drama about Eskimos on Little Diomede crying out about American glory to the inhabitants of Big Diomede, who sang of Marxist glory back to them, and of course, of love across the barrier, an ice-crossed Romeo and Juliet. A great political and ethnographic comic tragedy! The diabetic and bourbon-blighted indigenes of the States — for we had seen the gray, booze-ravaged faces at doors and windows as we set out for the community hall — in contest for the ideological laurels with the diabetic and vodka-blighted indigenes of Russia.

By mutual consent Angelo had lit the room dimly to suit the pale blue light of the day outside, and by now the other passengers on the *Nunatak* were landing in Zodiacs. I went out to meet up with Cath to protect her from falling on the skiddy seal guts at the landing. She was not in the first boat, from which the first off was the enthusiastic Professor Silver festooned with photographic equipment cases. To his credit, he helped an elderly couple ashore, and then ranged up the path into the township on its cold slope.

The last one to land was Cath.

After the filming, I met Cath back on the ship and we had a brief rest before we got ready for the evening meal. As we left, Cath said, "By the way, I asked your friend Louisa, the Californian woman, to have dinner with us so we can have a proper talk."

Whatever that meant. When we arrived in the dining room, Louisa was already there. I steeled myself, but after the greetings Cath and Louisa immediately launched into conversation. Looking around desperately for Angelo and the film crew, I heard Louisa start talking about her husband's job with Highgate Films.

"They do great work, of course," she said, "but he'd love to be an independent producer, even if the pickings are slim. He was executive producer on that Michael Chabon film *Wonder Boys,* and coproducer of *Bergman's Flush.* Just loves the business!"

"He's fortunate," said Cath. "And you're still working for the same crowd? Ocean, was it?"

"No, I'm on my own now," said Louisa,

with her lovely shy smile — a mile-long smile as I thought of it. "I've been working flat out for the last three years and recently I just realized I needed a break. I don't know what it is, but I've wanted to see these places since I was a kid. I'm a big fan of that very butch Arctic fishing show too, the one on cable. I had to really clear my books to do this." She grinned more broadly still. "I had to be selfish. I have an understanding business partner, but there's not a lot on at the moment, mainly festivals, and she's covering for me."

I indulged a two-second daydream, myself the Arctic cinematographer, she the Bering Sea publicist. Me Tarzan, you PR woman!

"And Cath," Louisa pursued, "I believe you have many production gifts."

Itching in my soul, as if condemned by a deity to wear an eternal spiritual hair shirt, I rushed in to answer. "She does a lot of my production scheduling as well as her gifts as an editor. I'm hopeless at it. In the past I hardly even scheduled things, just let what happened happen."

"Well, a production schedule is no work of art," said Cath in her flat, take-it-or-leave-it manner. Sometimes I found it admirable and even alluring. I didn't know what I thought about it now. I just wanted everything to come to a close and resolve itself into a quiet night. I improperly desired both of them, but not in a proximate, breathless way. I was, for the rare moment, their aesthete.

"How do you like your cabin?" asked Cath, changing the subject, for the truth was that she did think production schedules a lesser art, where to me anyone who could put one together seemed to have gifts beyond my imagining. But Cath, as always at sea, was very interested in cabins — we had had some hard ones off West Africa, great heat and a barely three-quarter bed, and closet space befitting a woman of only two kaftans and two shifts. That was when I was filming . . . Christ, I couldn't even remember. Oh yes, heading for Namibia after the Mali elections, 1992!

Along the way, Cath, as my companion, had learned to cherish a good cabin, and had one on this journey, and was willing to discuss it with people.

"Are you sharing?" asked Cath of Louisa.

Louisa laughed. "No, I splashed out on a full cabin," she replied. "It's an indulgence, I know. But I'm starting to get too old to share a cabin like a teenager with another woman."

I'm starting to get too old . . .

Her journey was thus costing her the equivalent of a midsized sedan car. That's how much the Arctic and the Eskimo meant to her.

I saw across the dining room, at a bigger table than ours, Silver had found a chair and was talking with Angelo. I noticed the professor's abnormally well-developed shoulders, although I suppose they weren't abnormal by Californian standards, where people "worked out."

"I do love my cabin," said Louisa with sudden exuberance. "I think I could live in it forever if they let me. All the Arctic explorers would have loved my cabin."

"I admire ours too," said Cath. "And I agree with you. A person could happily live in that ship-borne stupor . . ."

Across the room, Professor Silver was backing away from the camera crew's table with his arms raised in an appeasing gesture. The production assistant, Sue, seemed to be the cause, and our pleasant soundman half stood, as if to avenge a slur.

Louisa had noticed it too. "Oh God!" she said softly, as if she had a stake in what was happening.

Cath put a hand on my shoulder to prevent me rising to whatever offense had been given or compliment misinterpreted. Louisa said, "He's such a simpleton for a clever man. People get him wrong all the time."

"An idiot savant?" I asked cruelly. Across the room the potential for a fracas looked to have diminished, and I saw Silver with his hands extended begging for tolerance.

"He's brilliant," Louisa said. "But maybe not gifted at ordinary things."

Cath was examining not the drama across the room but Louisa, who shook her head tightly. "All I know is that he means no harm." And then she laughed. "I suppose George Bush would say the same."

"Kind of you, to be so understanding," said Cath. I was thinking the same. I was thinking: noble, kind, whimsical, gentle, ample-hearted woman! Divine legs, divine ankles too! A concatenation of the graces physical and spiritual! I was right to perceive in her a special deliverance for someone. The problem was that once I had convinced myself I was the intended subject for rescue.

When the dinner ended, I found I had in my nervousness drunk the main share of two bottles of wine and was exhausted. The strain of having thrown myself at, embarrassed myself with, Louisa, of knowing that I had once used her in a demented attempt at some sort of escape from my life, and of knowing that Cath did not know that, and of spending a night with both of them — all that wearied and jaded a man. And I realized that to allow Cath to talk to Louisa Wanstap from a position of ignorance was criminal. But how could I tell her here, on a ship in waters that were Arctic ice melt, in a place from which a brisk and angry departure was impossible?

The awful, desolate Chukchi Peninsula was our nearest port. The easternmost and least populated corner of Russia, it had no buses, no planes, not even a train, and nowhere to link up with a quick flight home. Not even an amiable bar to sit in, absorbing anger while waiting for the cab to the airport. Especially after they closed the gulags of the region, and decided that liquor was bad for the Chukchis, the mainland relatives of the people at Diomede.

If there was no escape for an outraged Cath off the coast of the Chukchis, there was no escape for me either.

Next day our landing was at dismal Cape Dezhnev, the easternmost snout of Siberia, from which we gazed out at the Bering Sea. It seemed spiritlessly empty in a way the Australian deserts never were. I would need to be a Chukchi to see its value, but the abandoned village on the foreshore seemed to say they didn't see much value in it either. The truth is that, as with King Island, the indigenes were sad to go and needed to be forced from this barren shore and its bounteous sea, and enter a state-organized indigenous village somewhere else!

I went ranging about the hill behind the cape, for the dinner had reacquainted me, even in Cath's company, with my infatuation for Louisa. My mind and this murky air were pervaded by her. Out of the blue, she had become the universal question.

Ashore, we filmed Yupik kids doing their best with the grim summer day, sliding and swinging on the play equipment in the grounds of the school. In the Palace of Culture, I got some footage of the Yupik and Chukchi dancing, then aimed my camera at ravaged Eskimos, men and women, looking hollowed and deathly as few alcoholics, even poor ones, did in the West, and who gathered by the door of a nearby communal kitchen.

And through it all I madly believed I was once again enchanted by Louisa. I was returning to the crime. Did other men of my generation do the same? Yes. But I had believed I had repented.

Laws of Hunting

Of so many of the animals, the mother is different from ours in the manner of bearing of the young. All our great companions on this earth beget a small wormlike creature which then makes its way from the womb to a pouch where it finds shelter and nourishment and protection while it grows. Then it appears in the world without anguish. There is a tale that as a punishment for the recklessness of one of our women at the beginning of time, women were deprived of this form of easy birth and that one day, when we have all fulfilled our duties, our women will bear less pain in their giving birth.

By way of furless wormhood and ripening in a pouch, the slicer who killed my son was born to the earth.

There are laws of hunting and there are customs nearly as rigorous as law. Dome noses are to be sought at special seasons of the year and can be approached by a party of no less than eight men, two harassers from the front, two flankers, two behind, and two to act according to chance. A dome nose can best be speared from the side, and when he falls, which is sometimes very sudden, it is better to be beyond the course and impact of that fall for the beast can crush a person simply in perishing.

The slicer is the worst and most testing of prey, and hunting it is the work of ten men. No one ever draws near the slicer alone, for this creature is too terrible to confront even if fading with disease or weakness. Slicers are skilled at seeming to fade, and then returning in a moment to terrible vigor. It is also the law that the larger beasts with young in their sac should not be attacked. One can tell when this is the case by the condition of their fur, the way it has been thinned to supply the unborn.

I have hunted many dome noses, but slicers are only hunted for one purpose, as a test for those who seek them out. You need to think slicer-wise, for they are secretive beings and do not easily show themselves. One of our ancestors, Ring-necked Parrot, a creature of scathing tongue, sings the slicers so thoroughly that they choose to keep to their boulders instead of risking another withering encounter with a bird that they cannot bring down with their huge forepaw and slashing claw.

Slicers mark their ground with an overpowering piss, and if you're traveling alone you can tell it's a warning and will run from it if you're wise. Slicers are great travelers too, fast and near invisible, a force in the world of the spirit as well as a presence in the land. But as private beings, they are torn between occupying remote rocks, which they cherish, and preying in the grasslands, where they are so potent and so wary, able to echo flickering light on grass and shrub on their own pelt.

If it's a woman's curse to bear a difficult birth, the slicer's curse is to live an unfriendly life from which it finds the need to strike into open ground only now and then. Yet a man is not fully a man unless he has been in a hunting party that sets out to encounter a slicer and then participates in the hunt.

When I set out from the Lake with my Son Unnameable, we had a hunting party of eight, Bandy being the eldest of the squad, then Dart, Stark, Baldy, Grass, and two new men — my son and a young man named Thorn — who were both to be tested by a meeting with the slicer, if that could be managed.

We sang our way on the line that followed the slanting rack from the direction of Nightside to Morningside. We were out there some days, and met some Upper Waters people out on a pilgrimage to the flint pits. We feasted together on a red bounder they had caught, and took the opportunity to rehearse with them some of the songs they gave us for their country in case we ever had to go there. They were good fellows, and pleasant to be with. We celebrated together, trading some Flower Eater songs and dances, and I thought how the outer strangeness beyond the camp was diminished every time we met people like that. But I noticed they carried emblems with them as protection. An old man who was the guardian of their emblems sat at a small camp separate from the main one, tending a small fire of his own.

The men from the mountains knew from our weaponry, and the care we had put into preparation of our spears, that we had an eye on the slicer. They realized then that it was a high hunt we were going to, and as we chewed thorngum they fell back on comic songs, inviting the slicer to give up and roll on his back, to forget his ferocity and his hunger, his unquenchable fire and his severity. They knew he could be invited by such tunes to come halfway towards us and to temper his magnificent fierceness to our weaponry and our souls.

When we left the Upper Waters, Dart moved at a shuffle as he sang the song for the path we were on. He was an excellent singer and his memory for songs was astounding. He sang, for example, about the perentie, divinely sly, only half-committed to making the world, wondering whether it did him enough honor or service as he gouged out the restless rivers and backwaters to entice the thirsty ancestor sisters.

We entered the trees around the first such lagoon. He sang and beat spear shafts against our shields in case the slicer had taken prey and was sheltering or drinking there. The slicer drank with a great delicacy, a humility, unexpected when you thought of his power. Leaving the thickets that marked the lagoon then, Dart sang us out into open country covered with bounder grass. The silver shrubs straddled a red plain where the leaves kept singing, with meaning, and so did Dart, as we got towards the places along the track of the perentie, where water had gone secret beneath the rocks and lay under each patch of clay. In his clear, incessant voice then, Dart sang us further forward on that slicer hunt so long ago and yet so sharp in memory. It was as if Dart drew the song from the earth up into himself and out into the air. The lines were holy in his mouth and praised the paradise to which the Heroes send us for a time as a mercy, so we may taste of it in the way of people, as the Heroes cannot. We must perish from this earth because the Heroes still have so many more children who are meant to be fruitfully placed here and entrusted with the country for *their* share of time.

We came to a water place, the lagoon named Brown Snake, and beyond it some hillocks where amongst the rocks my son and his fellow first timer caught a little hopper and brought it into the fire we had already set. We spent a pleasant night with all the stars to perceive and envy our brotherhood. A mild wind rose and combed the tall, lush bounder grass. It was the last night in the world for my Son Unnameable.

JUMPING THE RAPIDS

In a frenzy, I woke early to go on deck and watched an undying, vivid light drenching the sea and gracing the merciless Siberian coast. Then, bobbing like a habitual item in the sea, there appeared a gray whale, harpoon in its flank, floating in smooth sea with a marker buoy near it to identify the place. The indigenes, I knew, were permitted to spear leviathans on both the Russian and American sides of the Bering Strait. And here was the great beast, dead in slick water. Nearby was the Russian island we were going to today. I hoped with an automatic cinematographer's enthusiasm that the people would land their whale while we were there.

There would be a seal-meat picnic ashore today, and I met Angelo and confirmed that we would take track and an Elemack trolley and use them for a tracking shot of the seal-meat feast. And behind, a little way along the coast, stood a great avenue of whale jawbones, a ceremonial thoroughfare bordered not only with the huger arched uprights, but accumulations as well of whale skull plates and vertebrae. Whales had been ritually venerated and slaughtered here, and whale-meat storage pits were dug in permafrost. Meat could lie refrigerated there for Yupik ceremonies. We headed ashore early in the day, and two Russian policemen in their baroquely peaked hats watched us unload gear from the Zodiac. We filmed the setup of the seal-meat feast, capturing visions of women in thigh-long *kuspuks,* or dressed like Muscovite shoppers except for their sturdy leggings and boots, along with children helping or playing about the tables. A man who might have been a shaman stood on a knoll in a tall and flimsy frame-worked headdress as if ceremonial and magical events were imminent, though his cheap trousers were too mass market for full-on mystery.

We filmed the food but also the faces of those who served it. They put out bread and plates of boiled musk ox and seal meat, dried walrus and fish, with the fin of a killer whale, reddish and central to the feast, on its own small table. The police inspected this laying out of food with all the intensity of their boredom. The Zodiacs with the other passengers left the ship, and I saw them coming in past the killed and bobbing whale I had spotted that morning, which I'd hoped they would bring in for butchering before the arrival of the passengers. I got talking to a dark young woman who was a teacher on the island and asked her when they would land the whale. "I think this afternoon," she told me carefully as if passing a language exam. "But they do not tell me," she added with a laugh. She came from the far side of the Urals. She was as strange to them as was I.

The people from the ship landed and the feast began. I shot it with my discreet handheld while Angelo got tracking shots in light so strong that the production woman, Sue, had to walk beside the dolly with a black light-cutter held aloft in her hands.

I ate some seal meat when I could, and found it pleasant enough. Then, urged by a Yupik woman, and whether it was right for me to do or not, I tried a chunk of whale fin, chewing away at it, letting the whaleness pervade my mouth and imbue my face with the sort of satisfaction the Yupik or Chukchi woman wanted to see me display. Up the beach came a smiling Cath in a yellow parka, apologizing for not seeing me off. Far down the beach, in lilac top and black ski pants, I saw Louisa chatting to various folk from the boat as they all advanced towards the set tables. My sight endowed her, making her so thoroughly luminous and central in the broad scene that I was amazed Cath did not see it and fall into a rage of jealousy. I forced myself to focus on the passengers as they were intercepted by elders who called forth island dancers, girls in brown, some young men, who started performing a string of dances to the same walrus drums we had heard on the American side of things.

It was then that we were interrupted by the anticipated landing of the whale. Crews came down to the walrus-skin boats and lifted them off their racks. Some of the rowers were women, others middle-aged men. Were the young men away, working in factories, serving in Chechnya? With the rowers were men wearing the same framework ceremonial hats I had seen that morning. The walrus-skin boats, translucently orange this bright afternoon, were put efficiently in the water and pulled away from the shingle beach.

We shot the boats from behind the backs of the dancers, capturing footage of the Eskimo crew attaching the whale, the men in shaman hats standing in their places. Now the crews hauled away again, bringing in the great carcass. In the shallows, both crews slid over the sides and helped the dead creature ashore, the fatal harpoon still in place. An elderly woman, a bucket of water in hand, advanced down the shore and sang to the dead whale, while splashing water on its great head. Now there were even more intense dances by the feast. I climbed a hill and took in the scene with my handheld — the long shore, the bleak sea, the dancers, the whale, the cops, the schoolteacher, and the mass of passengers.

Coming down again, I met up with Cath on the edge of the feast.

"Are you enjoying this?" she asked, as we stood not so far from where the whale awaited butchery.

"I am," I replied with suspect emphasis, brushing my hand in a sort of caress along her arm. "Why wouldn't I?"

"Well," she said, "sometimes you don't seem to be all here."

"Here?" I asked guiltily.

"Here. At dinner the other night with the Wanstap woman, you barely had anything to say."

"I'm sorry. I thought I was . . . right there."

"It's not a complaint," she told me, "I just wonder whether you're well?"

I assured her I felt fine and promised I'd catch up on some missed or fobbed-off medical appointments when we got back to Sydney.

"Are you bored, then?" she persisted.

"What could I be bored with?" I was reckless enough to ask.

"With your job."

"What sort of ungrateful bastard would be bored by *my* job?"

"If you're bored, you're bored," Cath replied. "It's existential. I sometimes suspect you feel you can't say it because your father stuck out a boring job. But if you're bored and going through the motions, that's the reality."

"I do feel facile," I ventured. "But I'm not bored."

Certainly not in a world that contained Louisa!

"Outsiders are the best judge of your work. And they've already pre-bought what you'll shoot. Maybe your 'facile' is profundity to them. Why can't you just take what comes your way?"

I asked her would she like to come with me on a walk across the island later. It seemed to me to be a gesture of sanity on my part. "I think I'll stick to the lowlands for now, Shel," she replied. In fact, her right knee had a surgical wound down the middle where her kneecap had been replaced. I thought of our combined scars and atoms adding up to all this madness I was feeling.

Angelo and I conferred. He and his crew would film the avenue of jaws from the shore and then from amidst its ritual grandeur, and I would take my Sony inland and climb the hill behind and film the gigantic blob of whale and the village from above.

As I set out, the tundra growth looked shallow, but it soon proved to be a dense, waist-deep mesh of shrubs. The arctic flowers, yellow and purple and blue and tufted white, bloomed only six weeks a year and were a symbol of all things transient and ephemeral, which deserved to be lovingly filmed.

My path took me up the slope of the mountain and along the spur and down via a shallow valley to another beach just a little way from the village. I struggled through the tough tundra growth and I saw a line of passengers rising up the hip of the hill on a course bound to cross mine. An infallible thrill washed over me when I realized that Louisa was ahead of the others, though not far enough to promise we would have any privacy when she reached me. I kept forcing my way uphill and eventually she neared me, panting. After our greetings she asked a banal question about the filming, but every word was freighted with weighty meaning.

"This country is a test," she said, her blue eyes alight.

"I thought I'd get the long shot of the avenue," I said as everything vital in me seemed to crowd up into the base of my throat.

"The flowers are out too," I added as the others caught up.

"Purple saxifrage," Louisa remarked. "Very tough. Always the first to come out in the summer. Do you mind if we go with you, Shelby?"

I wondered if Cath would see my expeditionary orange parka blooming beside Louisa's lilac on the escarpment.

We all struggled forward, bending foliage and apologizing when it sprang back and lashed the walkers behind us. It took forty minutes of such wrestling to get to the summit, but it was worth it to see the whole compass of the island below, with the huge adornment of the thoroughfare with its great skulls, jawbones, and vertebrae. I began to film before we properly had our breath. Turning the camera west, I saw something unwelcome in the form of Professor Silver stumbling up from the blind side of the island.

"Ahoy there!" he called as if it were the most original greeting shipmates had ever given each other, carrying with him that air of being a man thoroughly happy. *Does he have a former wife somewhere who thought him the most boring and monochrome of men?* I meanly wondered. He was not puffing much either for a fellow who had forced his way across the tundra.

"Do you mind if I get some straight footage of the mainland?" I asked with suppressed irritation.

"Oops," he said, ornately lunging out of frame.

The other walkers sensed my annoyance and drifted away.

When it was time to descend, I followed Louisa and the others, and was soon wallowing in waist-deep bracken again. The sun was bright. There was heat and the vivid little flowers shone appealingly, and I sank down to plant level to film while, nearby, Silver chattered away.

I sweated plentifully on the lower slopes, trapped in the dense Arctic heath, struggling like a fly in honey. Out on the shingle, I went along the shore to reconnect with

Angelo and the crew and discuss whether we had enough. Angelo said he had shot four thousand feet.

Louisa and Cath had long since left the beach. That did not mean I would avoid doing something crazed when I got aboard again. It was not that I had every intention to do so. It was that I believed doing something crazed was unavoidable. I was a convinced lemming. I was in love with the precipice.

Back in our cabin Cath and I took turns in the shower. She was solid in her half-naked movements. Her breasts were gourds. On top of all my other grief, I was in a state of frantic grief that in recent times they had gone too infrequently caressed, thinking Cath deserved a better lover.

Back in our cabin after dinner, I told Cath that I had Arctic insomnia and knew I wouldn't be able to sleep. I apologized that I was going to sit up.

After kissing her treacherously I left the cabin and went forward past the lounge. I hoped Louisa would be in her cabin, but not profoundly asleep, as I paced up and down the starboard side and the stern framing my exorbitant speeches. I did not look at a watch, but at a given and emphatic instant, I turned inside, and waited awhile before reentering the soft hum of the interior of the ship.

Louisa's cabin was one deck below ours, and I took the stairs, every step feeling momentous and possibly irreversible. Standing in the slightly bilious fluorescent light at the head of her corridor, I breathed awhile, storing up oxygen for my bravery and planned eloquence. The seventh cabin was Louisa's, and I was about to make my way towards it when I saw someone enter the corridor from the direction of the aft stairs. I stepped back amongst the red curtains that screened the functional doors to the crew's quarters. And from here I saw it was Silver making his casual way down the corridor, without having seen me. He looked a little ridiculous, with both arms extended as if the ship were rocking considerably, which it was not on tonight's millpond Bering Sea. He was pensive and hesitant as he paused in front of a cabin and gave a discreet little knock. It was Louisa's cabin. Now I understood his almost sportive gait. The door opened to him, and I saw him touch Louisa's face, then he started kissing her. The door closed.

"Nooooooo!" I howled, without much sound, dropping to my knees. If anyone had seen me during these demonstrations, they

305

would have presumed I was suffering some sort of cardiac or vascular episode. And I found the necessary voice to plead, again over the murmur of the ship's engines, "No! Louisa! Louisa, no!" My mouth was in a rictus and I pounded the floor, carpeted here, with my hands.

After a while I got up with resolve and took myself to Louisa's door. But as I went to knock, all intention left me, all vigor, all plans, and all madness. I slumped against the opposing wall and slid myself along it. I had no idea and no care that anyone, observing, would think my dragging and stumbling in any way comic. It is painful to admit that I now considered pitching myself into the Bering Sea just to deal with this crisis of grief and emptiness. In a few breaths and a few seconds, however, I felt myself return to my flesh, and then I straightened and took the stairs thinking, *Christ, I'm tired.* And I remembered, as the first thing I could rejoice in, that tomorrow was a day of cruising towards the Aleutians, back to the islands of the American Inuit.

In our cabin Cath was deeply asleep in her bunk. I managed to take off my outer clothes before I got into my bunk, and allowed myself to be sucked into oblivion.

■ ■ ■ ■

We ended the journey with the shoot in the bag and the duty of editing ahead.

During the final stages of the voyage I would see Louisa chatting with the two friends I'd seen her with at the carousel in Nome, and with the older couple, but there was no hint of her Silver association, and no hint of what it meant — nothing, something, everything. These were illimitable questions I was sick of rehearsing. Had she chosen Silver recreationally? Or had she sought him out because I, who had uttered such exorbitant pledges to her once, was around playing the dutiful husband? Or did her turning to Silver represent something about her marriage, or about mine? Or did it all mean nothing? The way Silver had been drawn into the cabin did not seem to bespeak any grand impulse on his part, and suggested sexual opportunism on hers. Had he been co-opted like a servant at that door, rather than entering as an equal partner? He seemed to have blundered into a great gift, and been a sexual lottery winner. It might be Silver's very lack of gifts and charms and adornments that she had chosen. Or were there merits in the fellow I hadn't perceived?

Such were the grand issues that ran through my mind. I am afraid compassion for the Inuit had very little part of my conscious life. And when I was not engaged in those ridiculous, vain, and unrequitable debates with myself, I was a studied and guilt-struck valet to Cath.

Like all fools I thought I had managed the deception, until the ship docked, and our bus to the airport stopped for the toilets near a river up which red-flanked salmon were trying to ascend. I watched them, all at once more concerned for the salmon than I had been for most people on the entire journey. These muscular fishes attempted the leap up the falls below the bridge. I felt, of course, that I had a lot in common with the leaping, striving salmon, and thus a kind of dull fraternity with Silver, a leaper in his own right. It was wonderful to see the salmon make the jump successfully, but a dreadful thing to see those milling in the ponds beneath the falls, their skin turning perceptibly from rosy to gray. Every time they jumped and failed to make the falls, their coloration grew duller. They thrashed in the pools of denial. They seemed robust still, sinewy, and yet doomed.

I was thus mourning the unsuccessful

salmon, looking down on them from the bridge, concentrating on them and their graying flesh, when Cath came up, and stood beside me.

"Did you fuck her?" she asked in a falsely placid tone. "All of those times you were out of the cabin? Did you fuck her?"

"No," I hastened to say, hungry to be able to make an assertion. "No, of course not."

"Did you fuck her once?" she asked again with that air of wanting to tidy things up, to eliminate the loose end. "In the past, I mean."

I looked down at the dying gray salmon. They seemed so able, no less so than the ones that even now were clearing the falls. Perhaps they had cleared them last year. In their prime.

"I did," I said, feeling appalled for Cath. She was my love. It was as if I were a compass whose arm had swung back erratically to true north. "I'm sorry, Cath. It was lunacy. A misuse of her, an insult to you . . ."

"I'll let her look after her own grievance. But I feel violated. Do you understand?"

I told her I did.

"Well," she said, "you've been mooning around for the whole journey and we haven't had anything happening, and generally we do when we go away. Generally, it sets us off. Travel as the great aphrodisiac and all."

A robust red male salmon bounded over the lower falls and she couldn't help but applaud. "Some people would consider you've been pathetic," she murmured. "I think you've been *bloody* pathetic."

"I have been," I agreed. "I know . . . When I . . ."

"When you saw her again? You thought, *Ditch the old lady!*"

"You're no one's old lady," I pleaded. "But yes, both times . . . Lunacy, Cath. I went mad . . ."

Cath whistled, country girl at heart. "Mad. Well, it might be a psychiatric condition to you. It doesn't mean it's not life and death and betrayal."

"The truth is I'm terrified of how mad I did go. How easily . . ."

"Then," said Cath, "you bloody well know. If you let it happen again, it's the end for me."

Under her counseling, if this is what it was, and under the counseling of the gray flesh of the unsuccessful salmon, I could see I had been afflicted. But I was awake, all at once, to my dementedness.

"I'm over it all," I said, marveling at how the obsession had all sloughed away. "It was

310

ridiculous . . ."

I felt scarified, though, by the question I knew would never go away. If Silver hadn't gone to Louisa's cabin, would I still be suffering the obsession, and would I be considering disrupting the world for it?

"So, are you going to California to shake her loose from her marriage . . . ?" asked Cath. "Or are you coming home with me? If I bloody let you?"

Utterly humiliated, I said, "I'll come with you if you'll have me." An exquisite thing: three young salmon vaulted the falls in unison. It made the graying and the failed in the shallows more poignant. "I'll be lucky if you agree," I added.

"I wouldn't say that. I *am* a cold bitch sometimes. But you have humiliated me, and you won't get away with that again. In the end, we all have to live and die with someone."

"I don't deserve to live and die with you," I replied. And it was the truth, of course.

"Do you still like anything in me? Do you?" she asked.

"I like everything in you," I assured her.

"Ah yes? You haven't even talked to me for the last three weeks. You were too riveted by the banalities of your Miss Wanstap."

I frowned and thought, *She's right.* A

revelation: Louise had never said anything remarkable.

"What's happened to you men? The fifties used to be the age of gravitas. Now it's when you all revert to being bloody Labrador pups. Running round, banging into furniture with your erections."

She was right about that. Like Louisa's discourse, my passion was simply a commonplace.

"It will never happen again," I said. And I was sure of it, for Louisa had imparted a terminal education to me.

Cath looked down at the tragic salmon and up again and shook her head, and then went to take a seat on the bus.

A Death Before the Death: The Slicer

In the morningside when we woke, we could see aslant our path the place Dart knew from the song of that country to be the Creeper Hills. Their sharp stones rose above the plain separated from earth by a morning band of vapor which caused them to float in the air. This was where the slicers liked to make their secret home. We all grew hushed now and Dart ceased his song. My son and his friend went forward with part of the saved carcass of last night's hopper and laid it on the ground as the rest of us drew level. We looked at the meat sacrifice offered to the grand presence. This was the meat the slicer would be tempted forth with. The light on the rocks became sharper and all their clefts and cunning concealments were apparent to us.

Two of our party went beyond the rocks, upwind, to make a noise with spear against shield in the hope of flushing the slicer out.

The two young men stood with the slaughtered remains, waving the carcass about in the grass to make its scent go further. I remained in the line, as did the five others, making a shallow trap of men, flimsy so that it might entice the slicer to emerge. The two young men by the meat were, according to a long-honored plan, to pierce the beast beneath his armpits and then raise his body above us on their spears. I had seen it done in the past, and when the slicer was so raised on a spear point it looked very much like a man.

Now, as we stood, we sang a softer song of invitation, and after a while could hear the men from the far side of the rocks making their harassing noise to nag a slicer from its nest.

At last we saw, amongst the boulders, a tawny and spotted movement and the lash of thick tail — the moving creature we had been imagining for so many hours and days was beginning to take an interest, for whatever reason, in the wider world. The men with the spear and shield drew beyond the rocks, safe from the slicer's approach because of where they stood upwind, and grew louder, with great hoots and mockery. A crasser animal than the slicer would have been driven forward to us by them. But it

314

took a great deal of such clamor to overcome the slicer's preference for being aloof. Once a slicer emerges, it is willing to fill the earth with its fearsome presence, but to get it to choose the broader and more dangerous earth takes a gift for haranguing.

When the slicer came into the open, we saw it was a female, more awesome than the male we had expected. A male might fight for his lair and advantage and food, and his woman and young. A female slicer would be driven by something closer to her, the future of her womb and her pouch, of those she was still to bear. We on our side kept singing to her in a more flattering and cooing way than the men on the upwind side. She moved forward like a judge whose laws we did not know, her head swaying, her shoulders magnificent and potent. She advanced on four feet, but now and then stood back on her strong hind legs to assess the air. At such times she was a person, with the appearance of someone who walked two-legged all day. Though the wind ensured she could smell both us and last night's meat, she wanted us to believe she took no interest in us at all. Why should she descend to recognizing us or show any desire for the gross meat on our living bones? For she had a way of denying that it was a hunger for flesh that had brought her out. She sought to convince us that she had a higher purpose than appetite. And it was possible to believe that she had come forth with her heroic indifference just to show us what life should be. That it should be her. That in us was a failed and imperfect thing. And there was no doubt we were all humbled by her.

She sank to four feet again and advanced on us, then rose to full height once more before instantly letting herself flop, this time as if she intended to sleep. I did not trust the easy way she rolled on the earth, and I hoped the young men remembered from the songs the warning that the slicer could go from yawning to a terrible furor and speed in only a shudder of the eye.

And her other gift to us was that when she moved again and clearly knew we were there, she pretended to be unsure as to whether we were phantoms. She began to run now, pawing herself forward with tumultuous muscles in her spotted fur while pretending to be interested in a different horizon than the one we were now tied to.

So she arrived at a little claypan, where she bent down on her four mighty legs to drink some icy water pooling at the base of a rock, before rising to her hind legs and throwing off pretense as she eyed us with a sudden frankness which declared that she meant to have us. When she hurtled towards us, I wondered if the songs we had sung were adequate to have set up my son and his comrade for this splendid destroyer's attack. I saw my son calmly step a few strides aside from the path of the beast, and heard the gruff, manly sound as he and his companion beat their narrow shields with spear shafts as if each wanted to be the one to draw the slicer to him. Both of them were brave to show themselves without hunching, to demonstrate to the creature that we ourselves were beasts of honor. We were the only animal that sang at such length, but there was weakness as well as sinew behind the songs. If a young man showed a being who he was and lived, then no one lesser could question his worth. As for me, I let forth a cry of pride, exultation, and terror as she entered within spear throw, and the two of them crouched.

It was then that the creature's path changed and my brave Son Unnameable was chosen by her. I saw with dread that my son's task was to allow the being to prove its power to us yet again. As for my son, he stood and allowed the creature to vault and descend on him from the sky. There was just the narrow stick spear and its point and his leg planted back to answer the broad attack of the animal and its purpose. According to our desires, the desire of the people, the meeting about to occur was meant to lead to the expiration of the slicer and the gush of the beast's heart blood. This was supposed to be followed by the emergence of the young man on the verges of the Lake as a surviving hunter, grinning and shouting, sometimes with a venerated claw slash across his upper body!

In this case, though, my son's spear point was not correctly aligned for the slicer. The shaft snapped, its point broke off, and the beast landed upon my son before I could move, and took to devouring him in her mouth while slicing at his throat with her monstrous thumbs. I heard my son's brief terror uttered from within, his blindness as his face and eyes and nostrils were torn away, and the great wheeze of breath as his life gushed forth from his clawed-open neck. It happened with such awful quickness. My son's companion tried to sink a spear deep into the slicer's flank, but the spear did not accurately puncture the creature's heart, and she continued with her whole being clenched on my poor, dangling son's face.

We all moved in recklessly then as the

slicer released my son's head from its mouth and reared on its paws to display its own bloody face. It seemed that we killed it many times over. As frantic as I was, overcome with the vision of my son's bloody, meaty stump of head, I took account of where its forearm met its trunk and drove my own long spear exactly there and up into its soul. The creature looked up briefly, releasing her jaws as if to take a breath and a second of contemplation. Then she fell, one of her great slicing thumbs still in my Son Unnameable's throat. Having seen for the last time the meeting of the earth and sky, the slicer sank dead on top of my son, having taught us her legendary lesson.

The men helped me retrieve my son from under the great beast. He still had life in him, and I promised him impossible acts of cure. The other men now told me that he was dead. One of them had brought a pouch of ocher in case of a hunting death, and I wrapped my son's head gently in a sack of netting, of the sort his sister would become adept at making. Then the men lit a fire and sang the death songs for my son, songs ending in a growl to frighten his confused soul away from us for the sake of its own peace and embrace of its death. I had by then taken the time to wash his mutilated face and body, which we anointed to the waist with ocher. One of the men felled a small tree with his axe of flint, and we marked it with our knives, incising on it the symbols of his mother's god for him to seek. After that we buried him with the shield and spear with great reverence, again constantly consoling him and urging him back to the Heroes' world he'd come from by way of Girly's womb. I was gratified that, whatever hard designs the heavens and earth had for me, I did not have to present him to my wife, who would have lamented his devoured face.

ELDERS

There was to be a significant meeting between Heritage officers and elders to discuss the return of Learned Man to his country. I was considering ways to get to the Riverina, since it would be a chance to see Peter Jorgensen as well as to understand what might happen with Learned Man when the elders returned him to his country. The organizers and the elders told me that given my long-held interest in Learned I was extremely welcome to sit in on the proceedings. The plan of management was to be presented to the meeting, including to an elder of each of the three tribes. Despite all the arguing and activity of Learned Man's familiar, Jorgensen, I guessed it would be inevitably modest, because of lack of input and interest from the white side.

I called Jorgensen and was heartened to hear his sonorous, amiable voice.

"Have you been invited?" I asked after

we'd exchanged greetings.

"Yes," he told me. "More talk! But they've said I can speak to the elders. I think the bureaucrats want me to assure them that Learned is more than a Paleolithic freak. That he lived in country, and loved country, as they do. That he was a member of a whole community, which had a profound relationship to the land. Basically, I suppose, what you'd call stewardship for the earth. But love . . . that too. As if their land was a living relative." He paused briefly then growled, "Anyway, you've heard me say all this."

I agreed, of course. Who wouldn't?

"There are riches in what Learned could say to the world," he said almost plaintively. "But our crowd, the settlers, were not willing to listen. The process will be complete then. The circuit closed."

Jorgensen and I had often discussed the pictures of Aboriginal people in our school histories — a naked black woman and man and a few naked kids in front of a dead, hunted marsupial, a native dog, a miserable gunyah. People who needed a fire yet were implicitly unaware of the warmth of kangaroo fur. A primal nucleus. Learned challenged that picture, turned it on its head, spoke of a richer, more potent life.

"I'm pleased that Brendan Hayes, who's the new head bloke from Heritage, has asked me to speak," he said. "Even if I harp on a little, even if I'm a bit of an embarrassment by now."

I knew what he was talking about. A few months before, Jorgensen had attended a ceremony at the Australian National University to hand back Learned Man to the three tribes of the Lake Learned system. During the event the elders from the Riverina were welcomed to country by Waradjuri elders, and the remains of Learned were brought forth while young dancing men from the Canberra Ngunnawal tribe and from Learned's own country set a fire by the dais and smoked all ill will away from the place.

During the proceedings a new smooth-faced vice chancellor made a speech acknowledging by name most people who'd been involved with Learned Man except the late Professor Spurling and the embarrassing Professor Jorgensen. He made no mention of Jorgensen as Learned Man's first white encounter, making only a reference to the "discoverer" of what had not been lost. He also failed to mention the lack of archaeological protocols that had come to apply since Learned Man was discovered, which Jorgensen thoroughly agreed with.

To treat Peter Jorgensen as the Christopher Columbus or Captain Cook of the Learned Lake region, the embarrassing figure who proclaimed the discovery of what was not considered lost, seemed an undue sensitivity on the vice chancellor's part. And in any case, Jorgensen had not wanted to be named as Learned's vainglorious discoverer, but as his brother in an encounter, the man who had exchanged souls with him.

After the handover was complete, the three elders of the tribe gave consent on behalf of the traditional owners for the remains of Learned and over a hundred other of his people to remain stored at the National Museum while arrangements were made for their future resting place.

"Well, for better or worse, Peter, you're not the slightest embarrassment to me," I assured him now. "I won't say what you are because you'll get a big head."

But the longer I spoke, the more it felt to me as if I had swallowed something immovable. Something radiant with discomfort. Was the sensation one of pain? It was somehow broader than pain. It included pain as in a wrapping of furry unease. I had no appetite these days.

Jorgensen called me back again the same

day and asked me at some length how I was. After finally telling him about my health, we discussed it at length. He was far too genial a man ever to become a monomaniac and believe that his grievances trumped all those of others.

"I wanted to say, don't come to the meeting for my sake. I got a second email from Brendan. He says that he made a mistake when he said I could speak."

I made a sympathetic noise and was a little amazed. I assumed he was somehow entitled to speak on Learned in perpetuity. He had found Learned's gleaming skull bone. He had found the wonder, and as the old Barkindji woman said, the wonder had found him. Many other elders had since told him the wonder had found him because Learned Man had a message for us. A spacious purpose. Yet so far only experts and enthusiasts knew of Learned. Peter Jorgenson knew that the purpose of the encounter had not been achieved.

I realized all was inertia again in the future of Learned Man. Not for the elders. Learned Man, the patriarch, would go home to Lake Learned. And that was right. But all Peter Jorgensen wanted was to let humanity know the Hero was going home! When at last it happened, it was a day designed to be noticed in the world. Jorgensen believed the elders wanted that too. The bureaucrats wanted it. It was the powerful of the Commonwealth the news had not reached, in whom it had not activated any zealousness.

It meant I need not make that ten-hour drive to support Learned Man, or have Cath make it for me. I felt a wistfulness for Peter Jorgensen. Learned remained in a box, like a wedding dress the nation would not put on.

I had a number for Brendan Hayes, out there in the Riverina. And so I called him, advisedly or not. I felt I must, since to me Jorgensen possessed the holiness imbued by the antiquity of Learned Man.

"Look," I said, "not my business, I admit. But Jorgensen just told me you don't want him to speak at this meeting."

"He's not on the proposed program, no," Brendan replied with bureaucratic confidence.

"Look, Brendan, I'm going to say it. Peter Jorgensen is eighty-six. He is not going to be available to speak at some future event when everything about Learned Man is settled. We have him now. And he's the man who first clapped eyes on Learned Man since the old man's burial in the Pleistocene. And he loves the elders. In any language, English or Barkindji. Could you let him talk for ten minutes or so?"

"Please don't think he hasn't had many opportunities to talk to us all in the past. Or that we don't honor him."

"No, but he had that kick in the teeth from his vice chancellor. He's still recovering . . ."

Brendan took time now, word-choosing time. "He ought to understand, I think, that the vice chancellor felt he had to put Learned Man himself at the center of that event. That it was political. That it was time, pretty much, to talk about the tragedy of European occupation, not about Jorgensen."

I felt fraternally angry for my old friend's sake at Brendan's implication that Jorgensen was himself ignorant of or indifferent to that tragedy.

"Come on, Brendan! Jorgensen isn't an egomaniac. But he knows what he's done. Or, if you like, he knows what's befallen him." Silence came. As if Brendan were politely waiting to have what Jorgensen had done defined for him.

"The point is," I argued, "he chanced on the link, Learned Man and our shared humanness. Others defined the chain. He

327

was the one who found it there, in the lake sediments. And he always believed, from the first day, that Learned was *Homo sapiens.* Not some intermediate hominid on the way to being us. Jorgensen discovered *us.* Our ancestors were Learned's poor relatives in some cold Central Asia place, drifters. I doubt we lived as well, as majestically as Learned! But Learned is who we are and who we were, at a forgotten level. Peter Jorgensen, apart from anything else, gave us back our memory."

"But he might have just found what the traditional owners already knew was there," said Brendan. "At least implicitly they knew Learned Man and all his kin were there, and they were content to have them. They were a secret we had left them. Something we hadn't taken. There, buried in the lunette."

"Yes," I argued, my sternum burning with such discomfort that it blinded me awhile, "yes, but he wasn't some sort of thief."

"No," Brendan Hayes agreed. "He wasn't a thief and they don't think he was. Perhaps he was more like a trespasser. But they're a forgiving people, Shelby."

The burning of the sternum distracted me. I managed to say, "Oh sure, he called in his mates from the university and they took Learned Man away like they'd taken Miss Learned earlier."

"Without referring it to the elders."

"No, but we were dumb about those things then. But not malicious."

I knew it was a bad argument as soon as I said it.

"Well," said Brendan, "we aren't anymore. That's what the meeting is about. It's about what *they* want. I can understand Professor Jorgensen's sensitivity. But they have heard from him before."

"But on a human level, why not listen to him again? He's eighty-six, for fuck's sake, Brendan. These are his dying words. And he wants to give them to you, to the elders, fraternally. Without arrogance. By some lights, it's appalling if you don't let him have his say. I mean, did you ask the elders?"

I could hear the bureaucrat named Brendan. He was breathing on the line. After a while he said, "Have you ever thought that we whitefellas, Jorgensen and his friends, even me, even you, want to put Learned to rest on our terms? That at base we want to *own* Learned the way we thought we owned the land? And that might be the problem, you see, Shelby. I'm not being argumentative for the sake of it. What if Jorgensen tells them the way he sees it and they don't see it that way? They're polite people. They'll accept him as an existing factor in things, but they're too well mannered to tell him to stop pushing . . ."

"But they all say Learned came back for a purpose. What's the purpose? If it was to enlighten us, the enlightenment hasn't happened. So I don't see Jorgensen is pushing anything — or not in the sense you mean."

Brendan resisted, saying, "But . . . he says to them, 'I see it more sharply than ever before. Learned and his people kept the country through two ice ages. And forty thousand years or more — a span of time no empire lasts, no civilization. Except yours!' But they already know it. They know it in their blood and water. They know already that their culture was based on maintenance, not on ripping the shit from things. It's a triumph. But they don't need Jorgensen to tell them. And so he says to the three tribes, 'We'll build a great Keeping House according to your wishes. And it'll celebrate not only Learned but his heroic community who lived amongst the megafauna. And the nation and all of the world will come darkside and applaud what was achieved here, that continuity, that culture!' And believe me, there's nothing wrong with Jorgensen's oratory, Shelby. I have heard him at his best. The vision is splendid, believe me. And he's right, but he's also wrong. Because they, the Muthi Muthi, the Nygiampa, and the Barkindji, they always had Learned Man. They saw him in their dreams. They knew he was there and they didn't need Jorgensen to tell them."

"Come on, Brendan," I protested. "They keep saying Learned came back for a reason."

"Well, they might say that out of politeness. Have you ever thought of that? Because we bludgeon them with our intentions, Shelby. They have the good grace not to hit us over the head with theirs."

"*They* understand the wonder out there. But don't they want the rest of us to get the message too?"

"I'm beginning to think it might be more akin to their wishes if one day, a day they decide on, they just put Learned Man back to bed, out in the dunes somewhere. If they take us out of the picture, we can't complain."

"It's a bit bloody late to take us out of the picture," I said too heatedly. Why was I like that? Was it because my own place in the said picture was under question?

"Well, let me be straight with you, Shelby.

I used to think like you that the elders were waiting for the vision about Learned Man to capture us all before he was returned to his country. Now I'm not so sure."

"But all the jobs it would bring out there," I declared stupidly, like a rank politician.

"They've heard that song before. Live in any country town during an election . . . politicians sing that song best. It is simply this, Shelby. Jorgensen can unsettle them. That's why we didn't want him to speak. And no sooner had that been decided than I sent him an email accidentally saying the opposite."

The idea of Brendan as a hapless emailer appeased me a little. I had had my say. The knot in my esophagus throbbed and I was aware of tiredness. My argument deteriorated into random statements such as, "Why don't you give the poor old fellow a go?"

It was only as he was about to hang up that I remembered to say, "I've never spoken to him when the subject of Learned Man hasn't come up."

But I was aware that I'd failed in my advocacy of him.

WHAT THE STONE SANG OF

Amongst the disasters that abounded in the cursed stone Baldy had entrusted in me, deadly to women, was the misfortune of my son. It tipped the earth towards dark stars, towards the devouring of light by darkness, coming to ruin us with the same energy as that with which the slicer had devoured my son's face and slit his throat.

The stone evoked in me an urgency to speak to the ancestors. I wondered, of course, whether such communications would be denied to me as they seemed to have been denied Baldy.

"It is a bad thing," I confirmed uselessly to him. "We are in for a bad time."

"And daughters," he sighed. "I have no daughters."

"Mine is not with child," I told him, though I could not be utterly sure, and my daughter was of the age appropriate to have a son or daughter.

There was nothing much I could think of to do in normal daylight. Just as when the slicer struck and the only thing you could do was perform simple functions like washing and anointing, so now we simply wrapped the omens away with the potent emblems designed to steal at least a little of its own power from that dreadful stone.

When I returned to the Lake, somber and burdened by the idea of the stone, I saw Girly near the fire amongst a knot of potent older women, the wives of councillors. She smiled as if to herself when she saw me. Girly. She was suited to her name. Even as she came to join me, I saw the white painted faces of the bereaved family of a woman who had died giving birth to her first child that morning, and they looked as melancholy and sullen as could be required. They were meeting on the summit of the dunes to the Morningside to try to assess what forces, what curse from envious people, had brought an end to their daughter's life. She had had such a fearful time of going that it would turn out they meant to burn her and break up her bones so she would travel briskly from the scene of her pain to the full and glorious plain of the spirit. I could have told them exactly who and what had harmed

334

her, but I did not want to spread a general fear. There were already curses flowing in the air before Baldy had brought the stone back. For now only he and I knew that they had been enlarged and given new edge.

After greeting me, Girly said, smiling fully and honestly, "Our daughter Shrill is with child. She is slight, of course, but well into the path of motherhood. The little soul has occupied her and she feels it moving."

I looked at a stone, a normal slab of hard clay, and considered kicking it. In the face of what I knew, and out of fear for our child and her child, not wanting to see Girly make a fast fall from elation to affright, I declared this excellent news. But I knew my daughter had chosen the fatal season to carry a child through. I was annoyed and flustered that this news came now, though I understood I must react with joy.

The evening wind came up, churning the Nightside of the Lake in a way common at that time of the sun's circuit, the rain time of year. Lovely to see, it foreshadowed night in a way that caused Girly to lean against me, her breasts against my upper arm. But when night came, I did not sleep. And though Girly gave me her consolation, I was barely fit for it. Afterwards my sleep remained light and broken for some hours, and far too heavy at others, lacking in the qualities suitable for sky travel. I was not summoned by that ancestor who had been so concerned in recent time to demand my execution of the Sinner Unnameable.

Next morning, as soon as I was sure she would be at the fiber workers' place beyond the main fire site, I went to see Shrill. She was sitting on a great woven mat the women had made of lake grasses, and she was weaving an open-worked bag and conversing with another weaver, a young woman some paces away who was working on a similar bag. It was one of the places where, when the sun grew higher, the older women with weaving skills gathered, but for the moment only these two, more recent to the skills of weaving and dyeing, kept the space lively, persuading their supply of fibers to be compliant in their fingers. Seeing me come, Shrill stood up and pulled a skin cape about her shoulders, beaming at me as broadly as her mother had.

"A child," I stated rather than asked, looking as pleased as I could by trying.

"My husband saw him in the sky, of course, that's what happened," she confirmed. "As usual. And planted him in me."

"Is it a boy?" I asked, seeking as much

comfort as I could.

"Bass says he dreamed a girl."

"The father is sometimes mistaken," I said, though I had never been wrong. I had seen my two sons and daughter by the base of trees in heaven before I begot them and knew who they were before they came to earth.

I dropped to my haunches beside Shrill and she went on happily weaving, choosing strands of yellow grass and the Lake wattles, and fibers from the bark of the rough figs which she had dyed with flintwood. The weavers all had bladders of flintwood sap and dyed the fiber with it. I watched as her quick fingers wove wattles together and reached for a browner bark strand. She was a gifted maker of fishing nets to catch perch and scoopheads, using her long legs to serve as the frame for the weaving, then wrapping the string around them so that the mesh appeared between them as she leaned forward, working fast and making knots. Around her head was a band she had woven with thunderbird feathers and meshed the feathers of parrots in. It was not a piece for everyday wear. As for her work, there was a women's reason for varying the strands that I was not privy to.

"And you are feeling hale?" I asked. "Does

the child kick?" I added without waiting for an answer. "Your mother says the child kicks."

"Not yet. But it is as if she is waiting to do it. I can feel she has a plan to kick. And I am of a mind with this child. I have seen its face when I'm sleeping and it's the face of a child planning to kick."

I put my hand out to caress her shoulder and laughed with her. For it was always wrong to run counter to her happy disposition. There was something necessary flowing in her that prevented the expectation of sad eventualities, and it should not be quarreled with.

"You've told your aunt Scales?" I asked. Scales, elder sister of Girly, was a fortress of a woman, and might, by her good influence or her singing, be a fortress here against that foul stone.

"I told her first," Shrill asserted — and it was correct that she should have told Girly's eldest sister. For the child's totem would be that of Aunt Scales and the child's earliest instruction would come from that woman.

After that sweet conversation, though bitter to me since I'd had to pretend, I got up and said goodbye like a man without care and returned to the fire outside my hut, where Girly tossed tubers about on the coals with the fire-hardened fingertips our women had from their trading with fire. So too from dealing with the hot stones they built from the clay of termite nests, clay that drank in heat and was turned to stone by it, and thus made a hearth.

I crouched by her. She was cooking thin yams and green bulbs with mashed scarlet fruit. "I must go out again," I announced. "Away. On my own."

Girly's staring at the yams was as good as words. It said I was rejecting the bounty she was preparing.

"I'll take a skin of water," I assured her, as if that was the question.

"But you're just home. You're always going off," she complained at last, picking up a small yam and throwing it at my legs. It made a brief, fiery scald there.

"It must be done. It is work that must be done." I adopted an air of authority that would have persuaded any councillor but would not persuade Girly.

"Is there a camp of strangers out there, of Upper Waters women? With cunts of quartz to slice your pricks off. And you rush to them, as stupid men do!"

"You know it is not a matter of women," I assured her so wearily that she seemed to believe me.

"Take your skins, then, you fool. You know it will be cold without me."

"Of course," I agreed. "Certainly I will. But I must go."

"It's the child," I could have told her.

"Madness," Girly decided. "What it is you have in your head I would like to know. It's always there. You are always miles off."

I couldn't argue with her. "I am in the wrong place for dreams," I said then, not sure what I could safely tell her. "There is no dream path here anymore. It has moved on. I have to find it because I must dream for my own good and yours."

"And you talk to an ancestor," she complained, "and he gives you tasks he doesn't give others. And of course you do them to the limit. I wish it was some stony-cunted woman you were with! That would be easier for us all." She pushed the fruits and yams around the cooking stone. "I could beat all the stone out of her! But this . . . ?" She shrugged.

Girly was not happy.

SAVING LENSES WITH GRACIE

The news came into our living rooms in June 2000 that Ethiopia was in the overnight process of reinvading Eritrea. The border towns and fields were falling quickly to the Ethiopian army. Issayas's fellow old campaigner from the days when the Tigreans were also fighting Mengistu, Negasso — now the president of Ethiopia — claimed there had been offensive border activism by Issayas's troops and that, by the way, those Eritrean border provinces, Adi Quala and Senafe, were traditionally Ethiopia's.

The inescapable truth was that the Ethiopians were only about three hours' drive from Asmara, where Ted's lens facility was still producing optical lenses to European standards but selling them to the world for $7. If the Ethiopian army got to Asmara, the children of light, the children of the possible new moral evolution, would be defeated and Ted's lens plant would be destroyed.

At 9 a.m. on the day of waking to the news, I called the Department of Foreign Affairs in Canberra and spoke to a young official. Did the foreign minister know that the lens plant would be destroyed if the capital fell? Unless we used our diplomatic influence to let the Ethiopians know we considered it holy ground.

The official consoled me, as if I were the only one stricken with an eccentric conviction. He would pass on my concerns and telephone number to the minister. I could tell no one in government was galvanized, however, by the peril to Ted's lens workshop and I was unlikely to hear back from Canberra.

Regardless, I vowed that any destruction of the lens factory must not happen unobserved and that I must go to Asmara to document it. It had been paid for, after all, by *us*. By Australia. And it was part of Ted's legacy, and the tasks he had imposed had not ended with his death. I'm not sure whether it was Ted's rowdy spirit or a sharp memory of his pronouncements that was uppermost in my desire to protect and record. But I was not driven to win his posthumous approval. I was outraged about what might happen to the lens factory on my own account, and that of the Eritreans.

I spoke to Cath. She herself felt passionate but was limping and due to have a knee operation in three weeks. She expressed no doubt about me going to Eritrea if I chose to. The idea of Ted's lens plant being destroyed provoked a sort of familial courage or recklessness in us, and later that morning I received a call from Gracie, who'd recently graduated from the Australian Film and Television School. Cath and I had infected our children with regard for the image and for writing, even though I myself had been skeptical of the limits of both.

"I'm going to go and film what happens," Gracie said.

"You don't have to. I'm going. Just to shoot footage."

But in our ensuing conversation Gracie could not be argued out of her intentions, and I knew at her age I had been the same. I could understand this story might sing to her as the desert Aboriginal strike of long past had called to me.

Gracie and I made preparation to travel with our lightweight digital movie cameras. We were not primarily making a film. (Though a cynic might ask, "When weren't we?") We were to be witnesses. If Ethiopian soldiers retook Asmara, we hoped to inhibit them. And if we couldn't inhibit, we would provide the evidence of the crime. The idea that our cameras were God's eye in a naughty world was a temporary illusion of mine that had not fully survived Vietnam. It could be as misleading as the hands that wielded it. It also had an anodyne edge to it — in provoking outrage, it sometimes sedated it. There was a distance to it, as well. Even close-up could be, to the viewer, far away. But it was the only medium of protest I had.

Getting to Asmara presented us with problems. We couldn't go by way of Addis Ababa, for it was the enemy capital in this circumstance. Gracie, who wanted to be a producer and had her mother's practical skills, was energetic when it came to itineraries. She connived with the Eritrean ambassador in Canberra, and between them they worked out that we must first go to Cairo, where one of our old Eritrean guides would greet us, and then on to Sena in the Yemen, and next by Yemeni Air to Khartoum and so into Asmara at night. The pilots of Yemeni Air were robust souls, it seemed, ready to land in the less bomber-prone Eritrean evening.

So we had a pilgrimage on our hands, but we had expected to, and in the last months of my middle age I was content with that. I was not so pleased that Gracie was coming too, but I knew if I pulled out she would still go. Cath had faith that nothing bad could happen to me or Gracie whatever the peril, if the Eritreans were meeting us everywhere and conducting us.

We landed amongst splendid bare mountains in Sana'a, in the shadow of the old town of brown mud-brick, under splendid biblical mountains. Beneath another mountain, forty kilometers from Asmara, the Eritreans had flanked and halted the Ethiopian army on its till-then victorious path to Massawa. The stated casualties, fifty thousand wounded and twenty thousand dead, their number floated above the dishes of abundance, lamb and saltah stew and laxoox bread, brought tears to my eyelids. But who was I to weep at the relentless pity of it, after all the other relentless pity.

The Yemeni flight to Khartoum and Asmara was piloted by a tubby man with a full, rich prophet's beard. The flight was full of elegant young Eritreans from the US and Europe, all of them English speakers, who thanked us for going back with them. If Asmara was to fall, they said, they wanted to be there as witnesses and voices. So their motivation matched ours. They knew Ted's name and a few knew mine, and we were bound in a selfless fraternity. For these young people who had escaped the dismal statistics of the Horn by going to Europe or the New World had felt bound to return from profitable professions to stand before their cherished city. They were traveling in the only aircraft going there, and the sternness of their intention compensated for the fact there were not safety belts for all of the seats.

The city did not seem to be considered doomed by the young Eritreans aboard. As we spotted the lights of Asmara, permitted to shine for now by the lack of Ethiopian aircraft on the radar, our fellow travelers, unconstrained by seatbelts, began to dance in the aisles and were still dancing when we hit the airstrip, their knees buckling a little in the fraternal ecstasy of arrival.

We were met by two protocol officers, Ghebrehewit and Habtom. Of course, I knew Ghebrehewit from Ted's days. Our faces shone, theirs shone too, almost — I thought — as if we were some old-fashioned form of relief column. They asked after Cath, whom they had also met in the field, they said. In the old days. They had been fighters then, but bureaucrats now — their shirt collars were crisp. They had none of the edginess one might have expected in citizens of a city about to fall to a brutal enemy. They took us to the Ambasoira Hotel, where Cath and I had stayed when we last visited Asmara, in the hopeful days of independence. "We will show you Dr. Ted's eye facility first thing in the morning so that you can film as much of it as you like," said the one named Habtom.

"How far away are the Ethiopians?" I asked.

"They are held for now," said Habtom with a frown. "We are waiting for them to try again."

Gracie told me she slept profoundly that night. Dreamlessly. But she and I were still thick in the head when we approached the lens facility. We were met in the vestibule by a tall bald chemist, who led us past the display cases of plastic lens containers, Ted's face on each. He showed us the latest certifications, framed in a corridor, that the laboratory had been granted. "We are certified to European standards," he told us. "Of course, the Ethiopians aren't buying any at the moment. But elsewhere in Africa . . ."

He seemed as serene about the chance of invasion as the men had been last night.

Had I been demented to get so passionate in front of my TV in Sydney? I asked him, as if for verification, "Are you worried the Ethiopians will destroy the lab if they take Asmara?"

He expressed his breath in a sage, measured way. "If they do not know what the place means, it might stand more of a chance," he said. "But if they know what it means to us . . ."

I looked at my daughter; she had just seen evidence of Eritrean poise.

We filmed the laminar flow sterilization rooms into which we could look by way of mirrors. Beyond the glass, men and women wearing blue coats, masks, goggles, gloves, and plastic hairnets worked at microscopes or weighed materials for the plastic formulation for the lenses and their little filaments and armatures. The idea that if the city fell they might be hauled forth and shot, or else shot in their laboratories, did not seem to possess or delay them in their search for exact formulations and the minuscule smoothness required in lenses. In the various labs, they spun bottles of chemicals in separator machines, vouchsafed trays of lenses to autoclaves, inspected each lens individually, then loaded them en masse into the containers that carried Ted's face.

It was marvelous and it was noble and of course it was a manufacturing of light. But darkness was on its way.

In the afternoon, we chatted with men in the coffee shops the Italians had left in Asmara during the occupation that ended with World War II. No air-raid siren wailed. Perhaps this afternoon's pilots feared the same anti-aircraft guns I had seen firing on an Ethiopian bomber some years back. And now the Eritreans had their own fighter-bombers guarding the city, though there could not have been many of them. We had spotted their bunkers at the airport the night before.

One of the café dwellers waiting on war anew remarked, "We're a little short on aviation fuel."

Habtom said, a little like a bureaucrat, "Not short, brother. We're keeping all our reserves for operational flights."

Gracie and I were booked to leave on the tortuous route home in eight days, to allow us a few days' rest back in Sydney before Cath had her knee operation. In my world-spanning anxious jet lag, the fear of not getting back to be with Cath before her operation was combined with the dread of losing Gracie, who was happily filming my discussion with the Asmara café set. For though I had come here to film one thing, the lens facility and its fate, she was up for whatever presented.

"Doesn't Eritrea have its own airline now?" I asked. I had heard something about that.

"Yes," they said, a 737 chartered from the Russians and piloted by two Russian pilots. But it had stopped flying as soon as the invasion started.

"Well," I said, "Gracie and I will just have to go back on Yemeni Air. Whenever it visits again."

Habtom said softly, "I am afraid that all international commercial flights have ended for now, until we see what happens."

Ghebrehewit declared, "You got in yesterday because of the lull. The lull might last. I hope so." Yet I had a sense they were editing their words, which they had never done in the old days. Where had the old grandeur and certainty and spaciousness gone?

Given the lack of activity in the air, Ghebrehewit and Habtom took us on a reconnaissance south of Asmara. Near the town of Mendefera, where Tesfai, the man who had interested Ted in Eritrea the first place, had spent his childhood, we found the first encampment of those who were fleeing the Ethiopians. For the earlier arrivals from the south, some old Unesco tents had been pitched, and a vast supply of plastic basins were laid out like a bazaar in primary colors, all donations from the people in the capital. Nearby were some thousands of families who'd arrived too late for the tents and were living on patches of blue plastic. Men came up, the dust of their flight on foot clogging their *jellabiyas,* and shook or, more accurately, wrung our hands. Women, who looked to have taken to the road with their coffee-making sets wrapped in cloth and slung on their backs, kept house on these tarpaulins.

"No aid has come," said Habtom. "They think the aid will come after you. They see you and they hope the world is taking notice."

But only the Apples and ex-pat Eritreans were so far taking notice.

Children tottered everywhere, with young mothers shawled in bright cloth continually carrying their puking, projectile-shitting infants away from the living areas to try to prevent those areas from being fouled, like the good soldiers of primary hygiene, the doctors of the EPLF, had taught them. But it would not work, and later in the dusk, when we drove to a hill beyond, we could see families still on the way to the im-

351

promptu camp.

A man brought us tepid tea at one stage. "Has this been well boiled?" asked Gracie cheerily, her practical mother's daughter.

"At some stage," says Habtom. For him and Ghebrehewit this was research too, as we moved amidst the blue plastic hearths in this teeming site. Along the banks of a wadi, amongst acacia thorn trees, a wraith of a woman ran screaming. Other women ran after and surrounded her, and she knelt and gouged her cheeks with her nails and anointed the cuts that appeared and the Coptic cross tattoo on her forehead with handfuls of dust. Her friends tried to raise her to her feet again. Gracie moved amongst them, filming, though she did not know exactly what the phenomenon meant. "It is common," said Ghebrehewit. "Women raped at gunpoint in front of their children."

For her, no victory, no gift of tarpaulin and plastic basin and no return home could cancel that savagery. The other women were raising up their sister, caressing her. Gracie shot it with streaks of tears on her cheeks, for knowing by now what it was, she knew it to be yet unspeakable, and a defeat for what a camera could tell you.

At the Ambasoira Hotel, I woke Gracie next

morning, in a beautiful teal predawn, and she gathered her gear without complaint for a long drive south to the high front line in the mountains. It was a still dawn. As we drove past, those who had fled the south were just stirring in the refugee cantonments outside Asmara. Women with plastic basins or buckets in their hands were going towards the wadi for water, and men worried over little heaps of kindling, and it all seemed orderly — no women trying to claw their faces off, no young mothers running to intercept children who had lost management of their bowels. By early light, Ghebrehewit and Habtom had brought us up the dirt track that found its way, turning continuously on itself, up the sides of Emba Soira Mountain. They took us as far as you could go in a four-wheel Toyota before boulders blocked our way. At that point, we started out on the high track ourselves. Above us were the emplacements where trained soldiers were busy on the day's first fatigues. Some were already returning to their positions with jerry cans of water from streams below the mountain. Gracie and I filmed without plan, independently of each other, confident in each other's discrimination. Meanwhile the silhouettes of those Eritrean troops who had halted the Ethiopian army, at least for now, showed up against a ruthless stone ridge and a brightening sky.

Near the top of the ridge, short of breath, we entered a rough communication trench and all at once looked down on the Rift Valley, birthplace of humankind, where our mother, and Learned Man's as well, had lived. From this great altitude the Eritreans had outflanked the Eighth Ethiopian Army, which was trying to reach and reclaim the Red Sea coast. We could see below us, in the great arid declivity, in a majesty of geology and an ignominy of strategy and tactics, the clumps of khaki, like heaps of unclaimed washing. "They still fight like they did when the Russians advised them," said Ghebrehewit. "The Zhukov principle of overwhelming force."

In the trench line that ran along the ridge, a lean Eritrean machine gunner told us he had learned his English from BBC shortwave broadcasts, and claimed he had wept as he had harvested the youth below with his old-fashioned and dented machine gun. The gun's presence here could have caused more than the user to weep — bought from the Russians by Mengistu or the emperor, captured by the Eritreans, now used to shear away the boy children of Ethiopian hearths. It had been all too unequal, he told us. And though there was a local truce just now, no one had come to carry away the corpses that still reproached us from the floor of the valley. And who counted the numbers of dead on the valley floor, of a failed spring offensive like this? The tears of this machine gunner might be their only sure memorial. Or, to be fanciful, but not too grossly so, of the Eve who begot them all, machine gunners and targets, and who like an Aboriginal ancestor still traveled this grievous valley. But who counted them the way the Australians tried to count the dead of Gallipoli, a military enterprise as hapless as what had occurred here?

We stayed up there in that high, brown, sharp-edged aerie as the light became frank and full. We interviewed a company commander who had studied economics at Colorado State University, and a woman medic, a somber, reliable young woman with braided hair and the sweet oval face of the region. The soldiers looked so scrubbed. They seemed intelligent citizens, and the dead below, by contrast, were hapless kids Negasso had scoured from the streets and the high schools of Ethiopia.

On the way down to find the car, Ghebre-hewit said, "We have just taken back the town of Tessenai over in the west. It's been looted and some damage done, but we can go there in a helicopter tomorrow. Would you like to come?"

"Of course," said Gracie straight off, and she looked at me and uttered a little stutter of laughter, her eyes glistening beneath her mother's fringe of hair, but which in her case was brownish, from me. I saw at once that, of course, she was dealing with all of these events in terms of equal seriousness. She had been willing to be an inhibitor and recorder of any damage done to Ted's place, but apart from that she had documentary ambitions of her own.

"No, I'll go, and you can have any footage I bring back," I said to her. "But I think you're better to stay in Asmara."

Wisely she decided not to argue with my parental edict and began to discuss the state of the war and the truce we had heard about — was there really one? How reliable was it likely to be?

Ghebrehewit said, to reassure me, "There might be a general truce signed later today or tomorrow. We can't be absolutely sure about it."

Habtom asserted, "*They'll* certainly welcome it. Because of what happened to them on their way to the Red Sea."

■ ■ ■ ■

That afternoon a truce *was* negotiated by the Organization of African Unity. There were celebrations in Asmara in the evening — before going to bed Habtom and Ghebrehewit took us to meet some young Eritreans in a bar in the neighborhood of Kombishtato, and they were exultant, since their nation had survived and Asmara was safe. They were sure the truce would last, that the major ploys of this invasion had been made and negated. But for the first time I heard an urbane young officer arguing that the unfinished business was to expel the city's ethnic Tigreans, the people once considered allies but who were the same ethnicity as Negasso, the Ethiopian leader. There were posters in the streets calling for them to be rounded up, and on the way home from Emba Soira we had encountered busloads of them being shipped back to the border, to be let loose there.

Habtom had genial faith in this eviction. "It will be better for them back with Uncle Negasso."

"But aren't their homes in Asmara?" I asked him.

"Yes, we have been host to them for a long

357

time. But we can't afford them anymore. It's bad socially and in terms of security," Habtom replied. "But it's bad for them too. There's a lot of ill will towards them now."

"But how much can they take with them on those crammed buses?" I asked.

"It is sad," said the judicious Ghebrehewit. "But we did not start this war. Now the International Committee of the Red Cross is in charge of the evacuations, not us. Everything is being done properly. We can arrange an interview with the evacuation official if you wish."

The way he said it, it was as if no coercion at all were involved in removing the undesirables. I felt then I had discovered from the lips of Ghebrehewit, a fine fellow, that the Eritreans had turned as mean and human as the rest of us, no longer Ted's unique people, no longer men and women of exceptional enlightenment. And no longer the beacon Ted and I had had no right to look for, but believed we had found.

I was sick that night, and it wasn't the murky Kenyan wine Gracie and I had drunk at the bar. After coming home, we had been sitting in the lounge chatting with Ghebrehewit and Habtom and with a sheik from the Ethiopian desert region of Ogaden. This man, dressed in a dark suit with an open-neck collar, was impressive, an Oxford graduate, son of an important man amongst the semi-nomadic Ogadenians, who had been much misused and had suffered ferociously under Mengistu and in the famine. The man had a doctorate, and the Eritreans introduced him to us as head of the Ogaden National Liberation Front. As surely as eighteenth-century Scots had wanted their independence from England, this man and his Muslim brothers wanted independence from Negasso's Ethiopia, so now he and the Eritreans were friends.

As we sat talking, my stomach convulsed with very little warning, though the ten seconds of nausea beforehand were intense. I had vomit in my mouth and burning in my nostrils in the midst of a very urbane conversation on African affairs and Ethiopian minorities, all of whom took comfort from what the Eritreans had managed to achieve. I ran all at once from the room and so into the toilet, where perhaps two-thirds of the voided contents of my stomach landed acrid on the floor tiles. I continued to spasm, and then, aware of the mess I had made, began cleaning the floor with toilet paper. I was aware of the man from Ogaden standing behind me. He said, "Don't worry about that! Leave it for the servants."

It might be that Asmara was saved and my duty to the lens facility finished, but I had developed a new duty to Gracie, who wanted to take a helicopter carrying a general and some troops to Tessenai near the Sudanese border. She'd insisted on going even after I told her that it took only one Ethiopian soldier equipped with a rifle-propelled grenade who had not heard about the truce, or didn't give a damn, to end an aerial careen to Tessenai. Gracie believed that such considerations added savor to the expedition, so I'd insisted on accompanying her. As we waited to lift off, my mind was full, as always when it came to rotor-driven aircraft, of the neurotic but not far-fetched possibility that Cath might need to absorb a double fatality.

The helicopter was full of official-looking Eritreans, all of them in fatigues but none carrying arms. The three aircrew had an air of competence and toughness and wore pistols — that seemed to represent the extent of the expeditionary armament.

The seats were uncomfortable and ran along the sides of the fuselage, and the noise of engines was too loud for us to hear each other. It was a long haul before we began to see, squinting through the ports, signs of the recent Ethiopian advance in the form of great smudges of burned houses on a yellow-brown earth, and blackened rectangles of kraals whose cattle were gone, driven south or slaughtered. Those bitter thumbprints in the terrain seemed especially malign today, imbuing me with further nausea in this juddering, unkind aircraft. Gracie, by contrast, was on top of her game, conversing loudly with Habtom, and kneeling on her seat to film through the window and, for a period, from behind the pilots and into a limitless west. The Sahel — the line of transition between the Sahara and the savannah.

I was very grateful when we landed. There were military trucks at the airport to take us to town, though they creaked to a stop on the outskirts of Tessenai and we were shown the wreckage of a new cotton-processing factory, tall and of sheet steel. The Ethiopian troops who had taken Tessenai had not had tank support, so faced with this World Bank–funded cotton mill, with its storage silos and conveyor belts, they had undertaken the job of destroying it with grenades. On a freshly erected steel wall, they'd had time to write in Amharic script,

"Comrade Issayas, we know this mill cost you a lot. That is why we are so happy to destroy it."

I watched Gracie filming, thinking, *This is what would have happened in Ted's lens factory in Asmara if the Ethiopian army had got that far.* As Gracie moved energetically amongst the electric motors that had driven the belts and were now burned out or eviscerated with grenades, Habtom told me dolefully, "This mill had not processed a single cotton bud. It is utterly new."

The town of Tessenai was empty — the Ethiopians gone, the citizens not yet returned. Throughout the streets filaments of audiotape were draped across fences and down roadways that were not so different in appearance from semideserted streets in Australian country towns. Except this mass of thin green tape was from cassettes of Tigrinyan music and lyrics the invaders had found in the houses of the town. They'd pulled the tape out of the cassettes and festooned the streets with it, as if they were depriving their foe of their voice. Did the Ethiopian officers ask them to do this, or was the hatred of the uppity Eritreans as intense as this in the average Ethiopian youth?

The day seemed further yellowed with the

bile of this act, as with my own. We saw houses tumbled or wrecked, and cars assaulted with grenades, but the two chief objects of destruction seemed to have been Eritrean music and the cotton mill. Out of need or spite, the Ethiopian troops had also excreted in the operating theater at the abandoned hospital. In the emergency ward, where there was a chart of parts of the male and female body marked in the Eritrean language, they had assaulted the breasts and vagina of the woman and the groin of the man with their bayonet points, gouging large indentations not only in the charts but in the wall behind. And yet I had innocently imagined the Ethiopians would let Gracie and me give film witness of them blowing up the lens facility! I looked at the chart and thought that I knew nothing about humanity, that I was a mere visitor, and the sickness came over me and I went out into the hospital garden and vomited.

The following day there was still no aviation fuel for commercial flights. We visited Issayas himself, the trim, handsome president who lived in a normal house in the old village named Tselot outside Asmara. He had always disapproved of the cult of personality he had seen fostered on behalf of

Mao during the time he had spent as a student in China, so there were no posters of Issayas's visage on telegraph poles or walls. Gracie was permitted to film our encounter in a plain yellow-painted office block. Issayas spoke softly and with careful enunciation, telling me he would not let the Ethiopians take back, on the basis of some historic fiction, the provinces which were established as Eritrean by the Organization of African Unity. But they would try, he said, they would try.

I knew, didn't I, he asked, in a tone that was liquid and almost sedating, that the Eritrean people had just had an acute emergency? Of course I did, he assured himself, and Gracie and me.

My head swam under the impact of his silken delivery, his soft lips. You must be anxious to get home, he surmised. Asmara, meantime, should be a city of joy to you, he told us with a brief smile.

Three bedridden days later, at the end of which I declared myself better, lying through my teeth, on a gray morning we were taken to Asmara Airport. The hulking Russian pilots who had been waiting out the war in the Asmara Hilton near the airport came aboard in their uniforms and took us out of the temperate highlands of Eritrea across a sweltering sea to witheringly hot Jeddah and an airport full of Indonesian pilgrims coming from the Haj. They filled the aircraft cabin with containers of water from the holy Zamzam Well in Mecca.

■ ■ ■ ■

III
THE BOOK OF
SUBMISSION AND
RETURN

■ ■ ■ ■

THE LINE OF WOMAN

The harder nights, like this one, need to be confronted without recourse to thorngum, and without a fire to distract the sleeper and the Heroes with light. I slept, or failed to, by an old fire, a place where many-stem wood had been burned for years by people in the old times and where the repeated daily heat gave a gloss to the sand. You would see these fire spots now and then when traveling and know that the old people had eaten and laughed there. In a happier state of soul, I would have fixed my memory upon those lost scenes and borrowed from them an echo of their vanished warmth, and thus been warmer myself. I was not, however, in good spirits. I knew my daughter was doomed, that the line of our women was doomed, that all our clans would dwindle so that one day one old man would breathe out a last embittered breath and the trail of our blood would end. And if that was so, what was the purpose of things? It is a brutish point to think that all the singing of our people to sustain the grass and the great beasts and the plenty of fish, and the plenty of order and the rule of the law as well, is so soured that it comes to one old man sunk on his skinny arse bones by a lake of ghosts.

In some way I believed I was that old man or might as well be. It was so cold that I could barely bring my mind to the hope that our Hero would descend to me, or I ascend to him, to hear a heroic meaning given and a course of wisdom suggested. Not since the solitary nights of my manning ceremonies had I felt as desolate as this and lost faith that there were benevolent beings out there who might, after I had been tempered by solitude and cold, rescue me.

Though I hated it, and though my bewilderment was so sharp, I knew I must wait in this manner, in lowliness and misery. I came close to thinking how fortunate my defaced son was by comparison with me! How more fortunate was the Sinner Unnameable, the man punished by Stark's hand and mine. They, my son, and even the Sinner Unnameable, were restored to the greater world and to the Heroes, called thereto, and after a little confusion of spirit, flying on their way, while I was unreconciled and uncalled. One can ask oneself afterwards, and not for the first time, how was it ever established that unseen fibers as definite as the fibers produced by my daughter connect the hardest earth to the succulent and illuminating heavens? It does not present itself to us from virtue or from fasting or from taking thought or from any of our vain pleas and utterances. It comes as a gift, that line of ascent, that steep, scalable face of the intervening air between us and the higher them. And it was there now, that skyward track, open to me all at once and after I had despaired of ever scaling it, which I now did in ferocious though anxious joy. I will be guided, having been until now without a guide. My Hero will guide me. I will find a direction from what he says.

Almost before I knew it, the forest of stars loomed ahead and I entered its outer fringe, rushing through boughs of scalding light. At the first line of trees the Hero's wife, my aunt, was waiting for me with the luminous forest, of which trees of the ground, the thorn, and the split branch, and all the rest, are a mere whisper, a tracery of rumor.

My aunt smiled. Her kindliness is a great mystery that I should take cycles of days and morning upon morning to ponder. I wanted to tell her that and explain that life on earth deprives us of the hours of reflection and meditation. She had barely turned and led me only a little way before I heard men or Heroes, or men who are Heroes, shouting ahead. I heard the enormous thud of feet. I heard voices high and deep, and the shouts of joy that men and Heroes were finding in their communal dance, as if they were remaking the heavens as we on earth remake that place. It gave me an unexpected joy to know that the Hero would be surrounded by my ancestors up there, ahead of me, by heavenly brothers, heavenly fathers, heavenly sounds.

My great-aunt spoke to me. "You can find him now!" Because she could not take me any further. For even in heaven there must be territories secured to men, and other territories into which she and her sisters could advance, but into which neither I nor my Hero could.

I was alone now by the great trunks of light, and as a lesser being could not help but wait awhile, to delay, to indulge the old excuse of gathering oneself. I was shy, as well as anything else, to intrude into our high ceremony in which many worlds, not only mine, were being sung into continuance and into health. But in my world even now there was only one daughter above all. There was only one beloved net maker. There was, as well, our clan which died the more with that vicious stone in our midst, and delay did not suit its condition.

And so I went forward as if I were entitled to the ceremony occurring ahead of me. I entered into the most intense foliage of light. I had to struggle to go forward. Luminous arms held me back so thoroughly, giving me a reason not to persevere. I got through them and towards the great dazzling presences. Their features in remembrance defy any exact description. You can say of a man that his nose is broad or long or both or neither. You cannot remember all that you learned in the forests of the sky, however, for it was learned and understood and absorbed then, when you were there and can be spoken of only in terms of then and there.

I drew clear of the foliage of light and advanced into the columns of dancing and incantation and more intense light still. What was being sung in that holy place I can't remember, since it was a chant of such broad power. As it left those lips, it entered straight into that wing of the soul where unspoken meaning settles. The words of men and Heroes sang through the net of our words in that dazzling grove. As their song lodged in me, I was a happy man. For I could see my Hero dancing in the midst of the others. It was so pleasant to see his divine ecstasy and to be in the place of that happiness, and the seeds, the stalks, the leftover meat on the bone of his exultation reached me, and that was more than sufficient for me, given I was aware that the entire weight of his delight, if placed on me, would have killed me. I thought in that second, *He can't give me any command that is beyond me! I am ready for any demand.* This thought of mine must have passed straight to him since I saw his eyes now on me, and I went forward in his direction amidst the columns of dancers. I rejoiced in having returned to Bounder Man, the man above all of all such men. The dancers were gone in that instant, the thud of feet ended instantly, the chant that had supported the dancers disappeared into the pores of the sky. Only he and I were left. He was turned utterly to me.

Words had returned, as he wanted them to. "Hello," he said. "Hello, my son and brother." And in so saying he gave me back my place in heaven and earth.

"Hello, Father," I replied, mantling my shoulders forward to do him honor. In that greeting it was plain to me that he was still aware: my clan is under the curse, that he knows what curse it is and that every womb is blighted. For this was not ground on which things were explained. This was ground on which things were revealed.

"So, my man," he addressed me, this maker of my world and progenitor of the people. "You see the hostile force of things begin to eat your clan?"

"I see it. Wailing, they have buried the young mothers, and there is my daughter, the weaver and net maker, for whom there is no hope. It is bitter."

That was the plainest thing I could say.

He knew it all, yet the ancestors can well do with having these things repeated.

"But they are not in the same pain you are," said the Hero. "You know what the remedy must be. But it is so sour and so harsh that you do not want to hear it even from yourself."

Feeling dread now after the great rejoicing enthusiasm I'd felt earlier in that grove, I said, "You expect someone to swallow the curse?"

He looked at me, calm and level, though not saying anything.

I then said — and I am daring to challenge him, it must not be forgotten — "You want a man of the law to swallow it and bleach it in his body."

The Hero nodded twice, as if the idea had not already occurred to him, and he took me by the arm. "The thing would finish such a man. In taking it in he would be taken into it."

Despite his words, there was no doubt that he was suggesting it, and I was the only man of law in that place to hear the suggestion. So he was suggesting I should be the man?

It was settled in this way, right there, so clear. It was so dreadful that I could not have told it to myself, that he had been left to tell me in his way.

Instantly I woke in the cold place.

A Death Before the Death: The Postman's Shirt

The morning Gracie and I arrived home from Eritrea, we were greeted by Cath on crutches. We had barely caught up on our news over coffee before my mother called to say my father had been taken to hospital with a fractured pelvis.

So quickly I had been reminded that behind my own flimsiness of soul lay the sturdy souls of my parents, with their pride in stoicism through disaster, Depression, World War II, and all the rest. And their stoicism now bid fair to kill them, and last night's drama was typical. In the small hours my father, returning from the toilet to his bedroom, had gone to look out of the living room window, to see what "loud mongrel" was arguing with a woman on the footpath outside, and tripped on a rug. He'd obviously felt something structural break inside him, but he had a crazy bush theory that if you just stayed still, fractures and dislodgements would right themselves. It was a theory he had pursued while he was a rugby league player in our country town, his sisters begging him not to play while their mother was ill because they needed his unencumbered help. But he did play, and dislocated his collarbone. And he just pretended he hadn't been injured, keeping it a secret from everyone until it knitted again. Lying on his living room floor last night, he'd decided to play the same game, and had not disturbed my mother, passing out occasionally under the shock and wafts of agony. Mad old bugger!

When my mother found him, he had insisted she bring him around to our place, a quarter of an hour away, so he could sit and watch the sea and the "knitting" could commence. Mum suggested calling an ambulance, but he insisted that they were "needed for the sick." In his world you had to be near death to deserve an ambulance. His was the generation of the walking wounded. He had given mail out to the wounded and the hale in North Africa, pocketing that of the dead for return to their kin at some future time. Their arms in slings, their heads ringing and bandaged, soldiers had accepted letters from him with their free hands and opened them with their teeth.

Arguing against ambulances with my mother, he endured until he fainted. And now Mum was calling us for help, and she told us the ambulance had come and he could not help whimper and weep at last as they put him on a stretcher to take him to hospital, where X-rays showed the fractured pelvis.

In the little dairy and timber town where our family had lived when I was learning my letters in the sacristy of the town church — a classroom during the week, a vesting area for the priest on Sunday — my father had been the relieving postman. According to the men in his army postal section in North Africa, he was the ultimate postman, willing to die if necessary, though my mother and brother and I were waiting for him at home, to get a consoling and strengthening letter to the foot soldiers of the Australian 9th Division on the eve of desert action. Meanwhile my mother and brother and I had waited and prayed for his return.

Everyone seemed to attest to this when I was small, when my returned father took us to distant Sydney suburbs to meet his men and their young wives. All these men told my mother, "What a character! He'd get us up to a brigade headquarters waiting in reserve, and we'd deliver the letters by hand, company by company. Everyone knew him. Everyone cheered up when they saw us arrive in the truck."

My father once said that his great motivation as a postal sergeant was to get the letter in the hand of the possibly doomed soldier because "the poor buggers had been through enough." In my father's picture of things it was always the Depression, not imperial patriotism, that had driven men to enlist. Hitler had given these young men in the desert their job, and they were not to die at their work until all their mail was to hand. He himself declared that it was the Depression that had driven him to become a postman to the 9th Division. He believed it with considerable passion and might even have been testy to have the proposition challenged. But I know that my mother listened to the praise of his fortitude and determination with ambiguity. Because she was a veteran of the Depression too, and believed he had left her behind with two young children, myself and my brother, to voluntarily put his hand up for service overseas. And he was twenty-eight years old when he was sent to Africa, older than most recruits. The authorities had either dissuaded or ordered him away from his choice of being an infantryman, but he had still gone and seen the pyramids.

The question is, when leaving home could be justified by world events, why had he taken the choice of leaving home? In terms no outsider could condemn, nor, without being misunderstood, could his wife. This question still hangs over his bed now, and I cannot quiz him straight out about it because for me he is the ultimate uninterviewable.

No question that the stories abounded whenever we visited his men. Not only of letters delivered to retreating men in Benghazi under the great assault of Hitler's General Rommel in the spring of 1942, but during the great leap forward later in the year, running in letters to Ruweisat Ridge near Alam Halfa, where the world was beginning to prepare itself to turn against the great Teutonic tyrant. On one occasion, he and his men had all been caught by Stuka dive-bombers and huddled together on the vibrating gravel of the desert coast. Previously they'd been forced to shelter from a German barrage, devoutly nuzzling the earth.

Recently these tales of my father had made a late revival when a man came to our place to clean our carpets. He was the nephew of one of my father's men and said he had been raised on stories about my father. Because apart from the matter of delivering mail to the support areas, my father had been an expert in taking over bars that were supposedly open only to officers. I remembered those stories had also been popular on the Sunday afternoons of my childhood, my father finding a bar in Cairo or Alexandria and moving behind it to reassure the barman, "Don't worry about a thing, Hamid, I'll take over from here. Give yourself a break, son!" Even Shepheard's Hotel bar had not been immune from my father's endeavors, and this was always the cause of the truest and longest laughter. The bushrangers taking over the bloody bars from the Pommy officers, waging a cultural war against the English whether Rommel was on the advance or in retreat.

But the carpet cleaner's favorite story was about the day my father and his men had visited the pyramids from their nearby camp in the desert west of Cairo. And while they were at the pyramids they witnessed the arrival of an enormous, aircraft carrier–sized vehicle belonging to King Farouk, king of Egypt and the Sudan, sovereign of Nubia, Kordofan, and Darfur. Apparently, King Farouk was there to visit the site of some new archaeological discovery. Far ahead of him lay exile and death in Italy, but his biggest problem that day was that he needed the Allies to hang on to Egypt. He was nominally neutral and had covered his considerable hide by sending a note to Adolf Hitler saying that an invasion would be welcome. But he was not prepared for my father, who under pressure of a dare from his men approached the king and asked him to give them a lift into Cairo in his car. Farouk was famous for the scale and the elegance of his cars' carriage work. In any case, my father's approach to Farouk did the trick and his entire section got a crammed lift back in the super-cruiser limo to the center of Cairo, where they were not supposed to be anyhow.

When my father finally came home, we were living in Sydney, and I knew that behind his boisterous mien he was depressed. And though I understand it now, I didn't as a kid. All that driving about the desert, being shelled, being strafed, the sadness of delivering a letter to a soldier now dead, handing it instead to the man's lieutenant or captain, in the consciousness that it was economic turpitude that had driven the addressee here and to supposedly immortal renown as a martyr! Thinking, what did all that count for now? The brio of persuading a king, what did it account for in our suburb on the western line?

He had taken a vow, it seemed, not to have much to do with letters again. "I'm not going back to the bloody post office," I remember him telling my uncle Frankie as they drank beer together. I can well understand now that delivering a letter in a suburb could have only the most hollow meaning after he had managed to deliver one to a corporal newly arrived in Alexandria from the siege around Tobruk. What could plain suburban mail mean after that? And I remember my mother not liking him to see letters that arrived for us, especially bills to be paid, which induced in him almost a sense of being bullied. "Capitalist bastards!" he would say if he saw such an envelope.

He had wanted me to be tough and clever like himself, but after he returned from the war he could see that I'd cozied too closely to my mother, a bookish woman, insofar as any women from her hometown on the north coast were bookish. A woman who asked questions beyond that issue of delivering mail at all costs.

As for me, I was the elder son. I was not given to the style of manhood as practiced by my father in the desert. I did move around in a loose gang consisting of the kids on our block between Parramatta Road and the railway line. Meeting children from another block, we would organize a pair to fight each other, according to the traditions of the boxing films we saw at the picture house on Parramatta Road. One day my father saw me matched against a boy a year older than me, raising my hands unavailingly and, in his view, weakly. He did not understand that I was making a late attempt at negotiation. As I faced my opponent by a garage entryway on the pavement, my father came out of the house and said hello to all the boys, no animus in his voice, and then he bent to me and said, "You get into him, son! I don't want to see your arms stuck out in that way. Just remember, you only have to get in one good punch and he'll remember you for the rest of his life!"

My opponent was considering running, fearful my father would intervene yet and clip him on the ear. But my father again nodded to all the boys and went back inside. There were no favors for me. This was my education, and I understood he was right. He had always operated on the basis of getting in one good punch, and that was consolation for whatever else the world did to him.

I was right too, of course. Where was the sense of this one good punch if the world still battered you? I took the beating, and my equivalent of the one good punch was not to cry or cringe until, by some mysterious signal, the fight was considered concluded by both our groups. I am not sure that I landed my father's ideal punch, destined to be memorable unto death to the boy it impacted on.

When I started messing around with cameras in my mid-to-late teens, my father did not really approve. And yet, in the way I pursued my cinematic career, perhaps I was like him. Did anyone get in more than one good punch?

My father overcame the emergency of his fracture, but he needed perpetual care. We discussed whether his pleas to come home could be accommodated. Even his dream of sitting and watching the sea and letting things knit seemed a better thing than being the object of the tiresome functions of being nursed and monitored. "I just want to go bloody home," he would say again and again, and my mother would look stricken, and Cath would be brave enough to be the first to say, "You have to get better first, Frank."

My brother sagely reinforced Cath's advice. For one thing we knew the old man would accept help from no one but my mother. He could not abide strange nurses being privy to his functions. He was private and fastidious, and did not want to be judged not to be. In the past Cath had gone to a lot of trouble consulting me and my mother about helpers of all kinds, marshaled from Veterans' Affairs and the Benevolent Society, to help with the simplest processes of a household, but of each helper my father would proudly say, "Oh, I sacked her. We didn't need her."

The proposition we were living with was that he could not go home to die because it would kill my mother since she would be without helpers. So they put him in the section of the hospital to do with rehabilitation, and if rehabilitation was impossible he would go into palliative care. All of us tried to believe our line that we were getting him better so that he could go home, at least home to our place, if not to his own flat. But he must have known that he was in the ultimate process. This awareness that he was in anguish weighed with me. I was afflicted with an unfamiliar depression, as if the tragic conundrum involving my father were part of the same dismal fabric as the women of Serae border province now walking back to their desolated farms.

Dad was not always coherent during this time, and some of the things he did and said were influenced by delusional medication. Since he'd refused to go back to his old job at the post office, he had worked in stores. He had a gift for retail, and should have opened his own stores, except he had a terror of being in debt. Debt was a phenomenon. The weight of debt and the hefty thought of it were things in which he never intended to participate, or even land one good punch on the way to defeat. That was the other thing I hadn't noticed — that he took ultimate defeat for granted. And I didn't understand what made him like that when he was a child of Australia, the Lucky Country, the Disneyland of Affluence. In any case, being dapper, he was always well turned out to sell the manchester or haberdashery that was his specialty.

In the hospital with him one afternoon a little ice water I was helping him to was spilled on his pajama top. He was distressed by this, and motioned to his cupboard. By this stage he seemed to speak in affirmative or negative *mmm* sounds. I asked him what he wanted from the cupboard and pulled out the garments in it one by one, the threadbare inventory of the very sick — a dressing gown, a spare pajama set, his old gray slacks, and two laundered shirts. As I displayed one of the laundered shirts, he made urgent noises of assent and I realized he wanted his shirt changed. How I wished a nurse was there to do it, or someone who was a doer by nature. It would be hard, given his weakness, for me to change his shirt. But I felt that he wanted me to be the one who was humble enough to do it, and that I should stand up to events, and just bloody well do it for him. I took his pajama shirt off and saw the misshapen and "knitted" collarbone, and the cavities around it from which his now scrawny neck rose. It all hurt him, of course, as we began the process he seemed to believe so necessary, his *mmm* sounds warning me to be careful but also to know that what we were doing was essential. He was beyond lifting both shoulders at once, and so I had to engage in gently manhandling one shoulder, then the other, to slowly deprive him of one shirt, and the working of his arms and shoulders back into another shirt, an exercise that exhausted him. At last this task of re-dressing my father reached its close and I did up the buttons down the front of the shirt.

"There you are, flash as a rat with a gold tooth!" I said, though I wanted to howl with the pain he no longer had a voice for, aware that, as well as changing his shirt, I had exhausted him.

It was his final exercise. They upped his morphine that evening and he died after midnight.

The Sport and Joy
of Heroes

After that last conversation with the Hero, I awoke instantly on the cold earth, solitary and weeping. Because I was doomed. It is all very well to desire the great lake of heaven, but it must be earned by the dreadful ordeal of passage, of yielding up, as I was now commanded to yield up. No loud remand had come from the Hero, no threat of punishment for evading the thing. I had been condemned by the calmest authority.

Though I was a long walk from the women who slept at home by the Lake with their small travelers inside them, I went hobbling back home. The cold was in my knees and hips and ankles, and I was slow, but the cold air lay with the sheen, sharper than an eye and utterly lacking in ill will, over the Lake and the habitations. There was an old woman in skins standing at the edge of our habitations as if she were waiting for me and had avoided sleep to be in place for my convenience.

I had a question for her. "Aunt, are any of the women close to giving birth?"

"There are three," she told me. "The first is Shining of the Parrot clan, or so is my guess, but Blue and Sand of the Bounder clan are both heavy and ready to cast the babies forth."

"And there is my daughter," I told her, though I was not sure why I did.

"Yes. Shrill. But she has further to grow."

She considered me like the Hero had, letting the decision settle upon me, though how could she have known that I was in the track of a decision? That it was drawing near, as Stark and I had drawn near, to the Sinner.

"I must see my wife, Girly," I told her.

"That is all very well, my boy," she told me. "But you must not delay, you know."

I despaired that she was a wise woman. She had had a vision of me. She seemed to know that I had been selected. We said goodbye to each other and I walked towards my fire and my hut. The fire was of course embers, and as I entered the hut I was a creature of ice. There was time to work myself slowly into the furs around Girly, and when I touched her she said without complaint, "Oh, you are so chilled."

392

Her warmth soon spread into me and I wished to stay there easefully. She kindly disposed herself to me and — weeping secretive, restrained tears — I entered her a last time. This was the sport and the joy the Heroes had left to us as consolation for life's hard surfaces and testing births. The frightened animal I was, I wanted Girly to share my woe, but there was no reason to that wish. After our congress we lay still for a kindly spate of time. However, children were growing towards their calamity in the wombs of three women. I did not have a day for farewells. I did not even have a morning.

I rose at a normal time for our people at the Lake. From our fire I saw one of the women heavy with child stagger amongst her elders. There was barely time to seek out and chew the divine thorngum and compose myself with it. I went to the weaving ground, where I found my daughter talking to two of her aunts. These older women laughed as they asked after Girly, not least because they had probably seen her as late as yesterday and wanted to contrast my clumsy lame answers with what they knew from her. They were old weavers and warmed their hands by the fire to entice their skill back into their fingers. My daughter had already picked up a half-finished long bag of interlocking fiber, a beautiful work of skill. She watched me as if she did not quite know what to expect me to say. Her air of kindly wisdom said you never knew what to expect from men.

"Do you feel well?" I asked her.

"I feel well for a woman," she told me. "A woman who can foresee her child."

I put a hand on her shoulder and she raised hers, and there was a second's twining. A fiber as sure as any she wove ran beneath the earth, I believed, connecting us. Me and this sister of the boy destroyed by the great slicing beast. Little could be said of any of this. I could not tell her anything of my intentions for the day. That would need to be discovered. She would be consoled for my going when her child was born.

AGAIN THE CANCER

Cath and I were driving to hospital for further exploration of my esophagus and its postchemotherapy and postradiation condition when we heard, preposterously, radio news of the release of the UN's report of its investigation into Eritrea and its leader, Issayas.

The UN report paid tribute, said the radio news, to the "major feat of a people's fight for self-determination," as led by Issayas — a noble thing in itself. But these days, as a modern Eritrean refugee said, "If I die at sea, it's not a problem — at least I won't be tortured." The nation of heroes led by Issayas had now become the nation of the misused at his hands. People trying to cross the border to the Sudan were shot. Men and women were stuck for limitless years in the armed forces, the former army of light, if there was ever such a thing. Rapes of women were being perpetrated by members of an army that had once exalted the status of women and opposed genital mutilation. Indeed, according to the UN, women servants were kept in what amounted to sexual slavery.

Thirty-seven thousand Eritreans had fled the country in the past year, the report continued, and thousands had died trying to flee. Their flight was from a man whose smooth features I had confronted in bunkers, who had praised Cath for coming to the aid of his people, who had venerated Ted for saving the sight of so many of his people. Who spoke softly and who, even at this height of power, had not advertised his visage on the streets of Asmara. The personable, handsome Issayas of whom I used to wonder, on the basis of my high school knowledge of history, whether he would, after saving his people, start stringently saving them from themselves, as Robespierre tried to save the French by separating their brains from their spines in the Terror.

I remembered the Sunday during my visit with Ted and Fram, when I had first met Issayas in a bunker in She'b. A man then in his forties, he had spoken softly, like a scholar, about the US State Department's willingness to let the Russians have their way in Eritrea and see what happened. He claimed that the US hoped Eritrea would be crushed but the Russians mauled in the process as they had been in Afghanistan, with the Americans stepping in at the end to resume their influence in the Horn. As he spoke, a half window was open behind his shoulder and on the sill lay a nifty brown pistol someone had stashed there.

The rebel leader with the silken voice had not yet become a tyrant and could not credibly be depicted as one. And with his lack of stridency and his handsome restraint, he had enchanted everyone he met — including Ted Castwell, and I knew how hard that was. Issayas commanded a force in which men and women, Lowland Sunnis and Highland Coptic Christians, were as one in fraternity. A force in a movement whose cleverness in the tactics and strategy of war, but in the tactics and strategy of mercy as well, shone like a promise of evolutionary advance for the species, for a future society as utopian as could be hoped for amongst the flawed of the earth, God's fallen children. Tesfai, working in Australia, had subscribed too, and he was no one's fool. Someone had to evolve first out of the squalid polarity of our natures, out of the limits of our tribe. Why shouldn't it be the Eritreans?

"Look," Cath reasoned with me as we approached the hospital and the news report rolled on. "Don't go into this therapy with all *that* on your mind."

I pleaded, "But it's . . ."

"No," said Cath. "Just fucking stop it! You're the one in danger here!"

I had wanted to say how insignificant my medical excursions were by comparison with what we had heard today and seen in years gone. The young Eritrean women in their flak jackets and shorts and sandals, carrying automatic rifles, the most elegant thing they owned apart from themselves, walking across the earth with a grace you couldn't learn at schools for models. Revolutionary chic. And one way or another, they had been doomed, unless saved by some quirk of determination and good fortune, almost as rare as the good fortune that blessed a minority in the Holocaust. This or that lovely soldier girl who got away to open an Ethiopian restaurant in Frankfurt or Toronto!

I kept silence and thought of Ted's transcendent failed hope, but I could tell Cath was losing patience with what she saw as my chosen sadness at the report. "This is about you and *It,* for Christ's sake," she told me. "Simple as that. You'll live or you'll die.

Don't involve the whole damn world in it."

Her free hand sought my knee. I saw the opal ring on it — I'd bought it from a Serb in Lightning Ridge. She had dressed up for the day, a little generosity of the kind the target person often misses. The sort of un-noticed gift that women so persistently give. "I don't want you to bloody die," she said. "We haven't had enough *sane* life yet."

She was a woman for skilled emphasis.

We were soon in the cubicle where I met the anesthetist. He said he had been trained by my little brother in Melbourne, whom the Dancer had culled too early four years past. And in honor of this good man, the anesthetist treated me with a jovial frank-ness.

After frivolities with him, I was wheeled off towards the operating room, Cath run-ning after me. She did not dramatize events, but situations of departure in the hospitals were significant with her, and though the anesthetist assured her I was fine and that she would hear how the operation had gone within two hours, she trusted no one. That was her ancestral gift and limitation. I found it easy to listen to reassurances. She sus-pected them for the priestly certainties they tried to purvey.

When we got into the operating theater

and jovial nurses asked me how I was while briskly telling me how to lie on my side, I took special notice of my surgeon. Korean by birth, and Australian by choice or accident, her dark head in its theater cap was studiously bent and she looked young enough to be on study leave from North Sydney Girls High. I was a child of White Australia about to have my misery at least regulated, if not resolved, by a child of the supposed Asian Peril.

She rose from the desk in the theater. "Good morning, Shelby," she said with a tentative smile.

"Good morning, Doctor."

"Michelle, please."

"I don't put my faith in Michelles. I put my faith in doctors," I replied with a smile.

"You'll learn," said the anesthetist bending over me with a mouthpiece. "Just clamp your teeth on this."

And so I did and felt a brief warmth of oblivion enter my arm by way of the cannula and then a nothingness so profound I was not there at all to experience it.

My brother once wrote a scholarly article on an anesthetic so profound in effect that it altered the electrical polarity of cells so that atom no longer spoke to atom and the patient survived by machine. I had been fascinated by this article, since it meant that the anesthetist took the patient over the boundary of death and brought them back again. There was the world of the street and the traffic, and then there was the world of the surgical theater, and I knew where the sorcery lay and I passed out, content, in the midst of the sorcerers.

After the operation I did not wake instantly, for my sleep transcended time. Yet it is true that my waking seemed continuous with the insertion of the mouthpiece. The nurse in recovery declared, "You're with us, Mr. Apple!" And when I felt clear of head, Michelle was there. So was a sense of a blockage between my sternum and throat where her sophisticated little cameras had probed while she had worked at the tumors.

"I hope you're feeling well, Shelby," she said.

"One of the T3s seemed extensive," she told me soberly. "Too much so for me to remove it since it seems it has penetrated the mucosa. So, I'm afraid we can't rule out the involvement of the lymph nodes. I explained all that to you, didn't I? The relationship between the esophagus and the lymph nodes?"

I assured her she had, since she was frowning as if her Korean mother might be disappointed in her.

Michelle, PhD in the esophagus and fellow of the College of Surgeons, explained that only a PET scan could be definitive on the lymph nodes issue. She would have to talk to the professor, but it seemed that more chemotherapy might be indicated to prepare me for surgery.

I felt numbed and remote, and that was not entirely the effect of the sedative/anesthetic. "And, Michelle, could it also have spread too far to make an operation relevant?"

"We don't know, Shelby," she said briskly. "But I don't want to jump to unnecessary and unfounded conclusions. You should go home, and have a rest, and I will email these results to Professor Brown and to your GP. And I'll give your wife a diagram about what we did today."

"My wife likes a diagram," I assured her.

SWALLOWING THE STONE

So it could not be delayed now and I had to go and make the proposal to Baldy.

I found him by his hut, staring at the children who were feeding roots into the incandescent morning fire. He saw me coming and called out that I was his good friend and should join him by his own small fire.

I did. Drawing on the dust at my feet, I told him, "The Hero tells me I must eat the curse."

"What does that mean?"

"The Hero says I must swallow the stone."

"No," said Baldy, "that is too harsh."

"Well, there is no other way I can think of. Above all, no other way *he* can think of."

"Oh, brother," he said.

"I had thought of course that my Hero could think of another way," I told Baldy. "But he sees it as I see it, and it is the only way. If I wrap my body in thick furs and potent emblems and take it into myself . . . That's the way, dear person."

"I'll call the other councillors," Baldy promised me.

"No. Some of the women are ready to drop their children amongst us. The councillors must accept this, in any case. They can't exceed the Hero in wisdom. That's the reason he's the Hero."

"Oh," he said, "if we could split the thing in two parts I would take the first one. If we could reduce the thing to powder . . ."

"We lack a pounding stone adequate," I said. "Even in the mountains they have no stone suitable to pound the thing and powder it."

Dear old Baldy began to weep.

"It was made not to be pounded to powder," I told him. "If it were possible to reduce a curse to powder, we would be in heaven. Instead we are at the Lake amongst our clan and the other clans, and all their gravid women."

"Even flint," moaned Baldy, though not loudly enough so that others would be drawn to wonder what he was saying, "even flint cannot split it or powder it."

"That was what we always knew," I consoled him.

"You would do all this for the dear people?" asked Baldy in a way I did not have to answer.

"Take me there," I ordered Baldy. "And bring what we will need."

Watched by his silent wife, he began to gather thongs of dried bounder hides then wrapped himself in robust furs. I stood waiting for him, and then he was ready and we started out for the law ground. Would I come back here, to the huts, howling and not to be reconciled in the dead of night, looking for the utterance of my name, or for what of myself lay around the hut, a weapon, a knife of flint, a flensing stone, all a man might pick up and put down in the course of a day or a life? I could not promise myself that my ghost might not be discontented and lost in the middle air for a period of howling and anguish.

As we walked, I said, "You and I have to do this quickly. No pausing, no long periods of thinking. The thinking and all the pronouncing has been done. We will get to it in good order, as if we were doing something we might do every day."

"But it is hard," he insisted.

"I know in my blood that what I'm planning for today has been done before. That it's been done by someone in the past, a Hero, and that I'm just echoing."

"But don't think that if you do it you will become a Hero," he insisted as if I was suffering from vanity.

"Don't be a fool. I know I won't become a Hero. Who said I would become a God and Hero? No one has even talked about it."

He looked forlorn.

"Let's get there," I said with the irritability of one who is about to die.

We began loping along then, as if we were chasing a wrongdoer and had great distances in our feet. We got to the place of the men's law, and I sat down on the ground while Baldy went to the repository amongst the rocks. He took out the hardwood emblems of a number of Heroes and brought them to me.

"Yes," I said. "Good man."

He went back and found the crate of long stone that embodied the bounder ancestor, and he brought it to me.

"Oh, my Father," I said to it. "Make my journey merciful, both to me and to all."

I loosened the furs on my upper body and raised my arms, and Baldy began to strap the hardwood and the stone to my ribs, using the lengths of bounder hide to bind me in with power. I felt the cool divinity of the stone against my ribs. "Oh Heroes," I wanted to cry, "it is happening!" I also thought, *If I run free, no one can catch me.* But where was the point of running free in the dying world?

"Get the curse," I commanded Baldy with ill grace, as if he were the one delaying.

Baldy went and got the thing and brought it to me in its nest of fur. I saw the stolid yellow and blue and scarlet of its outrage and noticed that Baldy did not want to touch it in a direct way, with his own fingers.

"Lay it there!" I told him, nodding to one side.

He did so.

It gleamed at me from its roost of skins. It was naked. It could not be appeased.

I took it up in my bare hands, opened my lips wide, and placed it in my mouth. It was on my tongue before I knew it, occupying the space exactly as if honed to be mine. It felt too as if it was designed to be swallowed. Someone had swallowed it before me, or swallowed its brother. I was confirmed in the need for what I was doing.

After a time it affected my gorge and I wished to vomit, but this was a fatuous response from the animal I was, and I was engaged with the tasks of Heroes. I was furious at it. Such silliness. I began to swallow it, and all was changed.

At once I could feel the stone curse willing to take over my body and all its contrivances. I was gagging, and normal breath was gone for good, yet I was pleased in a way that it was in conspiracy with me, even if my purpose was to strip it of power. The stone indeed seemed to have an appetite for my throat, where it now lodged, and settled itself to destroying me.

As I gagged and groaned and made panicked motions with my arms and legs, Baldy pulled his hair in grief and raised his knuckles to heaven, knowing there was nothing to be done.

During the long afternoon the councillors turned up, Stark amongst them, and they solemnly lit a fire as Baldy told them what had happened, standing up a while, narrating the tale with stricken gestures. They looked on me with pity, but sang the songs of merciful death, for they could not argue with what I was doing.

I could feel the stone lodged in me with the weight of the sky, which I had not known to possess a weight until now. It was descending on my inner parts and choking them. And if I was choked by the sky, I thought, what would not choke me, and where was heaven in that weight? Sometimes I cried out in misery, but I knew it was useless.

My companions began to sing, "Oh, there he is, the man who took our suffering into him." They sang like that as if they had always known that one of us would have to perish in this way. With the weight of that stone crushing his heart. "Oh, you are the most worthy of men," they sang. "Oh, we will place you in the earth with honor."

But it meant nothing now that the stone was on my heart, crushing it like a little ripe pod. I must keep it in me, inside my rib cage. I must be put beneath the earth with it in me, so that if it was ever seen again, it would have been bleached of its color by the fluids of my body and would need to burrow its way like a little beast to the level of the earth. But it could not because I was taking its powers into me.

I must have choked for half a day, my heart surging, my breath of no value to me. Eventually I found the means to call to Stark, "Put the bone sliver in me. Give me the bounder shinbone."

The men stared at each other. It would not be normal, it had not been done in their lifetimes. But this, what I was doing, had not been done either. Nothing seemed to happen, and they resumed singing. With streaky sight I beheld someone put more wood on the fire near where Baldy wept. One of them stooped by him and put both hands on his shoulders.

Then I saw Stark go in the right direction, towards the stones where he and I kept it inside the hollow bone of a holy man — the blessed sliver. I saw him carry it secretively wrapped in its pelts towards me. He was howling, half joining in the others' song. "Oh, man who would ensure the birth of children . . ."

Then he stepped aside from it and gave it with all its power to my Son Unnameable, who looked like the young man who had not been defaced by the slicer. I was able to tell them, then, "Take it out again after . . . so that anyone seeing my bones will not think me a wrongdoer."

My Son Unnameable was all merciful decision. He produced the polished bone. Better him. Then, with an august grief but at the same time humor in his eyes, he displayed the thing to me. He knelt over me. I felt it penetrate my collarbone. It was divinely cool as it descended into me. I felt a freezing deep alarm and such gratitude.

"Aaaah! No pain. My Son," I cry!

SUBMARINE

I was ready for the esophagectomy now, and Professor Brown, the surgeon, assured me that if it went well I should return to normal life within a year. But just in case, I believed I must make another and most desperate attempt to reach the prime minister.

Dear Prime Minister,
I am scheduled to undergo a fairly serious operation for the removal of my esophagus. It will not necessarily cure the problem, and I have been warned it will present problems in itself. I can look forward to a long convalescence, even if no further cancer presents. I suspect it could come about that I will no longer be the Shelby Apple of old. I cannot bring myself to resent that, but it does place on me the need to talk to you without artifice.
Forgive me if, given the circumstances,

I speak directly, and say that in government you have appeared a mere shadow of the person you were when I first met you at Ted Castwell's house. You don't need me to say it, and it may be an unjust assessment, but that is the way it appears. In saying it, I do not parrot commentators. I express only my own assessment. You cannot even find the grit to progress us for fear of the gray neofascists of your right wing! Are you thus no more than a palace eunuch?

There is something you can do — and when I say this, please don't give me the usual constitutional excuses. The remains of Learned Man currently reside on a shelf in a repository of our National Museum and should be returned to the country of his people, in the spirit of healing between races and to the benefit of the traditional owners. The world could have a great center of healing in the Lake Learned country, a place of learning for some and of marveled fascination for all, an enterprise that succors the descendants of Learned Man and Learned Woman and puts paid to all mean argument about Aboriginals as the human initiators and owners. Ah, you say: we have to wait for the traditional owners. Of course we do. But what have you said to them? Are they aware that you have any vision on the matter, any intent to fulfill their desires?

The man Professor Peter Jorgensen, my friend and an old man himself, found or was found by Learned Man, and the Man himself is an inexpressible wonder, and all you and your minions can do is erect a little shack and invoke the piety of waiting to hear from the elders and traditional owners. I believe inertia suits you, and most of your colleagues. You didn't pursue the same nicety when it came to recently canceling native title in the Northern Territory. And what a pity we did not consult them in the nineteenth century before obliterating them with the Martini Henry carbine!

This is a chance to do something of unambiguous wonder. Please do it! And forgive the exuberance of this letter, or whatever it is, in this letter. If everything I write is misled, I am not misled on the Mr. Learned proposition. It is a world imperative!

Yours with closing respect,
Shelby Apple, Officer of the
Order of Australia

And that was what I sent off.

Selfishly, I did not want Cath to become, after the operation, in the manner of wives of the sick, a health handmaiden. I hated, perhaps with some vanity, to have her reduced from calyx of desire to medical attendant. That is, I was loath to enter the final phase of the relationship, when the hands that once tore at the flesh become wielders of wet cloths, or holders of the puke or blood bowl. It was not that she wouldn't be willing to do that or that she lacked the sturdiness of soul. She had all the sturdiness fit for deathbed nursing and widowhood. And she might need to be in the role as a means to distract herself from impending drastic separation. It was that I did not want her to be in that role, the last role I would see her in. I did not want my last glimpses to be of her as attendant, as nurse. But I knew I would not get my way on this. I was reaching the stage where you don't get your way on anything.

I had a sense even in the recovery room that this latest operation had not gone well. I felt diminished and remote, but somehow the surgeon had revived in me one memory. By the bones of Learned Man, there had been found the lump of milky hyalite. It came from far away, originally from the opal fields of Lightning Ridge. The cunning Dr. Brown had fetched it and, as I suspected, had implanted it in me. He had not told me so, and when he visited I said to him, "Cunning move, the stone." He did not admit anything, of course. He could not. He did not have to. There was a law operating here that made him do it.

The stone glowing in me, Learned Man's stone. I spent a lot of time after the operation, though sometimes I was confused enough to think I hadn't had it, on the *Mir I* submersible again. It had only taken up a few weeks of my life, filming the scientific vessel and its submersibles, and indeed, at the end, I had to make the most of the one long, long day in the darkness of the ocean floor by the hydrothermal vents off Costa Rica. Yet that dive recurred to me as if it was the model for all the days of my drugged afterlife.

I was frequently sure I lay stomach down, and never comfortable, what with the glowing stone within my body, on a leather bench, with the monitor and the controls for the external cameras to the left of me and at face level and, to my right, an easy-rig steadying apparatus for the small Sony. With it I would shoot activities inside the capsule — Sergei's brow bulging with Slavic intent, or Allan Trumball discussing the metabolism of the sea creatures, extremophiles, who had chosen to evolve at this inhuman depth and pressure. I could also shoot along the shaft of illumination from the *Mir*'s outer skin, radiating at depths that had never seen light, and amongst beings that had dispensed with the need of it. And I could shoot what that shaft picked up via my little tea saucer–sized window, 110 millimeters across. The cameras belonging to the ship (in pressure casings outside its shell) and my outer camera and its casing were not unrelated — in my delirium — to the incandescent rock within me, to its reach and its secrets. I could somehow sense it reaching its own focus in a dimension just beyond the limits of sight and working away at its own tasks. Because I could feel its sharp inquiry unreconciled to the rest of me.

Sergei, pilot and navigator, had believed in bonds between men. But he could not be told that the stone had been transferred to me. He disliked things that were too subtle and too demanding in the metaphysical sense. He was a man's man. He'd disliked female authority. He had designed this wonderful titanium orb as a place he could hide out with men, but these days there were too many women scientists for that to work. He had taken trouble to tell me and Trumball, the American who shared the orb of the *Mir I* with us, that he found it hard to tolerate bossy women scientists who filled his beautiful titanium orb with urgent requests and commands. Lifetime scholars of the hydrothermal vents at the bottom of the sea, they only had twelve hours or so, the limitations of our natural functions, in the *Mir* submersible to consider with their own eyes the clouds of bacteria emerging from the vents, and the creatures of utter dark who could live in their own way, without bladdery and collapsible lungs and cavities, at this murderous depth and in temperatures ranging from −2 degrees Celsius to 400 degrees. And Sergei, collecting samples at their, in his view, strident orders with the retractable arms of his machines. But he said that having got to know us in the ship's mess and during the preparations for the dive, he considered Trumball and me brothers.

Lucifers, light-bearers to utter darkness, we had on first reaching the bottom of the sea swept across a pavement of shining onyx. Newly coughed up and laid down by the vents in the sea floor and dark brothers of Learned Man's milky lump of stone.

"Sergei," I pleaded in a tone of Australian camaraderie, which — unlike the demands of the women scientists Sergei ranted about — pretended to expect nothing. "Mate, would it be possible to have the full halogens on?"

"You want the probe lights?" he asked, but not in incredulity, more like an indulgent uncle. Because he liked me, you see. He had declared on no evidence that I was brave. I was uncomplaining, I suppose. He seemed to be impressed by my polite inquiry, my "Would it be possible?" I had also apparently hit the right note of disapproval the night before, when Sergei told the tale of Colin Banter, famed film director.

Banter had always used the two *Mir* submersibles and their mother ship, the *Akademik Nikolai Alikhanov,* for his underwater features and documentaries. Indeed, Banter had discovered the *Akademik* and its *Mir*s in mothballs in the port of Kaliningrad after the fall of the Soviet Union, and brought them back into commission, his movies enabling them to pursue science again. But Sergei said he had begun to doubt Banter when the *Mir* Banter was in, with Sergei himself piloting, became stuck fast between the propeller and hull of the *Bismarck,* a sunken Nazi battleship, on the seabed of the North Atlantic, nearly five kilometers down. I thought Banter's reaction, to show reasonable fear, absolutely reasonable at that depth and in an ocean which there exerts a pressure of five hundred atmospheres. Indeed, being crushed and achieving instant, bone-liquifying oblivion was preferable to suffocating there. Banter felt a certain panic? I considered it valid panic. It wasn't as if they could call a tow truck. The *Mir,* with its inner globe of titanium, air pressured to an atmosphere of one, was in itself no guarantee of extended life if they were stuck there under the fathoms-deep hole or moved free but could not ascend. Sergei's bloody-minded calm as he played with the controls, bucking his bright tensile steel against Hitler's resonant old iron, would have made anyone sweaty with apprehension. So I secretly dissented from Sergei's condemnation of Banter and hoped that no minor crisis would arise and cause me to betray myself as fearful to our exacting pilot.

The great jet floors, lit resplendently now, became speckled with bacteria and colonizing microorganisms the closer we got to the volcanic vent in the sea floor, and there in the probe lights and on my monitor stood a chimney of saturnine black, for all the world like the industrial chimneys accursed of William Blake, black flues sending black plumes of smoke into the water under such pressure that one would have thought oneself in a dark evening in an industrial city. For the smoke rose like usual, terrestrial smoke, vast energies in it. The five hundred atmospheres down there failed to quell the power behind it! It became apparent that the earth was being made here, out of its own belly, and the chimneys were mere grace notes on the great slash in the earth we now slid past, hedged in by its banks of bloodred giant tubeworms gulping hydrogen sulphide and flourishing on it. And it occurred to me then that Learned Man wanted his stone here, back in the stew that began everything, amongst beasts that appeased it.

In the wet laboratory on the *Akademik* I had seen Russian biologists slice these worms open, finding no interior as in normal fish caught by normal humans. Brother Tubeworm lived off the bacteria from the vent, and bacteria made up half of a worm's body weight, and could convert hydrogen sulphide and carbon dioxide into its own organic molecules and into the red hemoglobin that gave it its rich color. All I knew was that on the laboratory bench, they smelled somewhat of ammonia. Their blood was full of nitrates. And the love of a tubeworm . . . ? They reproduced, I had been told, by the females releasing eggs into the surrounding water which floated upwards while the males simultaneously unleashed bundles of sperm. And when a larva was produced of this dark, deep love, it did not swim towards the light far, far above, since the suspicion of light was not in its system, but sought the rocks by the beloved sea vent, and there took longer than two hundred years to grow two meters in its white, keratin-like tubing.

As I lay here with my own willful cells, including the cancerous ones that had, like the tubeworms, with a chemistry as subtle as that, chosen darkness, I did not understand and had neglected to study why my cells added up to me, and why those cohesions of cells down there in the black hot poisonous deep added up to what they were. I seemed keenly to want to know why I was kin to these brachiopod fish who nosed amongst the thickets of red tubes and the skeletal vent crabs busy around the volcanic rocks. I asked Cath this question today and she thought I was feverish.

"Is it theology or biology?" I insisted on knowing. "Maybe someone could tell me."

For I felt the operation had made me closer to the deep-vent creatures. Certainly, given the great slashes in my back and front, I felt I was getting closer to the vent animals, that I was no longer a biped but a floating thing.

"It's because you're here and they're there," said Cath softly. "Life's all a matter of postcodes, darling," she went on to tell me. "You know that, don't you?" The idea was that I should concentrate on my own postcode and on an unlikely cure.

I know I am in the hospital bed, yet I am as well an inhabitant of Sergei's capsule, and by way of the cameras in the exterior casings, I am now getting wonderful, light-drenched footage of thickets of the worms in their white mucilage. Around them grow barnacles on stalks, living off the blizzard of visible microorganisms. I must acquire them by my camera, despite the claims the stone makes on my attention. Snails and navigating shrimp are incredibly here, looking like shallow ocean creatures, and blobfish, and fish with conventional fronts and flattened tails, and all of them modest about the triumph of their existence.

And this is what I see as I absorb the so-called cocktail of palliative care the surfer-surgeon has prescribed for me. And there

— there it is — the great gliding octopus, more balletic than anything at this depth should be, balletic at five hundred atmospheres, a hymn to the universality of grace, auditioning before us at huge gravity.

"Christ, Sergei," called Trumbull from his bench. "We are only the nineteenth, twentieth, and twenty-first humans to have ever seen that creature! They haven't even classified it yet."

The Americans who first saw it had called it Dumbo, and I wondered dizzily whether Disney's Dumbo was worthy of the compliment. Octopus in form, it played gracefully through the forests of tubeworms and of my delirium. It was the nymph, the form we were all seeking. I tracked it with my inside Steadicam. In the breathlessness of my dissolution, I track it still. It is the ultimate escapee of the light and thus of the malice of the gods. Even my cameras, internal and external, held it only for a second and a half. Nineteenth, twentieth, and twenty-first, I repeat in a haze of pain and fever. They are important numerals.

And then a party for Sergei and Allan Trumball and me. We have risen up off the bottom, we have emerged into the first intimations of the light-regulated universe through our little capsule portholes, the first great tinge of dazzle from the surface, which we break in a brilliant tropical sea. The ship beside our portholes blazes with flagrant light in the sunset.

The party aboard the ship started. It was feverish. Too much vodka in my blood. But we were apparently required to be drunk for brotherhood. For it was Sergei's birthday and we were not women scientists — they had left early despite me exhibiting my respect to them by engaging with them in front of Sergei and asking them about their work. Oceanographers and biologists, they were calm about the possibilities of what they had seen, calm even about their own research, but they were wearied already by the dreary, clogged testosterone in the mess, by men determined to droop, to stupefy themselves with vodka. Sergei was of course glad to see the women go, and when they had, he sang a song on the guitar, this inventor of titanium spheres that can hold up at depth. He sang a song of fraternity between honest brothers at the bottom of the sea, Russian, American, Antipodean, all great guys, unfussy, untemperamental, undemanding, and grateful for whatever Sergei showed us of the hydrothermal vents. This was a party I tried in my delirium of remembrance to get away from, for the vodka did not suit me and was clogging into a rock at my core. But Sergei sang along with his guitar to convince me, and poured me another of those poisonous little shots of vodka, in glass as thick as a curse.

I am under the hull. The air fades, the air devoured, used up. The *Bismarck*'s iron rump lies on my sternum. I can feel how intractable it is. I call out in protest.

"No," says Cath. "We're all here."

And I see their faces. My grandchildren have brought their blood-oxygen to my bedside. I tell my eldest grandson, Michael, "The breeding cycle of the tubeworm. The really deep ones. Hydrothermal vents. It's fascinating, Mick."

"Yes," said Michael in his sixteen-year-old basso. "You were telling me."

A beautiful boy with dark brown hair and a dutiful brow. And he looked at me knowingly. He *got* the stone. But he didn't mention it.

"You *get* these things, Micky," I tell him. "You always did. Good old Mick. My cobber."

The endearments I utter pierce me because the stern of that Nazi supership still lays athwart the route of my speech.

I see by my bed Brendan, Gracie's boy, seeking refuge from the ennui of the

425

sickbed/deathbed by fighting with Pokémon on his DSi XL. I approve mightily of this. In my own childhood I hated the sickrooms of the old. And I had to take them straight — too young for booze, and Pokémon and the iPad and the mobile phone as yet unintroduced as palliatives to the places your parents insisted you go.

"Hey, mate," I yelled to Brendan.

He looked up. His cowlick spiking free. I'd never met a cowlicked kid I didn't like, though they were generally a lot of trouble, with their reverse horn of hair, a warning to the earth's conventions that they would not hold up against the principle of chaos the cowlick stood for.

"Round up those Pokémon, Tiger!" I called.

"Yeah, Shelby!" he replied, calling me by my first name, something I always got a kick out of.

My wife and daughters hush me. Only because it's too much. Brendan's sage sister, little Sophie, eleven now, frowns at us, for she knows what is happening. She has her granny's frown of comprehending and she knows what the case is, that I'm stuck under the iron hull, between propeller and stern. She has already acquired a woman's taste for reality, reality being something her brother can face only with a soothing electronic device in hand.

Exactly as I've faced the world frame by frame, excluding with the rectangular limits of the lens whatever does not suit my case; now it is only fair that the world should strike back with the unframeable, the unfilmable.

This Brendan, just a few years back, would make me drive out on Saturday mornings to a place not far from where I grew up. And there, approached through artificial hills that reminded me of Teletubby Land, we came to a wonderful park which had been imaginatively designed for children. There was a great spinning disc on which children could sit or lie or else hang from by their fingertips, as Brendan did. Colorful tunnels ran through the hills, connecting one play pit with another. Great webs and funnels of rope were everywhere for the climbing. There was a flying fox, plenteous swings, and then, above all, a treehouse that was ten stories high. The way you ascended this tree house was by a series of internal steps, each about a meter tall, and from the top story you could see the river flowing as assertively as the Amazon. Brendan went up this structure of timber, concrete, and protective wire like an animal, for he was a young animal, and turned around occasionally to urge me on my way as I hauled myself from level to level, mainly by the strength of my upper body, or when that failed by simply rolling myself upwards, level by level, an undignified and painful method. And on either side of me children hurried and scuttled and bounded, ascending and descending, with the well-bred ones, of whom there were many more than the modern age was rumored to have delivered, pausing to say, "Sorry."

As a child of White Australia, the Australia that had battled to keep itself Caucasian at all costs and had even in my childhood considered Italians and Greeks the Aboriginals of Southern Europe, I was delighted to see turbaned little Sikhs yelling in an Australian accent, the children of the Prophet from Western Sydney, their hijab-wearing mothers anxious at the bottom of the tower, and Chinese, Vietnamese, Japanese, and Korean kids with no time to be wasted on their way to the Parramatta River apex, the top of this wonderful house amongst the trees. This obstacle course for me, a joyous, hectic ascent for Brendan and them.

When I reached the top and lay on the cement floor for a few seconds gathering my breath, I often found some young Chinese woman already there with her spry children, taking in the river view. "Oh," she would say, "are you well, sir?"

And though I wasn't sure about it, I'd assert I was.

"Do you need help?" she would gently ask. I was an object of mercy to her, and yet I enjoyed meeting these beautiful young women, their eyes softening, their Asian respect for the elderly deployed in my direction. So I would smile and say something banal like, "Getting up here was the hard bit." Even so, I didn't have the stone then.

And so I acquired what vanity I could from the exchange with the young woman who smiled and cautioned her children to make way for "Grandfather." I had fulfilled a small ambition I had, that of being the grandfather who was to be found in unexpected places. On that basis, I'd gone on a treetop adventure course with Brendan and his wise sister, Sophie, and as much as I complained to myself and grunted, as much as my feet slid off the wires or off the swinging slabs of wood hanging by ropes and providing steps forward, as much as I bruised my ankles with panicked missteps, I felt my own geriatric heroism also. And Brendan often turned back to yell to me,

"Come on, Shelby!" He was like me perhaps in that it was all life in the treetops or in the virtual world he liked. Ground level was a problem. Poor little fellow, I had passed that on to him.

And I had wanted until recently, indeed till now, to be Brendan's fellow adventurer and not a venerable figure. I didn't believe in venerable figures, especially not for children. I had never met one. I'd met the reserved, the careful, the self-regarding, who sometimes seemed to think of themselves as venerable. But there was no venerable creature around as I tottered, harnessed though I was — helmeted too — on some jungle treetop course. In uneasy balance, I'd fibrillate in the treetops as Brendan harangued me. "Hurry up, Shelby, we have to do the black course yet!" For the black course could only be attempted by children in the company of an adult. And he did not doubt that I, though the object of mercy of young, handsome Chinese-Australian mothers, should be that adult not only above the earth but above vertigo, and superior to limited stamina. I was aware he was doing me honor.

Did I do these things for love of children? Or was it for the absurd vanity I felt from the pathetic, momentary conceit? Or was I

430

willing to be a pretend child? It was all of these, of course. And so, now, under the keel of the battleship. The stone as big as the ship and indistinguishable from it. But I did not want Brendan's mother, Gracie, to say, or imply, "Put that Pokémon down and pay attention to your grandfather. He is very sick, and he's been good to you." A grandparent who can't be "good to you" is — what? — a less than human entity. A failed and *venerable* being.

Even with the *Bismarck* on my chest, and the serious octopus, crappily named Dumbo, gliding by for enchantment, I had time to remember how at the water slides Sophie lingered for me in the pool, and when I was ejected by the tube and rose up with my nasal cavities scalded by chlorinated water, she was there, smiling a complicit smile, child to child, joyrider to joyrider.

In this hospital room, beneath the *Bismarck*'s keel, my elder granddaughter Vicki kissed my forehead honestly — no peck — and said, "We all want you well, Shelby!" Her emotional deftness was apparent in that kiss. It was authentic. What a ferocious two-year-old she had been, an empress of diktats! Now everyone called her "the sweetest girl," which she authentically was, though of course she'd known from the womb how to torment her brother, the boy they called "poor old Mick," our first grandchild, friend and fellow explorer. Vicki embodied the conundrum of women. On the one hand fatuous enough to be enchanted by the boy band called Latitude Forty and their formulaic pop. And yet . . . here she was too, the eternal mothering healer, the woman as wise as her grandmother, the consoler above the capacity of boys to console. So, women — wise enough to transcend us; crass enough as an ill-advised majority to be charmed by us . . . My adolescent granddaughter. On her way.

I asked Vicki, "Do you know Sergei?"

"Sergei?" she asked.

"The Russian," I told her. "He's been here. Driving this thing."

"This thing," she said, but as if she knew what *this thing* was.

"He's somewhere around. Try the waiting room. I think he's there."

She nodded. Good girl. She did not let confusion or anything patronizing enter her gaze. "I can find out," she promised me. Vicki was the one in the hospital room best equipped to collaborate with Cath and get me out from beneath the steel ceiling.

"Look," I warned her, "he's a sexist.

They're like that. The Russians. But you can handle him. Okay?"

"Okay," she said and frowned.

I wondered who could define the frown of a fourteen-year-old, and why hadn't any of us, from Leibniz to Kant to Kierke-bloody-gaard, taken on such a supereminently useful and engrossing task?

"Ask him when he thinks he'll get us out of here," I instructed her, "because the air's getting thick."

Cath's face appeared in formidable but confused alliance behind Vicki's. "Sergei?" she asked.

"Trumball hasn't synthesized the enzymes yet," I thought of telling her. Therefore it was unlikely I could be altered from my extreme existence to one that would involve breathing on Mars or under the keel of *Bismarck*.

"It's all right." Cath intervened. "Because we're taking you to another hospital. It has better palliative care."

"Are you crying?" I asked sternly, because neither of us trusted easy tears.

"I'm just hoping you get better," said Cath as a nurse stokes my intravenous with some drug or other.

The nurse sees I notice. "It's just for your ambulance transfer, Mr. Apple."

I want to thank her, but the words lie above me like two whales. Then the ambulance arrives. There are tall men carrying me to the ambulance. One of them is Andy. I start laughing. "What in fuck's sake are you doing, you bloody clown?" But, Jesus Christ, by my head is a black hand, long in the palm and fingers, guiding. I feel a surge of gratitude and I confide in that man. I say, "Mum's the word."

IN PALLIATIVE CARE

My thoughts do not nest, they have no ledge to settle on as I go down. In the house made of sediments of the hills and dunes of the lake, its interlaced roof speaks to me like a brother through the mouth of a far-seeing, striped water lizard which has somehow appeared on my tray table in the palliative care ward. It says, "The world you swallowed is too big for you."

Well, I happen to know that and I think of telling him, "I ate it a rectangle at a time." Like oxygen, it was what I needed. Like oxygen, it will kill me. "But what sort of choice did I have?" I ask the lizard. After the death of Andy, how could I have stopped? "I owed him a record of the world he lost. I fed it to him in rectangles of film."

Since Andy was a gentleman and undemanding, I thought he needed this tribute all the more. He didn't ask for it. The air around us asked that he be given it.

As I make this argument to the lizard in the palliative care ward, Cath leans down from a celestial elevation and kisses me on the forehead. The kiss is distant, like a tremor in the chasms of the sea.

"He's a wise fella, that lizard," I tell her. But, like most of my statements, it doesn't have time to perch, it is gone. The hole in me is a tunnel in which time blows like a wind, all the time. There are no ledges and no purchase. A nurse has arrived to adjust my IV, frowning as if she is deciding what degree of mercy I deserve.

"Will it dissolve it? The rock I've swallowed?" I ask. It is an extremely pressing question. The biggest question. Does Learned want it back?

The fluid that now enters me stuns to silence the debate I'm having with myself.

"I've stopped arguing," I tell the air about my room, the new one. The one to do with hope of some sort.

LEARNED MAN RETURNS TO HIS LAKE

Some months after the death of Shelby Apple, the tribes whose traditional lands abutted Lake Learned returned their ancient hero, Learned Man, to his country in a wooden casket. The joy was visible in the faces of the elders.

A keen wind ran across Lake Learned that day. Peter Jorgensen, who was invited, thought that in Learned Man's day it would have shivered the surface of the water. It rustled the saltbush in a way that almost imitated the old lake as Jorgensen knew it had once been. He told the press that it was a day of immense history, but also a beginning.

"Learned Man," he said, "has not yet finished speaking to us all."

ABOUT THE AUTHOR

Thomas Keneally began his writing career in 1964 and has published thirty-three novels since, most recently *Crimes of the Father, Napoleon's Last Island, Shame and the Captives*, and the *New York Times* best-selling *The Daughters of Mars*. His novels include *Schindler's List*, which won the Booker Prize in 1982, *The Chant of Jimmie Blacksmith, Gossip from the Forest*, and *Confederates*, all of which were shortlisted for the Booker Prize. He has also written several works of nonfiction, including his boyhood memoir *Homebush Boy, The Commonwealth of Thieves*, and *Searching for Schindler*. He is married with two daughters and lives in Sydney, Australia.